The Kennedy Boys

Forgiving Keven

A Kennedy Boys Standalone Novel

SIOBHAN DAVIS

www.siobhandavis.com

Printed by Amazon.
Paperback edition © January 2019

ISBN-13: 9781792103865

Editor: Kelly Hartigan (XterraWeb) editing.xterraweb.com
Cover design by Robin Harper https://wickedbydesigncovers.wixsite.com
Photo by Sara Eirew
Cover models: Daniel Rengering and Jacqui Pogue
Formatting by The Deliberate Page www.deliberatepage.com

Note from the Author

While you can read Forgiving Keven as a **standalone** book, and it is a complete romance with a HEA for our couple, it is advisable to read the previous books in the series first to enjoy the full Kennedy Boys experience! Please note that this book contains spoilers to events from previous books. For those who are up to date with the series, Cheryl and Keven's story picks up straight after the end of Seducing Kaden.

Prologue
Christmas

Keven

Agent Dickhead shoves my head in the back of his FBI-issued SUV while the female agent—who has yet to introduce herself—gets in the other side to keep an eye on me. Jerkoff slides behind the wheel and starts the engine.

I stare out the window, at familiar landscape, as the miles eat away.

I've always known this day would come. Despite how careful I've been, some things refuse to stay buried. I knew the risk I was taking the day I sent the anonymous tip to the FBI about Kade and Eva's location. There wasn't time to put the proper precautions in place, and I knew it wouldn't take too long before they discovered where the tip originated from. I knew it would lead to further investigation, but if I had my time over again, I'd still do the same.

My brother and his wife would have died that day if I hadn't intervened.

And if I end up going to jail, I won't have any regrets.

My brother is alive, and that's all that counts.

The silence in the SUV is deafening, but I sure as fuck won't be the first to break it. So, I continue looking out the window, calmly awaiting my fate.

A short while later, we pull up at the back entrance of what I know is the local FBI field office in Chelsea, Massachusetts. I cooperate as I'm removed from the car and led into the building.

They deposit me in a small room, cuffing my hands to the table and leaving me alone.

Some time passes, and then the same two agents return with an older gentleman with thick dark hair. He removes the handcuffs from my wrists before dropping into a chair across from me while the other two stand in the corner like dutiful lackeys.

"Good evening, Mr. Kennedy," he says. "I'm Supervisory Special Agent Andrew Clement, and I'd like to have an off-the-record chat with you before your attorney arrives." Slamming a heavy manila folder down on the table, he eyeballs me with a penetrating stare. "We've had our eye on you for some time, Keven." He raps his fingers off the table while I stare neutrally ahead. "You've been a very naughty boy." He flips open the file, skimming through documents. "Illegal online gambling. Identify theft and larceny. Illegal wiretapping. Not to mention some of the undesirables you've been connected to in the past. The list goes on."

He has no idea.

Propping his elbows on the desk, he stabs me with sharp hazel eyes. "There is no denying how incredibly skilled you are with a computer, or your obvious intelligence, so I have a proposition for you."

I arch a brow, as the woman pulls a white screen down from the ceiling.

"Our analysis shows you have tried to mend your ways, and your most recent illegal activities have all centered on protecting family and friends. We know you sent us the anonymous tip which led us to the warehouse that day, and we're grateful."

He pauses momentarily. "However, your actions are enough to put you away for quite some time unless you agree to come and work for us," he adds.

Okay, what?

I eyeball the guy like he's crazy. "Work for you?" I splutter. "Doing what?"

"We could use a good technical analyst like you on a special high-priority undercover case."

"And what? If I do this, you'll rip up those charges?"

Extracting a document from the file, he slides it across the table to me. "That's a contract of employment which also confirms if you come to work with us we'll drop all pending charges against you and shred your file, subject to certain provisions, of course."

"What if I don't want to come and work for you?"

"Then you'll be prosecuted to the full extent of the law."

I say nothing for a few minutes. "I need some time to think about it."

The man smiles, as if I've just told a joke. "This is a one-time offer, and you'll need to make your mind up now." He clicks his fingers, and Agent Dickhead switches off the light as the screen powers up. "Perhaps this might help persuade you," Agent Clement says.

Photos of various well-known criminals appear on the screen, and he starts explaining. "Following the recent death of Jeremy Garcia, a drug war has erupted on our streets, as various interested parties battle to take over what was his."

More images fill the screen. "But that's not even the real problem. Most of the main players have their hands in several cookie jars. Narcotics is only one aspect of their business."

The images on the screen shift, showing several large trucks, open at the rear, with young girls spilling out of the vehicles, crying and in various stages of undress. "Sex trafficking is another lucrative source of income, and something that's been on our radar for quite some time, but we're struggling to find evidence to pin these guys down."

The images return to some of Massachusetts's most notorious gangsters. "The turmoil in the aftermath of Garcia's demise grants us an opportunity to infiltrate these organizations and start to build solid evidence against those responsible. With your background, and your skills, you could be a valuable asset to our team."

The screen changes again, and my eyes zone in on the pretty blonde outside the photography studio. My chest tightens as I examine the shot in more detail. She's looking up at a guy I don't recognize, and they're smiling at one another. "Who's that?" I ask, gnawing on the inside of my mouth.

"Daniel Stanten. A relative newcomer on the scene. He was being groomed by Garcia, and word on the street is he's the one to watch."

"And the girl?" I ask although I already know her name.

"Cheryl Keeland. His fiancée."

"I'll do it," I blurt. "I'll come and work for you." Light floods the room, and Agent Clement stares at me in surprise. I reach for the contract. "Where do I sign?"

Removing a pen from his inside jacket pocket, he hands it to me. I don't even bother reading it. Dan Evans, our family attorney, will string me up by the balls for this, but screw that shit.

I've spent years trying to get all thoughts and memories of Cheryl Keeland out of my head, to no avail. Torn through girls like they were a two-for-one special, but nothing or no one can erase the only girl who has ever owned my heart.

Cheryl was the love of my life growing up, and I never envisioned a future where she wasn't in it.

Until I fucked up.

And I lost her.

And I haven't been at peace within myself since.

I don't believe in kismet or karma or whatever the fuck you call it.

But right now, it feels like fate is sending me one big-ass message.

And I'm not going to fuck up again.

Cheryl may be engaged to that guy, but she hasn't married him yet, so there's still time to warn her.

Time to tell her what I should have told her senior year.

Time to win back the heart of the only girl who has ever mattered.

Skipping to the back page of the contract, I scribble my signature in the field provided, sliding the document across the slick surface to a shocked Agent Clement.

Grinning, I lean back in my chair. "When do I start?"

Chapter 1

March of the Following Year

Keven

I stare at the screen without really seeing it. When I completed my training in Quantico and returned to the Chelsea field office a week ago, I expected the SSA—Special Supervisory Agent Clement—to assign me to something more exciting than this.

When he initially presented me with his proposition, he mentioned a high-profile undercover operation, and I stupidly thought that meant I'd be in the thick of the action. Maybe Dan Evans was right, and I should have waited for him to arrive before signing my name on that contract. But I was too hyped-up at the thought of my high school sweetheart being in danger to think logically. Which is most unlike me because I'm usually meticulous in my planning.

Now I'm here—stuck behind a desk— instead of out there protecting the only girl I've ever loved.

Yes, I know my role is technically an intelligence analyst and that you have to be at least twenty-three before they consider you for a field agent role, but Supervisory Special Agent Andrew Clement recruited me to join a classified organized crime task force, and I thought that meant special exemption.

But I was wrong.

Ordinarily, sitting in front of a computer trawling for information for hours at a time is right up my alley but not on this occasion.

I only took this job to get close to Cheryl.

To protect her from that criminal she's engaged to.

To find out if there's a way to right the wrongs of the past.

But I can't do that if I'm trapped in this fucking office all day.

So, I've had no choice but to take matters into my own hands. One part of my plan is already in motion, and now it's time to make my second play.

My chair screeches as I jump up, causing a couple of my colleagues to jerk their heads in my direction. I stride across the room with purpose, bounding up the stairs to the higher level, and stalk toward the SSA's office. I rap on the door and wait to be called. Thirty seconds pass, and I'm conscious of eyeballs glued to my back from the lower level below. I'm about to knock a second time when the door flies open.

"Ah, Mr. Kennedy. What a coincidence. I was just about to summon you." He steps aside. "Come in."

I brush past him and sit down in one of the empty chairs in front of his desk.

"Make yourself at home," he deadpans before dropping into his seat and leveling me with an intense stare. I hold his stare, refusing to back down or show any obvious emotion on my face. He drums his fingers off the top of the desk. "Why did you need to see me?" he inquires.

"If surveillance hasn't been assigned to Cheryl Keeland, Daniel Stanten's fiancée, yet, then I'd like to request the job." I know no one is shadowing Cheryl, but it's best not to clue him in on how well informed I am.

"And why would I do that?" He arches a brow.

I clear my throat, preparing to admit some of the truth. "I know her, and I'm concerned about her safety."

His lips curve up ever so slightly. "I was wondering how long it'd take you to admit that." I can't hide the surprise on my face. He leans forward, propping his elbows on the desk. "Your reaction the first day we met completely gave you away. I'll admit I wasn't aware of the connection between you two the day I presented our proposition, but I knew your sudden agreement was something to do with that girl, so I ordered a background check."

"Then you understand." I fold my arms and wait for him to continue.

"If you joined this team expecting it to be an opportunity to reunite with your high school sweetheart, then I hate to be the one to disappoint you, but that's not going to happen."

"I joined the team to ensure she's safe, and I want to help bring down those pricks who almost killed my brother and sister-in-law. Those bastards who are kidnapping young girls from Mexico and trafficking them into the U.S. Those degenerates who flood our streets with drugs and guns, preying on the weak and vulnerable. *That's* why I'm here."

It's not a lie.

Yes, Cheryl was my initial motivation, but the more I've uncovered about the criminal underworld thriving in Boston, the more I'm determined to help bring them down.

"How very noble of you," he drawls.

I work hard to resist the urge to flip him the bird. "It's the truth," I calmly reply.

"I'm glad to hear it." He purses his lips as he stares at me. "And I happen to believe you'll make an excellent agent, in time, provided you remember why you are here. And that's not some personal crusade to protect your lost love. You have a set role in this team, and that's to provide intelligence."

"I don't see why I can't do both. It's not like one is completely separate from the other," I argue.

"They are not mutually exclusive, and that's the very reason why you won't be going anywhere near Cheryl Keeland. To do so could jeopardize our entire operation, and we've invested too much time to risk it. Our undercover agents have infiltrated both rival organizations, and we can't take any action which might undermine their efforts."

He stands, coming around the front of the desk. Propping his ass on the corner, he leans over me. "Besides, Daniel Stanten is only a minor player and not the focus of our attention at this time."

"I thought you said he was the one to watch?"

"Intel we've gleaned while you were in Quantico points to other parties with more controlling responsibilities, and that's where we're focusing our efforts, for the moment, so there's no need for any surveillance on Ms. Keeland or Mr. Stanten."

"That's a mistake."

The expression on his face is a cross between mild amusement and mild irritation. "Is that so?"

I sit up straighter. "Yes. Something is off about that guy. He grew up on the wrong side of the tracks in Roxbury, yet he went on to graduate with honors from Harvard Law, and then he set up his own legal practice pretty much straight out of college, funded by Jeremy Garcia. We both know it's not legit and that Garcia was grooming him for a bigger role, you said that yourself, but the question is *why Stanten* in the first place? What connects Garcia and Stanten that would have him choosing a newbie to take care of his legal affairs? It doesn't add up. There's got to be some purpose behind it."

"Maybe. Maybe not." He shrugs. "Garcia's own son died at birth, and he'd taken a number of young men under his wing over the years. It's not inconceivable to think he was trying to find someone worthy to replace him. Someone who would succeed him at the helm of the organization when the time was right."

"I don't doubt that, but why Stanten? Why, and how, did he come to Garcia's attention?"

"It sounds like someone has been doing some moonlighting on the case."

I hold up my hands. "I admit I've been digging into his background, but it's all been on my own time."

He scrubs a hand over his jaw. "Perhaps you're right, and it ties into the reason why I wanted to speak with you." He pauses briefly. "I need to speak to Eva Garcia."

"Eva Kennedy," I correct, quickly cutting across him. Eva's married to my brother now, and she wants no reminders of that monster she was once forced into marrying. When Jeremy Garcia died that day in the warehouse, Eva wasted no time cutting all ties with him. He's a part of her past she's trying to put behind her.

"I meant no offense, and I've called you in here as a courtesy. I could bring Eva in for questioning at any time, but I thought you might like to mention it to her, and we could schedule a mutually convenient time that suits both parties."

"Is there anything specific you need to talk to her about, or it's more of a general conversation?"

"I'd like to talk to her about her time with Garcia. To find out if she has any information that might help with our case. Agent Wentward seemed to think she'd be predisposed to help."

"Agent Wentward?" Disbelief bleeds from my tone. Agent Dickhead, as I prefer to call him, doesn't have any knowledge or right to make such sweeping statements. There's no love lost between the two of us since my arrest, that's for sure. He hasn't done anything to hide his disdain for me, and I love returning the favor. "How the hell is he qualified to cast judgment on Eva?"

"Colin was part of the team at the warehouse the day of the shooting, and he helped escort your sister-in-law to the hospital."

Why the hell didn't I know that? I'll be having words with my brother. He should've told me the guy who showed up at our house Christmas Day was the same guy who assisted Eva the day everything came to a head in that abandoned warehouse.

"I'll talk to Eva. When do you want her to come in?"

"Ideally, as soon as possible. We need to explore some new angles. Our undercover agents say it's going to take time to infiltrate the highest levels of the organizations, so we need to explore all other options in the meantime. Cracking this case sooner than later is my priority. If we cover several bases, we stand a greater chance of success."

"Which is why I think we should put more effort into Stanten. Let me dig deeper. See if I can find the link that connects him to Garcia."

The phone rings on his desk, but he ignores it, looking contemplative as he stares at me. "Okay, Kennedy." He nods with a resigned sigh. "Take a closer look at Stanten but strictly from the confines of your desk." He narrows his eyes at me. "And you're to have no contact with Ms. Keeland. That's an order." He picks up the phone, holding the cradle to his chest. "Have I made myself clear?"

"Crystal," I lie as I get up and walk out of his office.

Chapter 2

Cheryl

"Can I open my eyes yet?" I plead in a voice that betrays my excitement.

Dan wraps his arms around my waist from behind, pressing up close to me. "You are the hardest person to surprise. Do you know that?" Amusement underscores his tone.

"I know," I readily admit, "because I get too excited and I'm way too impatient." I laugh. "Please, Dan. I know we're here. Let me see."

Since he woke me up this morning, telling me today was a big day and that he had a huge surprise for me, I've been wracking my brain trying to figure out what it could be. I know I drove him insane on the journey here. Especially when he put this blindfold on me and made me promise not to peek.

All I know is we've left the city behind, and we were driving for about a half hour until he stopped. I heard little beeps as he punched in some code on a keypad and the creaking of gates. Then we were on the move again before coming to a complete stop a minute later. I'm guessing he's brought me to some lavish hotel and I'm practically jumping for joy, too excited at the prospect of spending alone time with my fiancé, in luxurious surroundings, to worry about missing a few days of classes.

Not that I need extravagant gifts, but Daniel Stanten sure knows how to spoil the woman in his life. I keep telling him to stop it, that he should be saving his money, but it goes over his head.

Dan helps me out of the car with strict instructions not to remove the blindfold yet. I hop from foot to foot, impatiently waiting for him to put me out of my misery. It's unnaturally cold out today, but I'm cocooned in my thick bubble jacket, so I only feel the sharp, icy sting slapping my exposed cheeks. A gentle rustling sound in the background is the only noise I can hear. Wherever we are, it's unbelievably peaceful.

"Welcome to your new home," Dan says, sliding the blindfold off my eyes and hugging me from behind.

I blink for several seconds until my eyesight has adjusted to the light, and then my eyes bug out of my head, and my jaw drops to the floor. "What?" I splutter, unsure if I heard him correctly.

We're standing in front of a massive modern two-story property with wide cherry-framed windows and a stylish cream brick façade. The roof is split into various sized triangular-shaped peaks, and a professionally landscaped lawn stretches along the front of the house. All around us are clusters of tall trees, some still snow-capped from the recent light snowfall.

"I bought it for us. Surprise."

I twist around in his arms. "You bought us a house?" I squeak.

He waggles his brows, grinning. "I did good, right?"

I turn back around, staring at the huge house. "How could you even afford something like this?" I mean, I know Dan's new business is doing well but not *that* well. He's only been running it a year, and I don't see how he has the money to make such an ostentatious purchase.

"Business is booming," he says in a clipped tone, his body turning stiff against me.

"Baby." I spin around and cup his face. "I'm not criticizing. I'm just blown away, and I don't want you to get into debt when you're only starting out. A smaller house would be totally fine with me."

He takes a step back, removing himself from our embrace, and a muscle clenches in his jaw. "Most women would be screaming and throwing themselves at their fiancé if he surprised them with this house."

"Dan." I move toward him, but he takes another step away from me. I soften my tone. "I'm only thinking of you. I don't want you to put yourself under too much pressure." I grab his hand so he can't move away from me anymore. "I love the house. It's absolutely stunning. And I'm overwhelmed you've bought this for us, but I love you for *you*. Not the things you think you have to buy for me. I would be happy living in a shack once I was with you."

Dan doesn't talk about his childhood that often, but I know they didn't have much. It was just him and his mom, and they grew up in quite a rough part of Boston. He's worked really hard to claw his way to where he is today, and I respect him enormously for his ambition, his drive and determination. But I don't want him to kill himself working to provide for me. Or to feel like I expect the best of everything. He's already working crazy hours, weekends too, and with his business trips becoming more frequent, I'm worried about his stress levels.

His handsome face relaxes, and he reels me back into his arms. "You have a good heart, Cheryl, and sometimes, I forget you're not like most women I've known." He grabs my ass and squeezes. "But you have to stop worrying. Trust I have everything under control." He slaps my ass firmly before taking my hand and leading me toward the house. "And get used to this, because this is only the start." As he winks at me, I try to ignore the anxious churning in my stomach.

I walk around the opulent living room in a bit of a daze, unable to take it all in. The whole interior of the house has been professionally designed and decorated. It's literally like stepping into a showhouse. There isn't a single thing left to do—it's in pristine walk-in condition.

A fluttering sensation takes up residence in my chest, and I'm even more uncomfortable than I was outside. This must have cost a fortune. And, while it's tastefully furnished and decorated, it doesn't feel like a home to me.

"It's killed me keeping this a secret from you," Dan gushes, tugging me into the massive well-lit kitchen. "But the place was a wreck when I first bought it. It's why I got it for such a good price. I demolished most of the original structure and hired contractors to rebuild it, and then I hired one of the leading interior designers to create the perfect family home for us."

Next, he drags me into an exquisite dining room with a long walnut table that seats twelve. A massive chandelier hangs overhead, and the room overlooks the sprawling back yard with a wraparound deck, patio, pool, and manicured lawns.

Dan draws me back into his chest while we both stare out the window. He rests his chin atop my head. "I wanted to have it ready to walk into before I brought you here. I know you're busy with college, the studio, and your volunteer work, so I didn't want to burden you with this. You're not mad, right?"

I kind of am, but I don't articulate that sentiment. I don't want to appear ungrateful or dampen his obvious delight, so I keep my thoughts contained this time even if I am disappointed that he didn't allow me any input into the project. I would have loved helping with the design and overseeing everything, but he didn't give me the chance. "I'm not mad. It's beautiful. Thank you, Dan."

His lips latch onto my neck as his hands slide up under my sweater. "Want to christen this room first?"

"He bought you a freaking house?" Hayley's shriek is so loud that several heads in the auditorium swivel in our direction.

"Shh. Keep it down! I don't want half the class to know."

"Where is it, and do you have any pics?" she asks, fiddling with her new Tiffany bracelet.

"It's in Lexington, and no, there wasn't time this morning. I got a quick tour, and then Dan drove me back to the apartment to collect my car." I don't mention the quick fuck because I'm not one to divulge details even if Hayley doesn't hold back in telling me about her conquests. Girl has an insatiable sexual appetite. I'm no prude, but some of her stories make my ears burn they're that hot.

"You're such a lucky bitch," she pouts, slapping her notepad down on the desk in front of her like it's personally insulted her or something. "First, he buys you a brand-new Audi A3, and now a house?" Her lips curl into a sneer. "And you don't even appreciate it."

"I do appreciate it," I protest, quietly opening my notepad as the professor gets ready to start the session. "But I don't need extravagant gestures, and it's a little unnerving at times."

"Dan strikes me as the type who likes to spend money on his woman. If you're not careful, you'll lose him to someone who lets him indulge his generous nature."

My brow wrinkles as I turn to face her. "Why the hell would you say something like that to me?" It's both hurtful and bitchy, and I've noticed Hayley making a lot of snide remarks lately that I don't like. I'm not sure if I've done something to upset her or if she's jealous of my relationship with Dan, but she's been off with me the last few months, and I can't figure out why. And, it's not as if she even knows him that well. They've only met one time.

When I first met Hayley, the first day of class last September, she was a Godsend. Transferring to a new college for the last year of my degree was hugely daunting. I've left all my family and friends back in Delaware, and having lost touch with most of my old friends from Wellesley, I was very much alone when I initially moved back here. Making a friend the minute I stepped foot on the MassArt campus was more than I could have hoped for. But Hayley literally barreled her way into my life.

We ran into one another outside the auditorium that first morning, both of us tumbling to the ground, the contents of our book bags spread out on the floor around us, and an instant friendship was formed in between our laughter. We gelled, instantly, and we were super close those first few months.

But something has shifted in our relationship recently, and I don't understand it. I've asked her what's wrong, but she constantly tells me everything is fine, almost leading me to believe I'm imagining it.

"I'm just looking out for you, Cheryl." She pats my hand, and the gesture strikes me as condescending. "I know Dan is the catch of the century, and I'd hate anything to come between you. What kind of friend would I be if I didn't try to warn you?"

Chapter 3

Keven

My brother Kaden is waiting in the lobby of my Chelsea apartment building when I return home from work. I'd messaged him earlier, asking him to meet me. "Hey." I jerk my head in acknowledgment at the security guard in the lobby at the same time I greet my brother.

"Hey, man. How are you?" Kade slaps me on the back, almost dislocating my shoulder, but I pass no comment. Since Kade decided to bulk up, a subtle competitive rivalry exists between us, and he loses no opportunity to try to remind me of his physical strength.

All my brothers work out, but since that shit went down between Cheryl and me senior year of high school, I've thrown myself into the gym, and lifting weights, as a welcome distraction. It was that or continue with the self-destructive path I was on.

I also took up running a couple years ago, and I jog at least five miles a day. It served me well during my FBI physical. They place huge importance on fitness, and if I ever want to move to a special agent role, I need to maintain peak physical form.

Kade started working out seriously about a year ago, and he's more obsessed than I ever was. As the eldest, he likes to think he's better at everything, and I know it kills him that this is one area where I excel. In every other way, my brother is a far better man than me, but I'm not handing over this crown to him too. This one is mine. So, yeah, he can keep snapping at my heels, but he won't win this battle.

We don't speak as we ride the elevator to the top floor, but this isn't the type of conversation you have in an elevator. Once we enter the penthouse I now call home, I dump my duffel bag on the floor in the hallway and head straight for the kitchen. "Beer?" I inquire with my head stuck in the fridge.

"Just the one. I'm driving."

I smirk as I uncap both bottles, handing one to him. "Look at you. All responsible and shit."

"Says the FBI agent," he retorts with a knowing smile, clinking his bottle against mine. "How's that going?"

"It's okay." I walk into the open-plan living area, and he follows me. We sit down across from one another on the new leather couches.

"Not what you were expecting?" he asks, crossing one leg over the other.

"I thought it would be more hands on, but they have me stuck behind a screen all day."

"Because that's your skillset." He tips the bottle into his mouth. "And that's what they recruited you for."

I shrug, not really wanting to get into it with him.

My entire family was shocked speechless when I told them I'd agreed to join the FBI. I guess it's ironic. I pulled tons of illegal shit in the past. Was mixed up in lots of shady stuff before I copped on to myself. So, it's funny that I'm now on the other side of the law. I understand why it was surprising. But they don't know the real reason why I joined—they don't know I'm doing this for Cheryl.

"Mom did a good job with the place." Kade casts an appreciative glance around the stylishly decorated room.

"And Mrs. McConaughey," I add, because Mom and Brad's mom set up the interior design business together. I bought this penthouse before it was built, seeing only the blueprints, and hired them to furnish and decorate the place while I was training at Quantico.

Brad is my younger brother Kyler's best friend and practically a surrogate Kennedy. He's grown up with our family, and my parents took him in when shit hit the fan and his family had to leave the country without him. He's had his fair share of crap to deal with in the last couple of years, but things have turned a corner for him now his family is back on American soil and he's with Rachel. They've been good for one another, and I'm glad to see both my friends in a happy place. God knows, Rachel is well overdue it too.

"I hope their new business venture works out," I say, because I know how much they've both put into it.

"I'm sure it'll be a success with Mom at the helm. If she could run a successful multi-billion-dollar fashion empire, she can run a boutique interior design business."

"True."

We both sip from our beers. "How's college?" I ask. "And plans for your new business?" Kade and Eva are in the process of setting up an online golf business.

"Senior year is tough. You're lucky you had enough credits to graduate early. I'd kill to be finished now."

I *am* lucky I had enough credits, because if I didn't, I would have walked away from Harvard without my degree, which would've sucked. The FBI pulled some strings while I was at Quantico, and Harvard allowed me to graduate early. Now, I've got a nice framed certificate on my wall and a new potential career path.

"I just want to focus on the business," Kade continues. "Eva is making great progress, and I really want to be doing it alongside her."

"You only have a few more months until you graduate. It'll pass before you know it."

He nods, and I scrub a hand along the back of my neck as awkward silence trickles between us. While it's great we're back on speaking terms, I hate the formality of our conversations these days.

Things are still a little strained between Kade and me.

We had a falling out during a family vacation to Ireland the summer before last, and we didn't really speak for the best part of a year. But since he got together with Eva, and in the aftermath of the shooting, we resolved our issues, and I got my brother back, but it hasn't been quite the same, and I wonder if we'll ever truly reconnect.

Perhaps it's just he's moved on with his life. He's married and thinking about starting a family, and I don't even have a steady girlfriend. Our lives are moving in different directions so maybe losing the closeness we once shared is inevitable.

"What was so urgent I had to drop by?" he asks after a few beats.

"My boss wants Eva to come in. I thought it best to ask you first because I know how much Eva hates talking about her prior life."

He puts his beer down on the coffee table, sitting up straighter and resting his elbows on his knees. "Why do they want to speak to Eva now? She already gave a statement after the shooting."

My brother and his wife have a complicated history. Eva was Kaden's professor for a while, and they had a short-lived affair behind her gangster husband's back. Eva broke things off to protect Kade, not that he knew that at the time. They spent years pining for one another before eventually caving to their feelings last year. In November, Kaden and Eva attempted to flee the country together. He was going to sacrifice everything for her because they both knew the monster she'd been forced into marrying would never stop looking for them. But my brother has loved that woman from the moment he met her, and he was prepared for a life on the run if it meant being with her. Only her husband found out about their plans and kidnapped and tortured both of them.

I'd been worried when I discovered Kade had taken up with Eva again, so I'd planted some GPS trackers in his shoes. If I hadn't done that, I wouldn't have been able to locate their whereabouts and tip off the FBI. They arrived just in time. Gunfire was traded on both sides, and my brother was shot, but thankfully, it wasn't serious, and he made a full recovery. So did Eva. But I know she's still haunted by the events of that day and the abuse she suffered at her first husband's hands. I doubt Kaden wants her to relive any of it, but like my boss said, they'll just take her in for questioning whether she likes it or not. At least this way, Kade can prepare her for it.

"They are looking for more general information this time," I explain. "Things are escalating on the streets, and we've seen a rise in gun violence and the supply of drugs and women to the city. The SSA wants to cover all angles, and he wants to see what Eva may know that could help."

"I'm not sure she'll be of much help. She deliberately stayed away from Garcia's business."

"I think he thinks she may know stuff unwittingly that could help."

Kade drags a hand through his hair. "I hate that we can't leave the past in the past." He shakes his head. "We still have bodyguards because I'm terrified of retaliation. That bastard may be dead, but that doesn't mean the threat is."

"I'm still monitoring both of you and keeping an eye out for anything suspicious. I'm not about to allow anything to happen to either one of you again."

Kade looks up at me, and I'm surprised to see tears in his eyes. "I didn't know you were doing that."

I shrug, downplaying it, tipping the last remnants of beer into my mouth. "I'm still watching out for everyone in the family. I've set up one of the bedrooms as a special surveillance room. Got a bunch of new equipment. Have it set up to automatically search the net and underground chat rooms for any mention of our family and extended family."

"Can I see?" he asks, standing.

"Sure." I put my empty bottle down and lead him out to the bedrooms, bypassing my master suite and the guest bedroom and stepping into the last room. It's the smallest of the three bedrooms but still a sizable space and more than fit for its purpose. Fitted desk units rim the perimeter of the room on all sides, and wall-mounted cupboards and storage space lies overhead. The rest of the room houses all my new tech.

"Fucking hell, Kev." Kade stares at the multitude of screens and computers, all displaying different feeds and images. "This looks like some hardcore shit. And not cheap either."

"It is, and it wasn't." Not that money is any issue. I came into my trust fund when I turned twenty-one last year, and I've more money than I know what to do with, so even though this equipment cost a huge chunk of change, it's only a drop in the ocean.

Kade presses his face up closer to one of the screens. "Is that Cheryl Keeland?"

Fuck. *What was I thinking bringing him in here?*

He leans in so close his nose is touching the screen. I slump into a chair, preparing myself for the impending interrogation. No point lying. "It *is* Cheryl."

He turns to face me, folding his arms and propping his butt on the side of the desk. "What's going on, Kev? And no bullshitting me."

I rub a tense spot between my brows. "Cheryl is the reason I took the FBI job."

"Go on," my eldest brother prompts.

"She's engaged to a guy who was working with Garcia although I'm guessing she's no clue what her fiancé really does for a living."

He plops down in the seat beside me. "Shit. That's not good. I wonder if Eva knows him?"

I sit up straighter in my chair, cursing myself for not thinking to ask her before now. "His name's Daniel Stanten, and he was apparently being groomed to take over from Garcia. I'm betting Eva's at least heard of him."

"Okay. I'll ask her about him and Cheryl. And go ahead and set the meeting up with your boss."

"Don't you want to talk to Eva first?"

He shakes his head. "No need. I know my wife. She hates what that bastard was involved in, and if she has even a tiny piece of information that might help the FBI, she'll want to share it."

Kade turns his attention back to the screen, watching the images of Cheryl coming out of the photography studio where she works. I set up software recognition searches for her online, and I was also able to hack into a few local camera feeds, one near MassArt and one outside the studio, and it now automatically transmits and records any images featuring Cheryl.

Yep, I've got Stalker 101 down to a fine art form.

"I'm guessing your boss doesn't know about this little side operation?" Kade pins me with a serious look.

Hell, no. SSA Clement would bust my balls if he knew about this setup. He has specifically told me to stay away from Cheryl, so he can't find out I'm working my own game plan on the side. "Nope, and I'd prefer it stayed that way, so don't mention this to anyone. Not even Eva."

"I don't keep secrets from my wife, Kev." He sighs deeply. "But I'll do it on this occasion. For Cheryl." He eyeballs me with a grim expression. "I want in. Whatever you're planning, I want to help."

Kade always liked Cheryl, and he looked out for her back in high school when she was getting bullied over her dyslexia. Ultimately, it's what led to us dating back in ninth grade, but that's a story for another day.

"I don't want to drag you into this shit. Getting mixed up with Garcia almost cost you your life. And it's worse now because a notorious New York criminal mastermind is trying to encroach on Garcia's old turf, and Garcia's old rival is embroiled in a war with this New York crowd and remnants of Garcia's organization still loyal to him who are fighting to hold onto their patch. It's messy out there, and it's only going to get uglier. I don't want you or Eva anywhere near that."

He slaps me on the shoulder, and I silently curse him. "Eva won't be anywhere near it, I can promise you that." He scrutinizes my face. "What are your intentions toward Cheryl?"

"I need to open her eyes to that asshole she's engaged to."

"And that's it?" Kade quirks a brow, and I shrug. I'm not one for openly discussing my feelings. "Come on, Kev. Just fucking admit it. You never got over losing Cheryl, and now you've been given a second chance."

"You've forgotten the part where she hates me."

"That was then. She's older now, and the past is in the past."

"I can't get my hopes up," I quietly admit.

Kade nods. "I understand that more than you realize, but what you two had was too special to let an opportunity like this slip through your fingers. And you don't have to say it, Kev. I see it written all over your face. If you love her as much as I think you do, then you need to fight like crazy to win her back. There's no room for complacency or doubts or second-guessing."

"I'm not you, Kade. I don't know how to do that."

"Sure, you do." He grips my shoulders. "Out of all of us, you are the most loyal and the most selfless when it comes to those you love. True, you're the least vocal, but that doesn't mean you don't know how to love or how to win back your girl. Just open your heart and tell her everything."

"What if she doesn't want to hear it?"

"Then you make her listen."

My lips curve up at the corners. "I can't believe we're having this conversation." His grin matches mine. "You've changed."

23

"Not really," he says, shrugging. "I'm just a different version of myself now that I've found my person. And you will be too if Cheryl is that for you."

"She is, Kade. I've never been able to forget her." I'm quiet for a minute before admitting the truth. "For a long while after she left, I kept tabs on her."

He rolls his eyes. "Why doesn't that surprise me?"

"It's always been easier to watch over someone remotely than show how I feel."

"Don't beat yourself up, man, because what you do counts just as much. You look out for those you love. You protect those you love. And everyone knows it."

Chapter 4

Cheryl

"Maybe I'll ask Hayley to come stay while you're gone," I muse as I lounge on the humongous bed in our new bedroom. We moved in a week ago, but I'm still trying to get used to the sheer size of the house, and I'm a little freaked out at the prospect of staying here for the next four days all by myself. I love how private the property is, but it stretches for miles in all directions, and while I enjoy walking in the woods that border our land, it's a little spooky at night.

Dan groans. "Not Hayley, babe. You know how I feel about her."

Dan isn't Hayley's biggest fan. He thinks she's trailer trash and taking advantage of me. I usually defend her, but she's really gotten on my nerves this past week. It's clear she's been sulking over the house. I had thought this weekend might be an opportunity to patch things up, but maybe Dan is right.

"Why don't you ask that nice girl you work with at the studio? Belinda, right?" he suggests, closing his overnight bag and placing it on the floor.

"I could ask Lin." I bob my head, smiling. "She just broke up with her girlfriend so she's probably at a loose end."

"Problem solved," he says, pulling me up off the bed and into his arms. He glances briefly at the expensive TAG Heuer watch on his wrist. "I have a half hour before I need to leave." He grabs my ass, pulling me flush against his hard-on. "Want to demonstrate how much you'll miss me?" He leans in, nipping my earlobe. "Because I'm definitely going to miss you."

I stroke his hard length through his pants. "Of course, I'll miss you. You know I always do."

"Then prove it, sexy." He starts unbuckling his belt while pushing me to my knees with his free hand. "Work your magic, baby."

"Holy shit, Cher, this house is amazing," Lin says, later that night, as she glides around the living room with her eyes out on stalks. She pauses in front of the window, glancing out over the magnificent grounds. "We could take some incredible shots here."

"I've already snapped a few," I admit, pulling my Nikon D850 out of my bag. "Here, look." I thrust the camera at her and she scrolls through some of the exterior shots I took earlier today. "We could explore a bit more tomorrow morning before work."

My mind automatically wanders to tomorrow's lunch date. I nearly fell off my chair when Eva Garcia reached out to me this week, asking if we could catch up over lunch. I'd only met her a few times, in the past, but I'd instantly warmed to her. She's career-orientated, like me, and she was extremely welcoming when I was feeling completely out of my depth at some of Dan's business events. I was shocked to discover her husband—the man my fiancé looked up to—was involved in tons of illegal activities in the Boston area. Dan was flabbergasted to learn that the man who invested in his legal practice was using legitimate business enterprises to hide such heinous crimes.

According to the news reports I saw, Jeremy Garcia was involved in bringing drugs and guns into Massachusetts, and he was also heavily involved in sex trafficking. I almost threw up at the revelation.

This was a man who had welcomed me graciously into his home.

Who spoke so highly of Dan.

Although, if I'm being honest, there was always something creepy about him that was off-putting. The media said Eva was unaware of her husband's activities, and I believe it because Eva doesn't strike me as the type of woman who would ever condone such deplorable things, but they also claimed she was forced into marrying him so maybe she was aware but had no way out.

Anyway, I'm curious as to why she wants to meet me, and I'm looking forward to seeing her.

Lin and I order takeout, and after eating, we move to the home cinema with a bucket of popcorn and a bottle of wine.

"Damn, girl, your man certainly knows how to woo his woman," she says, shaking her head as she takes in the massive screen and twelve-seater home theater.

"He thought of everything," I deadpan, settling into a seat as I pull up the menu on the screen.

"I agree with you though," Lin adds, kicking off her shoes and curling up on the seat beside me. "He should have consulted with you. Allowed you to have a say in your own home. But you can't really fault him for his reasoning. You lead a hectic life, and you would've been stressed trying to fit in a project of this magnitude."

"True, but it still would've been nice to be asked. Anyway," I say, scrolling through our options. "There's no point dwelling on it. It's done, and the house is beautiful, and we're very fortunate."

"I love that about you," my friend says, tucking her slender jean-clad legs underneath her.

"What?" I toss some popcorn in my mouth.

"You always see the positive in everything. You don't let negative shit drag you down. Unlike me." She sighs, pulling her long dark hair back into a ponytail. "All I've done since Summer and I broke up is over analyze every little detail and berate myself for not handling the situation differently."

"Hang on here a sec." I put my glass down in the little cupholder attached to my chair. "Why are you beating yourself up over *her* betrayal? *You* didn't do anything wrong."

"We both know that's not true, Cher." Her brow furrows. "I'm married to my job, and I neglected my girlfriend. I drove her into another woman's arms."

"That's the biggest load of bullshit I've ever heard." I shake my head. "Summer should've talked to you, told you how she was feeling. My God, you've been together six years. You deserved at least that much. How could you fix something if you didn't know it was a problem? And if she wasn't into the relationship anymore, she could've ended it before sleeping with someone else. There is never any excuse acceptable for cheating. None."

"Wow." Lin sits up straighter. "Who cheated on you?"

"Who *hasn't* cheated on me is an easier question to answer," I joke, even though it's not funny, but I don't want to think about the disastrous decisions I've made with my love life. Old fears are never far from the surface, and I don't like where my mind goes sometimes. The last thing I want to be thinking about, at a time when my fiancé is away, is *that*.

"Well, they're all fucking idiots," she loyally proclaims, instantly backing down. And that's one of the things I love about Lin. She knows when to push it and when to leave it.

She joined the studio where I work seven months before me. She's a few years older, and she graduated MassArt three years ago. Like me, she came to the attention of our boss when she won an award last year for one of her photos. Sara extended an offer of employment, and Lin jumped at the chance, exactly like me. When Sara Lewis, renowned award-winning celebrity photographer, offers you a job, you don't refuse it.

"And Summer's an idiot too. I'm betting she'll come crawling back."

"I hope she doesn't," Lin says, her tone more somber now. "Because I'm not sure I'm strong enough to say no, and I want to have more respect for myself than that."

I empathize because I've been in her shoes, and it's not easy, but I'm proud of myself for holding firm to my principles even though it ripped my heart to shreds and I've never truly recovered.

But I force those thoughts aside, settling in to watch the movie before my mind wanders to forbidden territory I dare not let myself think about.

"What's that place?" Lin asks early the following morning when we're exploring the woods that surround my house.

I crane my head in the direction she's pointing in, my eyes popping wide when I spot the focus of her attention. "I've no clue." I sling my camera around my neck and walk purposely toward the large barn. "Let's take a look." We wade through muddy, leaf-strewn brush, pushing stray branches out of our path as we approach the large barn. It looks newly painted even if the area around it is densely overgrown.

I trudge up to the doors, curling my hands around the heavy padlock securing the structure. "That's weird." I frown as I trawl through my memory for any recollection of Dan mentioning this place, but I'm pretty sure he didn't breathe a word.

Lin has wandered around the back of the barn, so I trail after her wondering if there's another way in. When I round the corner, Lin has her ear pressed to the side of the barn. "C'mere." She gestures with her hand. "Do you hear that?"

I press my ear to the wall and listen. A faint rattling sound tickles my eardrums, and a shudder works its way up my spine. "Yeah. I hear it." I pull my cell out of my back pocket. "I'm going to message Dan." I tap out a quick text, and then we listen for another few minutes, but the sound is gone. We walk the full way around the structure, wading through the long grass, but there's no other visible entry or exit point.

I check my cell again, but Dan hasn't replied. Not that I was expecting him to. He's notoriously non-communicative when he's away on business. At first, that fed my paranoia, and I spent countless nights tossing and turning, wondering what he was doing and with whom. But I spoke to him, and he allayed my fears, so I try not to dwell on it even if my brain is automatically wired to think the worst.

He explained how he lines up back-to-back client meetings, so I usually don't disturb him while he's gone. But something about this place gives me the heebie-jeebies, and it warrants contact.

"We'd better head back to the house, or we won't be ready for work in time," I say. Saturday is our busiest day in the studio, and it's all hands on deck.

"Yeah. I need another shower after trekking through this jungle," Lin jokes, grimacing as she surveys her mud-splattered jeans.

"I must look for a gardener or someone to come clear out the more overgrown parts of the woods," I muse as we start walking back in the direction of the house.

"I'm sure you could hire a couple of teenagers locally who would be more than happy to earn some extra pocket money," she suggests.

"That's a good idea. I might put a notice up in the local store."

After we shower, change, and grab a quick breakfast, we set off for work in my Audi.

The schedule is crazy today with every spare minute of studio time booked out, so I'm lucky to make it to lunch, but I hate canceling on people at the last minute, and I'm determined to find out why Eva has made contact with me.

She's already seated when I arrive at the Italian restaurant, and she stands, waving her hands in the air to capture my attention. I'm smiling as I walk toward her. She steps out of the table, pulling me into a hug. "Cheryl. It's so good to see you."

"Likewise." I unwrap my scarf and remove my jacket, hanging them on the back of a chair before sliding into the seat alongside Eva. "I was pleasantly surprised to hear from you. I've wondered how you are."

"I'm sorry it's taken me this long to reach out to you. You've been on my mind," she says, tossing her gorgeous, long, thick, dark hair over her shoulders.

"I have?"

"Yes." She looks over my shoulder. "Let's get our order in, and then we can chat."

I quickly peruse the menu and order a chicken salad with a side of garlic bread. Eva orders a bowl of ravioli and a bottle of Pellegrino for us to share. The large diamond on her ring finger sparkles, throwing dazzling streams of light in my direction. "Wow, that is some ring, but Kaden always had amazing taste."

"I wasn't sure if you'd heard I remarried," she says, sliding our glasses to the waitress so she can fill them.

"It was splashed all over the news, and Dan told me." Apparently, her and Kaden had been having an illicit affair, but after I learned the truth about Jeremy Garcia, I couldn't fault Eva for seeking happiness where she could. And I know Kaden. He's a great guy, and I've a lot of love for him.

Her smile falters at the mention of my fiancé, and I frown a little, but she quickly recovers. "Kade says hi, by the way."

"Tell him I said hello too. And congratulations. To both of you."

"Thanks, Cheryl. I never thought I'd get to be with him, and I never take it for granted. He's given me the life I've always dreamed of, and I have to pinch myself most days to believe it's real."

"I'm really happy for you." I take a small sip of my water and wonder if I should say anything. "I read about Jeremy, and I was shocked. I'm sorry you went through that, and I'm glad both you and Kaden were okay."

When I first heard the report on the radio, my initial instinct had been to go to the hospital to check if they were both okay, but I know how close-knit the Kennedys are, and I knew they would all be there. I just couldn't face seeing them.

Seeing *him*.

I couldn't trust myself not to fall apart, which is ridiculous, because after all this time, and after what he did, I shouldn't feel anything for him. But it's hard, because when I pictured my future life as a teenager, Keven Kennedy was always a fixture in it. And I adored his family and the way they welcomed me with open arms. They made me feel accepted at a time when I felt so lost and like an outsider.

When I broke things off with Keven, I didn't just lose my boyfriend. I lost the future I'd had all mapped out and a family I'd grown to love as much as my own.

"I wanted to warn you," she says in a gentle tone. "I hated the thought of you getting mixed up in that."

The memory of the night Dan and I had dinner at her house returns to me, clear as day, and I instantly recall the conversation we had when we were alone. "You did try to warn me." I fix my eyes on hers. "That's why you told me to contact ... Keven."

She nods. "I couldn't risk saying anything. Jeremy had men and cameras all over the house, but I couldn't not try either. I didn't want you to become trapped like I was."

We stop talking for a couple minutes while the waitress places our food in front of us. "I appreciate that you did that for me, and I'm very grateful. Dan was utterly horrified when he found out what Jeremy was really up to." A shiver creeps up my spine. "It makes me sick to think he could've gotten ensnared in that world, but that's what would've happened if Jeremy hadn't died."

At first, when I heard the news, I was plagued with doubts. Jeremy and Dan were so close, and I wondered how much Dan was aware of. It's not that I wanted to believe that of my fiancé, and I didn't want to outrightly accuse him, but I needed to know he wasn't mixed up in criminal activity.

I shouldn't have doubted Dan though.

The second he walked through the door that night he collapsed against me, sobbing and blaming himself for not realizing his mentor was hiding his true persona and masking his operation behind legitimate businesses. He felt like a fool for not realizing, and he was utterly distraught and so obviously shocked that it helped put my concerns to bed.

Eva looks away, quietly eating. Wondering where the sudden tense atmosphere has come from, I pick at my salad. I'm sure Eva doesn't like to think about that time, let alone talk about it, and it's obviously upset her, so I change the subject. "How are things at Casa Kennedy? I'm guessing they've all welcomed you warmly."

She shoots me a grateful smile, chewing slowly and taking a sip of her drink before replying. "They most certainly have. I was worried because they didn't know anything about me. Kade had to keep it a secret from his family, and then I worried because I was older, and I was his professor at one time, but they weren't judgmental at all. This is the first time I've had a proper family, and I really like it."

"They're a tight bunch and it's good to have them in your corner." I want to ask her to pass on my good wishes, but I don't want word getting through to Keven that I'm back in Boston. Although, I'm probably being egotistical. I'm sure he's moved on and that the Kennedys have long since forgotten me.

I stab a piece of chicken with my fork, abnormally frustrated at my thoughts. If I'm being honest with myself, since I've returned to the area, Kev's been on my mind a lot, and I hate it. It feels like I'm disrespecting

Dan any time I think of my childhood sweetheart. I shouldn't still be thinking of him. I hate that I am, but I seem powerless to stop it.

"Can I ask you something personal?" Eva says, bringing me back into the moment.

"Okay," I say, a little hesitantly. I put my fork down and give her my undivided attention.

"Why didn't you contact Keven?"

A muscle clenches in my jaw, and tension cords my shoulders into knots. "He's a part of my past I'd prefer to leave in the past." I take a quick drink, watching warring emotions play across her face. "Besides, it wouldn't have been fair of me to reach out to an ex when I'm engaged to Dan. It'd feel too much like a betrayal, and I won't do that to him."

Eva opens and closes her mouth in quick succession. She spears another ravioli, popping it in her mouth, looking contemplative as she chews. I force a piece of chicken into my mouth, but it tastes like sandpaper.

"Screw it." She tosses her napkin on the table, shoving her plate aside. Then she moves in closer to me, lowering her voice. "He can be mad at me. I don't care. I can't sit here and say nothing."

"Who, Kaden?" I surmise, setting my own lunch aside.

She stiffens, jerking her head up at the same time the scent of his cologne invades my airspace, throwing me back in time. My hand shakes as I clutch onto the edge of the table. My chest tightens, and blood pounds in my ears.

No way.

This *cannot* be happening.

I refuse to look behind me.

I'm not ready to see him.

"You set me up." I eyeball Eva, challenging her to disagree.

"It's not what you think," she pleads.

"Cheryl." His deep voice causes goose bumps to sprout all over my arms, and tears prick my eyes.

"Go away," I toss over my shoulder. "I don't want to see you or speak to you." I keep my eyes locked on the table. If I look at him, I'm not sure how I'll react, and I refuse to do this in a public place.

"Cheryl, please. Just hear me out," Keven beseeches, moving closer. I know because his body heat knocks into me, rendering my insides to mush. No other man has ever held power over my body like Keven Kennedy. Unhelpful memories surge to the forefront of my mind. I squeeze my eyes shut to ward off the painful reminiscing, but invisible hands ghost over my body, alerting my libido to his presence.

Snatching my bag, scarf, and jacket, I jump up out of my seat, knocking into Keven in my haste to get away. Firm hands land on my waist, and terror combines with anxiety and longing as I feel his touch all the way to the tips of my toes.

"Leave me alone," I shriek, and I'm sure I'm drawing attention. I wouldn't know because my eyes are glued to the ground as I desperately try to avoid catching even a glimpse of him.

"Cheryl." His tone is more determined this time, and he tilts my face up with his finger, forcing my gaze to meet his.

And it's every bit as painful as I thought it would be.

Looking into his pale blue eyes is like traveling back in time. To a moment when he was my everything and I believed I was that to him too.

His hair is a little longer than it was back in high school, and he's sporting a thick layer of stubble on his chin and cheeks.

God, he's even hotter now—how is that fair?

His lips part slightly, and my eyes fixate on his mouth as I remember how amazing it felt to be kissed by him. Keven's kisses had a way of touching every single part of my body. We used to spend hours feverishly making out, both of us addicted to the high. Butterflies scatter in my chest, competing with the dull ache in my heart.

We were so unbelievably good together, and I was crazy about him. I completely adored him, and he was my equal in every imaginable way.

Until the start of senior year when everything changed.

I still don't know why, or how it happened, and it's haunted me for years. Yet I never sought him out. Rejected all his attempts to reach out to me. Because what's done is done, and there can be no going back.

Keven showing up here will achieve nothing except send me into a new world of pain.

His eyes penetrate mine as if he wishes he could uncover all my deep, dark secrets. My skin is hot where his large palms hold me at the waist, and my body trembles underneath his touch. His face is awash with feeling, and I'm losing control of my own emotions, but I won't give him the satisfaction of knowing how much he still means to me.

"My God, Cheryl." His voice cracks, and I'm shocked to see tears welling in his eyes. "It's so good to see you."

Out of the corner of my eye, I spy someone taking a pic with their cell, and that's my cue to shut this down. The Kennedys are infamous in Massachusetts, and well-known nationally; therefore, it's no surprise someone's recognized him. The absolute last thing I need is to be papped with my ex and have Dan call me out on it. I snap out of the reminiscent haze I've been wallowing in, piercing him with a venomous look. "Get your hands off me, Keven, or I'll scream so loud every single person in this room will turn in our direction."

He removes his hands so fast I almost laugh. As much as I loved the Kennedys, they were very precious about their reputation. Kennedy Apparel was a big deal back then, and the whole family was celebrities around Boston. It was one part of being with Keven I disliked. He wasn't fond of the attention either, and it looks like some things haven't changed as I watch him pull up the hood on his hoodie, sheltering his face from prying eyes.

"Can we go somewhere private to talk?" he asks, and his simple request rubs me the wrong way.

"I'm not going anywhere with you. I don't know what you hoped to achieve here today, but I have nothing new to say to you. In case you didn't get the memo last time, I despise you," I lie, summoning my darkest look as I glare at him. "Stay away from me. I mean it."

I glance over my shoulder at Eva, upset that she'd do this to me. "I thought you were my friend."

"I *am* your friend, Cheryl, and I'm begging you to hear Keven out."

"No. I don't owe you or him anything, and I'd appreciate it if you'd lose my number, Eva. Both of you, just leave me the hell alone."

Before either of them can say another word, I race out of the restaurant, desperately fighting the tears that beg to run free.

Chapter 5

Keven

"Fuck." I watch Cheryl's retreating form with a heavy heart.

"I knew this was a bad idea," Eva says, dropping some bills on the table and grabbing her coat. "You should've let me do this my way."

"Not now, Eva. I need to go after her. Wait in the car with Rick. I'll be back."

I don't stick around for her answer, racing out the door after my ex. "Cheryl, wait!" I shout, sprinting down the road after her. She hasn't gotten far in her heels, and I catch up to her in no time, planting myself in front of her so she can't escape. "Cheryl, please. Just stop for a minute."

She has no choice as I'm blocking her path. "Why are you doing this, Kev?" She pins me with those sad, beautiful, big blue eyes of hers, and I melt. Teenage Cheryl was my every wet dream, but this grown-up version is the stuff of fantasies.

She is absolutely stunning.

Even more beautiful than I remember.

The epitome of a classic, natural beauty.

In school, her hair was straight, landing just below the nape of her neck. It's much longer now, falling in soft waves down her back. Her plump lips look every bit as kissable as they were back in high school, and I'd trade everything I have just to taste her on my lips once again. Her flawless skin is devoid of makeup, which was something I always liked. Although I can't risk a full body scan—not with the daggers she's currently sending me—I got a good look at her before I made my presence known in the restaurant. It's clear she's filled out in all the right places. She's still slender but curvy, and her body is just how a woman's body should be.

"We have unresolved business," I tell her, purposely keeping my eyes locked on her face.

"No, we don't," she argues, her lips turning all pouty, and it does nothing to quell the craving to kiss her.

I lean in closer, putting my face right up in hers. "Yes, we do. You wouldn't even let me explain, and then you were just gone!"

"There wasn't anything to explain," she grits out, and I hate the hurt glimmering at the back of her eyes. "I had a front row seat."

"I'm so fucking sorry about that, and if I could rewind time, I'd do everything differently, but there is stuff you don't know. Stuff I couldn't tell you back then. I wanted to, believe me, I did, but I didn't know how."

"What does it matter now, Kev?" She shrugs, and her hair falls over one shoulder, exposing the delicate column of her neck. "It's in the past. *We're* in the past. I've moved on."

"I heard." A muscle clenches in my jaw like it does every time I think about that lowlife she's engaged to. As much as I want to tell her to stay away from him, I've got to play my cards right. If I try to warn her now, she'll only dismiss it as jealousy, and I can't take the risk that she might tell Stanten. If I do anything to fuck up the FBI investigation, I'll find myself out of a job and behind bars. So, my best option is trying to worm my way back into her life.

Even if it's just as friends.

I need Cheryl to trust me again before I spill the beans on her darling fiancé.

I know I've my work cut out for me, but I'm determined to win her over.

"Then what is this about? No good can come from dredging up the past." She grips onto the strap of her bag, shuffling awkwardly on her feet. She's doing everything in her power not to look at me, and that fact alone gives me hope. If I meant absolutely nothing to her anymore, she'd have no trouble looking me in the eye.

"I need to tell you, Cheryl. You need to know the full story. And who knows? Maybe we could become friends again. We were such good friends before we became anything else."

She jerks her head up, and I hate the anguish etched across her face. "I'm happy and letting you back into my life will only make me miserable."

Her words cut through me like a knife. "Tell me how you really feel," I deadpan.

She sighs softly. "What do you expect, Kev? You shattered me. You broke my heart and destroyed my faith in men. I'm finally in a good place in my life, and you show up expecting me to hear you out? You're a part of my past, and you don't belong in my present or future. I'm sorry if that's blunt, but that's the way it is. Whatever you think you're doing here, just forget it."

She moves to step around me, and I reach out, gently taking her arm. "I only want to talk, Cheryl. You may have moved on, but I can't."

I'm not playing fair right now. Cheryl has the purest heart, and she never denies anyone in need. I don't want to fight dirty, but I can't let her walk away from me either. "I can't leave the past in the past until I've told you what I should've told you back then. I know you don't owe me anything, but all I'm asking for is one hour of your time. Please. If I ever meant anything to you, please just meet with me."

Pain lances across her face, and I hate that I'm manipulating her. But it's for her own good. She might not know she needs me, but I damn well do, and I'm not going to stand idly by and watch her make the biggest mistake of her life.

"One meeting. One hour. And then you'll leave me alone?" Her voice shakes a little, and I know I've gotten to her. I nod, reluctantly letting go of her arm when her eyes flit to my hand. "Okay."

Air whooshes out of my mouth in grateful relief. "Take this and text me. We can make arrangements from there." Her fingers brush against mine as she takes my fake business card, sending fiery tingles zipping up and down my arm. She jerks her hand away as if electrocuted, and I'm pretty sure she felt it too.

We still share an intense connection whether she wants to admit it or not.

It's not like we ever fell out of love or lust with one another.

My stupidity drove a stake through the heart of our relationship, but the feelings were all still there.

"I've got to get back to work," she says, looking flustered. "I'll text you."

"Let me walk you," I offer, moving into step beside her.

"No!" Her tone is firm. "Just drop it, Kev." Her chin tips up defiantly. "If *I* ever meant anything to *you*, you'll do as I wish."

Nodding, I shove my hands in the pockets of my jeans. She casts one last lingering glance my way before joining the crowds heading in the opposite direction. I watch her until I can't see her anymore, and then I turn around and head back to Eva.

I slide into the backseat of Kaden's Ford Expedition beside my sister-in-law. Rick—Eva's bodyguard—is behind the wheel, waiting on instruction. "Can you swing by Harvard, please, Rick," Eva says. "Kade is waiting for us."

I slam my head back against the headrest, exhaling heavily.

"What happened?" Eva asks, lightly touching my arm.

"She still hates me."

"I very much doubt that." Eva smooths the wrinkles out of her skirt. "She couldn't even look at you in the restaurant because she's terrified of how it'll make her feel."

"Or she just can't stand the sight of my face."

"I know you're not as handsome as Kade, but most girls wouldn't kick you out of bed," she teases, trying to lighten the atmosphere in the car.

Rick has skillfully maneuvered his way into the busy Saturday traffic.

"I really hurt her, Eva." I turn and face my brother's wife. "And I still see the hurt on her face. I should have listened to you. I should have let you try and talk to her first. I just feel so helpless. If anything happens to her ..." I twist my head around to the window before she sees the emotion building behind my eyes.

"Nothing will happen to her because you won't let it." She squeezes my hand. "You excel at protecting those you love, and you won't fail her."

I face her again. "What if I can't get through to her? What if she really does love him?"

"Maybe she does, but I don't think so. She told me it was a whirlwind romance and fast engagement. She hasn't been with him long enough to really know him, and he won't be able to hide his true self from her forever. She won't stay with him once she finds out."

"How can you be so sure?"

"Because she's smart and sweet and too damn good for that asshole. She'll see the light." Her mouth kicks up at the corners. "Especially if you give her a helping hand. Don't let her tell you no for an answer."

"Is that how my brother did it?" I arch a brow.

"That was part of it." Her smile is nostalgic. "Mostly it was because we loved each other too much to stay apart, but Kade *was* relentless in his determination to win me back, and though I was scared to let him into my heart again, I couldn't resist long-term. Prove yourself to Cheryl, Keven, and don't ever give up. Not until you've exhausted every possible way of showing her how much you care."

After picking Kade up from Harvard, Rick deposits us at the entrance to my workplace, and the three of us step inside. I'm like a hobo in my jeans and gray Henley next to my brother in his custom-fitted suit and Eva in her tailor-made skirt and blouse. We pass through security and walk in the direction of the elevator. None of us speaks as the elevator soars toward the tenth floor.

I subtly watch my brother, smiling to myself as I watch him with his wife. He has his arm wrapped protectively around Eva's waist, and he's pressing little kisses into her hair. It's a side of him I'd never seen before, but it suits him. They adore one another, and I'm glad they got their HEA.

My boss is waiting in the hallway when we step out of the elevator. "Mr. and Mrs. Kennedy." He walks toward them, extending his hand. "It's good to see you both looking so well. Thank you for coming in today."

"I want to help in whatever way I can," Eva says, shaking his hand.

"We really appreciate that." He eyeballs me. "Thank you for setting this up."

I nod. It's not like I could refuse. I'm still the newbie around here, and everyone knows it.

"Before we begin," Kade says, leveling a solemn look at my boss. "I wanted to ask you something."

"Okay." The SSA straightens his shoulders.

"What is the risk to Eva of retaliation by associates of her former husband?"

"Kade." Eva's voice is soft as she plants her hand on his arm.

"It's fine, Mrs. Kennedy," the SSA assures her. "And I can't fault your husband for his concern." He eyeballs Kaden. "Nothing we have gleaned so far indicates there is any threat to your wife's life. The families are too busy battling for control of the streets to concern themselves with Garcia's ex. I believe the threat is minimal and that you have nothing to fear."

Kade nods, and I can almost see the stress lifting off his shoulders. "Thank you."

"You're welcome. Now, if you'll follow me." His smile is tight as he leads us to the large conference room at the end of the hall. The rest of my team is already seated, and I slide into the vacant chair beside Agent Cunningham. She's the friendliest on the team. Unlike that dickhead sitting on the other side of her. Agent Wentward doesn't even acknowledge me, getting up and shaking hands with Eva and Kaden like he deserves special treatment just because he helped them the day of the warehouse shooting. I swear, every new encounter with that douche only heightens my intense dislike of him.

SSA Clement makes the necessary introductions, and then we get down to business. Kade sits protectively by Eva's side, ready to jump in if necessary.

Agent Wentward asks Eva a ton of probing questions before Agent Mead flips on the screen, pulling up the photo slideshow I compiled before I left the office last night. He goes slowly through the photos of members of the crime families and known associates of Garcia's, asking her if she recognizes anyone.

"Stop there," Eva says, pointing at one particular photo, her face twisting sourly. "I know him."

"That's ah …" Agent Wentward rifles through his files, but I don't need to look at the paperwork to identify the douche on the screen.

"That's Jesse Roberts," I confirm.

"I wondered what'd happened to my former colleague," Eva says. "I guess now I know."

"He's recently started working with Daniel Stanten in his bogus legal practice," I say.

Agent Wentward glowers at me, but screw him. It's not my fault he hasn't done his homework properly. I've spent the past week digging into Cheryl's fiancé's background, and I know plenty about that asshole by now.

"Who is he to Daniel Stanten?" The SSA directs his question at me, but it's Eva who answers.

"They're friends. They went to college together, and Jesse was instrumental in the warehouse shooting. He used Kade's ex to feed information to my former husband, knowing what he would to do me. It was retaliation for all the times I'd rejected his advances. He's a horrible human being and a pathetic excuse of a man with no moral compass whatsoever. It doesn't surprise me in the least that he's taken this route."

"And what about Daniel Stanten?" the SSA finally asks Eva. "What do you know about him?"

"Not a lot," Eva truthfully replies. "I only met him a handful of times, but I never trusted him. Jeremy almost idolized him. I think he reminded him of himself at that age. It's only after everything went down that I realized Daniel was obviously manipulating Jeremy, and I've wondered why."

"I think I know why." I sit up straighter in my chair, focusing my attention on the SSA. "I haven't had time to apprise you of this yet as I only received confirmation of my suspicions just before we came here."

"Okay. What have you discovered?" He rests his elbows on the table.

"I knew there was something about Stanten's background that didn't add up, because the only kid of an impoverished single mom doesn't attend Harvard Law, without a scholarship, unless he has some powerful connections. I followed a link which led me from Stanten to the Mancusso crime family in New York. It seems Stanten is Carmine Mancusso's secret son."

Chapter 6

Keven

"Who is Carmine Mancusso?" Eva inquires, her gaze bouncing between me and the SSA.

"He's the capo crimini—the head boss—of an infamous New York crime family," SSA Clement explains. "His organization is trying to infiltrate Boston in the aftermath of your former husband's demise and the collapse of his criminal empire."

"What proof do you have?" he asks me.

"I followed a few leads and found a PI he used back in the day. Guy's a jackass. I hacked into his system in seconds. Seems he decided to go digital, and all his files are scanned onto his cloud drive. Found a ton of interesting intel, and I've sent the rest to the organized crime unit."

"Good call." The SSA bobs his head enthusiastically, and Agent Dickhead doesn't even attempt to hide his displeasure, scowling at me as if he wishes I'd evaporate into thin air.

"It appears Stanten's mom was one of many mistresses Carmine had over the years. She was paid to disappear with the kid. She's a known prostitute around the Roxbury area with a heavy-duty drug problem. It didn't take her long to squander the money Mancusso gave her. Stanten was basically dragged up, but he kept his nose clean. Graduated high school top of his class. I don't know when or how he connected with his dad, but Mancusso paid for his college education,

45

bought him a place, and he makes a healthy deposit in his bank account every month."

"Mancusso's son Frankie OD'd eight years ago," Agent Cunningham says. "He was the only legit heir to his throne. The rest of the kids he has with his wife Rose are all daughters."

"I'm betting Stanten isn't the only male bastard kicking around," Agent Wentward supplies. "So why choose him as the heir apparent?"

"Because he's smart, ruthless, and he looks the part," Agent Higgins suggests.

Eva clears her throat before speaking. "If Stanten is really the son of Carmine Mancusso, why would he align with my former husband? Aren't they rivals?" It's an intelligent question. One which reminds the boss that we have civilians in the room.

"That's the million-dollar question and something we need to explore further," the SSA says, standing. "Thank you so much for coming in, Eva. If you think of anything else, let me know." He hands her his card. "I'll escort you both out."

He turns to me. "Stay here. We're not finished with this discussion."

Kade nods in my direction, and I signal him with my eyes.

"Wentward will really hate your guts now," Agent Cunningham whispers into my ear, and I smirk.

"He already hates my guts. That's nothing new," I reply in a low tone.

"That's very impressive investigative work," she adds with a wide grin. "Boy's obviously got mad skills."

I shrug her compliment off just as Agent Dickhead decides to interject himself into our private conversation. "What do you expect of someone who spent his formative years illegally hacking into financial systems and skimming millions off unsuspecting account holders."

"It wasn't millions or anything close to it, and it wasn't by choice." I work hard to keep the anger from my voice, but I'm seething. He thinks he knows me, but he knows fucking nothing.

"That's what all the criminals say," he snarks.

"You're coming across as an even bigger asshole than usual," Sinead says.

"My issues with Kennedy are nothing to do with you." He leans back in his chair, glowering at her.

"Tension in the office affects all of us," she says, turning to him with fire blazing from her eyes.

"Well, don't blame me." He jabs his finger in my direction. "Blame Boy Wonder over there."

I grind my teeth down to the molars, jerking upright in my chair. I'm not proud of my past, but I'm not going to keep quiet and let Agent Dickhead continue to hold it over me every time he feels like it. Time to put the truth out there.

"I found out the man who raised me wasn't my bio dad the day I turned eighteen, and it sent me into a tailspin," I start explaining, capturing the attention of everyone around the table. "Then I lost my girl and sunk even lower. Got caught up with a bad crowd, racked up a huge amount of gambling debts I couldn't pay without involving my family, so I made a stupid deal instead. Those lowlifes I owed money to gave me a list of powerful, wealthy names, and I skimmed cash off their bank accounts as payment in kind. It wasn't my finest moment, and I hated every second of it, but they weren't the type you double-crossed."

A muscle clenches in my jaw as I stare at Colin's unyielding face. I don't think even the truth will alter his poor perception of me. "It wasn't millions although it might've been if my dad, James, hadn't figured out what was going on and paid my way out of the mess. He loaned me money to pay off my debts and repay the money I'd siphoned out of the bank accounts. When I got my trust fund last year, I paid him back." I eyeball Colin, challenging him to continue fighting me on this. "I fucked up, but I tried to make it right."

He snorts. "Yeah, by using your *trust fund*." He shakes his head, his mouth curving into a sneer. "You have been sheltered and mollycoddled your entire life. You've no business being here."

SSA Clement returns to the room at that exact moment, and he wastes no time hauling Agent Wentward out of the room for a private chat.

"Are you okay?" Sinead asks me.

"I'm fine," I clip out. "He's not the first guy with a chip on his shoulder because of who I am and where I come from, and I doubt he'll be the last. Once he doesn't interfere with my work, he can think whatever the fuck he wants about me."

The two men return to the room, and Colin slithers into his seat like the slimy snake he is, avoiding eye contact with me, which tells me all I need to know.

The SSA continues with the briefing. "This new intel changes things. If Stanten was cozying up to Garcia, it can only mean he was a plant. He's still involved with those associates of Garcia's who are fighting to maintain control of their patch. Most likely he's feeding information back to Daddy Dearest and they must be planning something big."

He walks to the whiteboard, scrubbing it clean, before scribbling new content. When he's done writing, he faces the team, jabbing his finger around the room. "Higgins and Mead, stay the course with the DeLucas. We can't forget or underestimate the rivalry between the Boston families. Garcia eliminated DeLuca's second in command, and they didn't have a chance to retaliate before he died, but I doubt they've forgotten. Agent Cunningham, you continue to liaise with the organized crime unit here and in Federal Plaza, explore any and all leads."

He turns to Wentward. "You're assigned to Stanten. Shadow his every move. If he stops to take a piss at the side of the road, I want to know about it."

The SSA stands, gesturing me forward. "Kennedy, I'm altering your assignment. Come with me." I stride after him to his office. "Sit," he commands, dropping into his chair while I claim a seat in front of his desk. "Ignore what I said before. I want you on this full-time. Continue to dig up whatever you can on Stanten, and feed it to Cunningham and Wentward. I trust that won't be an issue?"

"It won't be an issue for me."

"I've spoken with Colin, and it won't be an issue for him either."

That's laughable, and completely unrealistic, but I bite my tongue.

"And I want you to reconnect with your ex. Ingratiate yourself back into Cheryl Keeland's life. Gain access to that house, and see what you can discover."

I sit up straighter. "Hold up. I thought you said I was to stay away from her in case it jeopardized the case?"

"I know what I said, but I've changed my mind." He pulls out a file and starts leafing through it. "You have an in and we need to use that."

Glancing up from the file, he drills me with a deadly look. "She can't know you're FBI."

Not a problem. I gave her a card which seemingly confirms I'm a freelance technical consultant. It's the same line I told my family to feed anyone who asks. I don't want anyone outside my immediate circle to know I'm working for the Feds. Especially not certain undesirables from my past. It took a lot of effort to extricate myself from the mess I got myself into a couple years ago, and I've no desire to rub shoulders with any of those assholes again.

"Understood."

"I see you passed pistol qualification. Good. I'll email the relevant department and organize a firearm for you. It'll be ready for you to collect Monday morning. No heroics before then."

"Of course, sir."

"Okay. Get out of here. I'll talk to you Monday."

I check my cell as I make my way out of the building to my car, but there's no message from Cheryl yet. I hope she hasn't already changed her mind. Given the conversation that's just taken place, I really need this meeting to go ahead with her. I need to apologize in order to get things back on track.

Let the boss man believe I'm doing it for my job.

But I'm doing all this for her.

I let Cheryl down once before, and I'm never making that mistake again.

My brother Kyler is the only one of my brothers waiting when I arrive at the Armani men's store a couple hours later. "Isn't Kade here yet?" I ask, raising my fist for a knuckle touch.

"He got delayed but he's on his way," Ky explains.

I sit down beside him. One of the store assistants rushes to offer me a beer, but I decline. I roll my eyes as I survey the large empty store. "Kade asked for the celebrity treatment, huh?"

"Nah, man." Ky leans back grinning. "Wasn't Kade."

"Shit." I scrub a hand over my prickly jaw. "Mom has definitely taken on the role of bridezilla in place of Eva."

"Eva is as laid-back as Faye when it comes to wedding planning," Ky says, his face lighting up at the mere mention of his fiancée. "Mom's the one flipping out."

"Doesn't it make you want to elope?" I ask. Faye and Kyler got engaged at Christmas, and they've set a wedding date for August.

"No point. Kade and Eva did that, and Mom's still insisting on the big white wedding."

Truth. I was the only one from the family who attended the registry office ceremony last December. Kade and Eva had waited years to be together, so they wasted no time getting hitched once they were free to do so. I was honored Kade asked me to attend and even more honored he asked me to stand as best man at their forthcoming May wedding.

It's going to be a lavish affair with over three hundred guests in attendance. If it's freaking Eva out, she's not showing any evidence of it. Kyler is right. She's just taking it in her stride.

"Maybe, by the time you get around to finding a girl, Mom'll have worked it all out of her system," he teases.

I thump him in the arm. Hard.

"Shit, Kev. Relax." He shakes his head before straightening up, turning to me with a strange look on his face. "Weirdest thing happened the other day."

"Keep that kinky shit to yourself. I'm on a strict need-to-know basis, and I don't need to know what you and Faye get up to in the bedroom."

Now it's his turn to thump me. Man, he's so easy to wind up where Faye's concerned. "Asshole," he mumbles under his breath. "I'd never discuss my sex life with you or any of the fam, and you know it."

Faye is technically our cousin, but only Kal and the triplets share a bloodline with her. James, the man who raised us, the one we all call Dad, is Faye's uncle, and he became her legal guardian when she was seventeen.

Ky, Kade, and I have a different bio dad, so she's only our cousin by marriage. There is nothing that prohibits Faye and Ky from being together though that didn't stop some of the tabloids from spewing a ton of crap when they announced their engagement.

"Okay, I'll bite," I tell my brother.

He rubs a hand across the back of his head. "Faye asked me to set up an appointment with this photographer, and the girl who answered the phone sounded really familiar. It wasn't until after I'd gotten off the phone that it clicked. She said her name was Cheryl, and I'm convinced it was your ex, Cheryl Keeland."

"Was the photographer Sara Lewis?" I ask, and Ky nods. "Then it was Cheryl," I confirm. "She works there part-time, around college." Kyler's jaw slackens, and he opens his mouth to speak, but he's interrupted before he gets the chance.

"You're tapping Cheryl Keeland again?" Kent asks, stepping into the room flanked by Keanu and Keaton. The triplets are the youngest of my brothers, but they're not little kids anymore. They're eighteen and graduating high school soon, and it makes me feel old.

"I thought she moved to Ohio or something," Keanu says, perching on the edge of the couch beside me.

"Delaware," Keaton corrects him, leaning back against the wall.

"She did, but she's back in Boston now," I supply.

"And you're fucking her again?" Kent says, sprawling across the other couch like he owns it. Asshat has no boundaries and no manners.

"No, I'm not," I growl.

"Pity. She's hot. I saw her blowing you this one time and got loads of ammo for the spank bank." He cups his crotch, rolling his hips, and we all groan in frustration.

Kent loves to provoke controversy, and he craves the spotlight like a true media whore. Sometimes, I wonder if he'll ever mature. If he'll ever find someone to love, because putting up with his shit isn't easy. He's constantly in trouble, and I know Mom is consumed with worry for him. It doesn't help that it looks like Keanu is following him down the rabbit hole lately. Keaton's the only one of the triplets with his head screwed on, even if something doesn't seem right with him at the moment.

"Jesus Christ, Kent." Kade swats him across the back of the head as he arrives, shaking his head. "Have you no filter?" He subtly gestures toward the four store assistants standing off to one side.

"Just keeping it real, man. And speaking of hot, where's that sexy wife of yours?"

Kent's a little shit, and Kade will kick him around the room if he starts talking crap about Eva, which is the last thing he should be focused on right now.

"Cut the crap, Kent. We're here to get measured for suits for Kade's wedding. For once in your life, can you think about someone else?"

He flips me the bird, but he keeps his mouth closed, so I'm counting that as a win.

We all get measured and wander to a nearby restaurant for dinner afterward. This is the first time in a long time that we've all been out together, just the men.

"Sucks that Kal lives in Florida," Kyler says after we've placed our orders. "He should be here with us." Kal attends UF where he lives in a family house on campus with his fiancée, Lana, and their son, Hewson.

"He's meeting us in Nantucket for Easter," Kade says, swigging from his beer. "He's staying at his place with Lana and Hewson, and I think John and Greta are staying there too, but they're all coming to Mom's for dinner." John and Greta are Lana's parents, and they used to work for my parents, looking after our Wellesley house and grounds.

"I didn't know we were going to Nantucket," I say, frowning, because this is the first I've heard of it. "How come?"

"Mom said she wanted a change this year," Keaton explains.

"Is Dad coming too?" I ask, figuring they must have decided this while I was away at my FBI training program and just forgot to update me.

"Yep. Everyone's going," Ky supplies. "Including Adam, the twins, and Whitney."

All gazes swivel to Kent.

"What?" he snaps. "Don't look at me like that."

"What's the deal with you and Whitney anyway?" I ask. "I can never figure it out."

Faye only met Adam, her bio dad, when she moved to the U.S. Adam never knew she even existed until Faye's parents passed. He's become a permanent fixture in her life since then, and Mom usually invites him to our place for the holidays. He shares custody of his other three kids with his ex-wife, and he brings them along if it's his year to have them.

Whitney is Faye's half-sister. She's a year younger than the triplets and the female equivalent of Kent—as in, she likes to be the center of attention, is always in trouble of some sort, and thrives on drama. They are drawn to one another like moths to a flame, and it's combustible every time they get together. Last Christmas, they were caught fucking in Kent's room, and Adam was close to murdering my brother, or so I've been told. I wasn't around to witness it, thanks to an unscheduled visit to an FBI interrogation room, but Kade said it was like World War Three erupted in the house.

"She's hot, and she sucks dick like a pro," Kent supplies. "But it's nothing serious. We fuck around when we see each other, but it's not like we're dating or exclusive or any of that shit." He shudders as if the very thought makes him ill.

"Does Whitney understand that?" Kade asks.

Kent shrugs. "She lives in New York. I live in Wellesley. We see each other two, maybe three, times a year. What else needs to be said?"

Ky sighs and I sense his frustration. "If you don't have feelings for her, and it's only a casual fuck buddy scenario, do me a favor and stay away from her? Because I honestly think Adam will strangle you if he finds you screwing his daughter again. And I'm not sure Whitney sees things as casually as you do. This has the potential to be a major fuckup and that's the last thing I need before my wedding."

"Christ." Kent drags a hand through his hair. "You're all so damn serious. Lighten the fuck up." He eyes my beer like it's crack cocaine, and I know he'd kill for a drink.

"Sucks to be you," I tease, gesturing at my beer before I lift the bottle to my lips.

"Maybe I'll invite Cheryl as my guest," he retorts, deliberately trying to wind me up. It's his usual M.O. when he gets defensive.

"Go for it, bruh. I'd be surprised if she even remembers you."

"Girls *never* forget this face." He points at himself, puffing out his chest. "And once I'm fully tatted up they'll be fighting in droves for a piece of this Kennedy." He rolls up his sleeves, showing the considerable ink on both his arms.

Mom blew a gasket when the triplets came home the day after their eighteenth birthday sporting tattoos. It wasn't anything new for Kent—he's been getting inked since he was sixteen. There isn't any law you can't flout, or anything you can't buy, once you have money. But I was surprised at Keanu and Keaton. Keanu claims his tats are getting him new modeling gigs because that look is all in right now, but it was really out of character for Keaton.

"Do you ever listen to yourself?" Keaton asks, shaking his head. "I swear you're getting more immature as you age."

"Screw you and your boring fucking life." Kent flips him the middle finger.

"My life isn't boring," Keaton protests.

"Sure, it is," Kent says, smirking. "You've stuck with the same pussy since you were sixteen, and we all know you're going to marry Melissa and knock her up as soon as you get the chance. You'll be old and gray before your time, I'm telling you, man. You want to take a leaf out of Keanu's book, and start experiencing the world of pussy out there for the taking."

"Don't fucking drag me into this," Keanu says, glaring at Kent.

Kev, Ky, and I share knowing looks. Things are gonna get interesting once the triplets start Harvard in the fall. We know there's plenty of crazy mayhem to come and that we'll have to look out for them, like we've looked out for one another all our lives.

Kent may drive me fucking insane, but he's the one who needs the most guidance. Lately, Keanu has shown signs that his world is spiraling, and I'm guessing it's something to do with Selena, his on-again, off-again girlfriend. And despite what Kent just said, I think Keaton's in a very unhappy place in his life.

All three of my youngest brothers are trying to find their way in the world, and things are going to get messy.

But I'll be there for them.

Because they're my family.

And family is everything.

Chapter 7

Cheryl

"Do you want to tell me what's wrong?" Lin asks later that night as we share a bottle of wine while watching the latest episode of *Survivor*. "You've been in a funk since lunch. What's happened?"

"I'm not sure I'm up to talking about it." I top my glass up and take a healthy glug. "I'd rather just drink to forget it." Which is the truth because since my disastrous lunch date with Eva, I can't keep the trip down memory lane from replaying on repeat in my mind. Not even the #HotCop, Daniel Rengering, the guy I'm rooting for on *Survivor*, has managed to distract me tonight; usually I'm glued to the screen, silently cheering him on.

"Is this something to do with Dan and the barn?"

I shake my head. "Not really, and I haven't heard from him since I got that text." Dan texted me to say he's storing some equipment for work in the barn and I'm not to go in there. I don't like his explanation and it reeks to the high heavens. *What kind of stuff does an attorney need to store in a barn of that size?* I fully intend to probe him about it when he comes home Monday night.

"What does *not really* mean?"

I sigh, tucking my hair behind my ears and stretching my legs out on the couch. "Don't mind me. I'm probably just projecting because of ..." I stop myself from saying his name in the nick of time.

Lin slides off the recliner chair, sinking to her knees in front of me. "Babe. Spill it. What's on your mind?"

I take another glug of wine for courage. "I met someone from my past today, and it's thrown me," I finally admit.

"Someone like a friend or an ex?" she astutely surmises, rubbing my legs.

"An ex, although calling Kev that doesn't come close to conveying how much he used to mean to me."

"Oh, this sounds juicy." She jumps up on the couch, placing my feet in her lap. "Tell me more."

"You've heard of the Kennedys from Wellesley, right? Their mom used to own Kennedy Apparel."

"Girl, everyone knows who the Kennedys are. They've kept the whole country entertained these past couple years with all those salacious scandals. Those boys are seriously hot."

"I thought you didn't swing that way," I tease.

"I don't. Doesn't mean I'm blind though." She bolts upright. "Hang on here a second. You don't mean *your* Kev is Keven Kennedy?"

I nod. "Yep. I went to the same private school as the Kennedy boys although they didn't even notice I existed until midway through ninth grade."

She rubs her hands together. "Take your time explaining." She winks. "I want all the details. Every single delicious one!" She's only short of dancing a jig, but I can't help smiling. If I'm going to unburden to anyone, it's going to be Lin. She's the most nonjudgmental person I know, and she doesn't sugarcoat things either. She'll tell it to me straight.

"Try and contain yourself. It's a long and complicated story."

She leans back, folding her hands under her head. "I'm going nowhere. And I love long and complicated, so let's hear it."

Her eyes shimmer with excitement, and I roll my eyes, but I'm grinning despite myself. This is going to be painful, so I'll take any lighter moments where I can. "I was pretty shy back then and really self-conscious because I was a late developer compared to most of the girls at Wellesley Old Colonial High. I wore braces until I was sixteen, and I'm dyslexic, which made life challenging at times. I crossed paths with Kaden first. He was a year ahead of me, but he rescued me one day when a bunch of girls were getting up in my face, calling me dumb and teasing me over my dyslexia. I was attempting to defend myself, but I was seriously outnumbered, and they were pushing me around. Kade showed up and told them to fuck off. Then he insisted on driving me home. He knew those girls would wait for me outside, and he was right."

My mind drifts, and I smile as I remember meeting Keven for the first time. "When we got to his SUV Keven was already there. He was a freshman too, and although he was in a couple of my classes, he didn't have a clue who I was."

"Ouch." Lin grimaces in sympathy.

"Ouch indeed." I slurp my wine. "But he was really sweet and instantly every bit as protective as his older brother. Sat beside me in the back and demanded I tell him which freshmen had been picking on me. Then we chatted about school and my passion for photography, and he was really interested in hearing about the projects I was working on."

I sigh, and a goofy grin slides across my mouth. "Kev has this way of looking at you that's incredibly intense. When he puts his mind to something, he applies himself two hundred percent, and it's like that when's he talking to you. You get his full attention. His mind never drifts. I'd never had someone focus on me so completely, and I know I fell a little in love with him that first day. It was so easy to talk to him, and before I knew it, Kade pulled up in front of my house. I remember how much I wished I lived farther away because I didn't want to stop talking to Keven."

"When did you start dating?" she asks, clearly eager to get to the good part.

"Not until tenth grade. We were best friends from that day on, and both Kade and Kev looked out for me in school. Once the bullies realized the Kennedy brothers had my back, they changed their tune. They all wanted to be my friend purely to get to the guys."

"Wow. I had no idea you even knew them. You never mentioned it."

"Because I had to put it behind me, and I don't go there for my sanity."

"Don't even think about not finishing the story," she warns, her eyes flashing darkly.

I laugh. "This isn't a book, Lin."

"Could be. You'd make a fortune. Especially if you included photos." She bolts upright, her eyes popping wide. "Did you see Keven on the cover of *Men's Fitness* a year ago?" She fans herself. "Damn, that man is a fine male specimen. If I was going to try straight with anyone, I'd try it with him. Fuck, that man has an incredible body. Such sculpted abs, and he has an eight-pack! Eight! I tell you—"

"Oh em gee. Enough! I'm almost sorry I mentioned anything now. If I'd known you were a fully paid-up member of the Keven Kennedy Fan Club, I wouldn't have."

"Stop getting your panties in a bunch. I'm just saying I understand. I'm not into boys, and he even gets me all hot and bothered. So, go on. How did you end up dating Mr. Sexy?"

I throw a cushion at her head, and she giggles. "I had a major crush on Kev from that first day, but he didn't see me as anything more than a friend. I loved spending time with him, but it killed me when he started taking other girls out on dates. I was upset for months but tried to hide it from him. I consoled myself with the fact he never went out on any second dates, but it still hurt, ya know?"

"I do." Lin purses her lips. "My whole high school dating experiences were a disaster, but obviously something changed with you two."

"I got to a point where I was so hurt and mad that I decided to do something about it. I'd been asked out on a few dates but had always said no. I told myself I'd say yes to the next guy who asked me. So, I went out on a date with Asher Monroe. He was one of the most popular guys in school, and I couldn't believe he'd asked me out. You should've seen Kev's face when I told him."

I chuckle at the memory. "But he didn't try to stop me, so I went out on the date, and it was a good date, so I agreed to another one. I decided if Keven didn't share my feelings, then I had to at least try to move on."

"What happened next?" She's chomping at the bit, and all she needs is a bucket of popcorn to complete the look.

"If you'd stop interrupting me, I'll tell you." She flips up her middle finger, and I throw back my head, laughing. "Kev was all moody when I told him I'd agreed to go out with Asher again. He kind of ignored me that week, which made me even madder, so when Asher moved to kiss me at the end of our second date, I let him, even if I was sad because I'd been saving my first kiss for Keven."

The biggest grin spreads across my mouth. "I'd only just gotten into bed when there was a loud rap on my bedroom window. It was Kev. He'd scaled the tree outside my room." I shake my head, smiling profusely at the memory. "I let him in, and he stalked toward me with this fierce look in his eye, grabbed both sides of my face, and slammed his lips down on mine."

My eyes shutter as the memory replays in my mind's eye. "It was everything the kiss with Asher hadn't been, and I knew it was a branding, that he was claiming me, that we were making a commitment." My hand moves to my chest, right where my heart is beating furiously as the recollection of that first kiss takes hold of me. I'm not surprised my eyes are watery when I finally reopen them.

"No one else has ever kissed me like Keven," I whisper, finally admitting something I've been scared to acknowledge, even to myself. "The way he kissed me, touched me, held me, it was this all-consuming sensation. Every time it was infused with a silent "you're mine," and he always made me feel so safe and so loved. Keven isn't big on words, but he's big on gestures. I fell for him so hard, and we were inseparable from that night. We did everything together. We couldn't bear to be apart. I attended all his basketball games and went to every family event with him. We were permanent fixtures in each other's homes. He's the one who taught me how to play COD. He's the one who got me hooked on superhero movies. I was really into photography by then, and he modeled for me. I have hundreds of photos of him, and he even got permission for me to shoot all the official basketball games. Several of my photos adorn the walls in my old school, and every time we'd pass them, he'd smile proudly."

I pause for a breath, barely able to speak over the massive lump wedged in my throat. Lin reaches out, squeezing my hand. My voice is choked when I continue. "He'd walk me to and from class where he could. He picked me up and dropped me home from school. He drove me to my photography and dance classes and waited in the car for me. He showered me with kisses, and I was scarcely out of his arms. He was the most devoted boyfriend ever, and I was the most envied girl at school."

"Wow."

Tears roll down my face. "Yeah. It was wow. For almost two years I walked on a cloud. Nothing seemed insurmountable once I had Kev by my side. I thought we'd be together forever. We made firm college plans. I was going to MassArt, and he was going to Harvard, but we were going to live off campus together in our own apartment. So, when my dad announced, the summer before senior year, that we were moving, I was devastated. Dad had been promoted at work, and they wanted him to move to Delaware to oversee their new plant there. I cried buckets, begged my mom to let me stay behind. Mom loved Keven, and she could see how much in love we were. She also knew how much I wanted to study photography at MassArt, so she fixed it for me. She arranged for me to live with my aunt during senior year, and I was so relieved. But it was short-lived."

I grab a cushion, hugging it to my chest. Pain barrels into me from all sides. It's been over three years since we broke up, but it still hurts every bit as much as it did back then. I don't think I'll ever get over it.

"I was so preoccupied with my family's move and making sure things worked so I could stay at Wellesley that I didn't notice something was up with Kev. It became obvious a couple months into our senior year. He was acting strange and distancing himself from me. He forgot to pick me up a few times, and he started partying hard. We were fighting, which I hated, because we had rarely ever fought up to that point. It was our senior year, and I didn't want to party hard. It took extra effort for me to maintain a decent GPA with my dyslexia, and I needed to focus on my studies. I didn't have time for partying, so Kev would go by himself. It hurt me that he was apparently throwing all our plans away, and I couldn't figure out why. Kade was at Harvard, so I couldn't ask him what was up, and I wasn't as close to his other brothers, so I didn't feel like I could confide in them. Every time I asked Kev what was wrong, he'd shut me down. We'd lost our virginity to each other during summer break, and I began to wonder if that had changed something for him. If I wasn't good enough for him. I was plagued with doubts."

I bury my face in the cushion, and wracking sobs heave from my chest. *I don't know that I can say this out loud, and how awful is that? I should be over this. I'm engaged to another man, for God's sake, so why does my ex's betrayal still cut me up so badly?*

Because you still love him.

I punt kick that nasty inner troublemaker off my shoulder. No good comes from thinking thoughts like that.

"Cher." Lin moves up beside me, wrapping her arms around me. "What did that boy do to hurt you so bad?"

"He cheated on me, Lin. I walked in on him fucking the head cheerleader at a party." I break down completely, sobbing into her neck as all the hurt and pain resurfaces. I might as well be back there now, standing in the doorway, in utter shock, my heart rupturing in my chest, wanting to disbelieve my eyes, but unable to ignore the truth staring back at me.

"He betrayed me in the worst possible way, and he shattered my faith in men. Kev broke something in me that day and I've never healed. I don't think I ever will. And I can't ever forgive him, because he tarnished every good memory of us, he left me heartbroken and bitter, and, worst of all, he stole part of my heart and soul. Parts I'll never get back because he still has them, he still owns them, he always will, and I fucking hate him for that."

Chapter 8

Keven

I walk toward my front door with my heart thudding wildly behind my ribcage. Cheryl always had this effect on me—the ability to twist my insides into knots and render me speechless. I was pleasantly surprised when she texted me this morning asking to meet today, but it means I've had no time to prepare.

To share the same air space with her again and not be able to touch her is going to kill me.

I yank the door open and suck in a breath. She has her hair pinned up, and it serves to further highlight her stunning features. Loose strands of wavy blonde hair frame her heart-shaped face, and she looks so fucking beautiful. Goodness radiates from her every pore, like an angel.

She arches one elegantly shaped brow, and I realize I'm staring.

"Sorry, come in." I step aside, ushering her in. Light notes of lavender and jasmine waft through the air as she passes by me, sending me tunneling through time into the past. "You still wear the same perfume," I blurt, closing the door and moving to her side.

"Yes, but I'm sure you didn't ask me here to talk about my perfume."

She's sassier than she was as a teen, and it only adds to her attraction. "No. And thanks for coming to my place although I would've been happy to meet you any place of your choosing."

"And, like I said on the phone, I don't want to risk meeting anywhere public in case someone spots us and posts a photo online. I'd never be able to explain that to my fiancé." She pulls off her soft calf-length gray coat and pink cashmere scarf, and I take them from her, hanging them up in the hall closet with a heavy heart. I hate hearing her call that thug her fiancé. Although I'd hate those words coming out of her mouth in reference to anyone but me.

I lead her into the large open living space, and she whistles under her breath. "Wow, this is gorgeous."

"Thanks. I only moved in a short while ago. Mom and Brad's mom have an interior design business now, and they decorated the whole penthouse for me."

"Your mom always had exquisite taste."

In everything but men. I think it, but I don't say it.

"Would you like a coffee? Or anything else to drink?" I ask, trying hard not to rake my gaze over her beautiful body. She looks delectable in heels, figure-hugging skinny jeans, and a pale yellow silk blouse.

"Coffee would be good. Thanks."

I gesture toward the couch. "Why don't you take a seat, and I'll fix the coffee."

I head to the kitchen area and power up the Keurig. She's quiet as I fix our coffees, and when I head into the living area, she is standing by the floor-to-ceiling windows, staring outside.

"If it wasn't raining right now, I'd suggest we drink these outside," I tell her. "I haven't even had the chance to use the outside terrace yet."

"I'm sure you'll get plenty of opportunity once summer rolls around." She takes the offered cup. "Thanks. You have a great view of Mystic River."

"I know. For a last-minute purchase, it was a good buy." I guide her toward the couches, and she sits down on the one across from me, removing her keys and cell from the pocket of her jeans and placing them on the coffee table in front of her. "Eva tells me you're in your final year at MassArt?" I lie.

I'd discovered that fact for myself after I'd learned she was back in town. I also know she built up enough credits to skip junior year and move straight into senior year when she enrolled. Not that it surprises me because Cheryl has a natural talent when it comes to photography. She has this way of looking at the world that's unique and awe-inspiring.

"Yes, and it's everything I always imagined it would be." Her comment guts me, because it was always her plan to attend MassArt while I went to Harvard, but I fucked that up for her with my stupidity. "I'm guessing you graduated Harvard early if you've already set up your own tech consultancy?" she adds, blowing on the steam arising from her cup.

"Yeah. There isn't much about computers I don't know."

"Still as cocky as ever I see."

"It's the truth, and it if makes me sound arrogant, so be it." I shrug.

"Wow. Still big on apologies too." Her eyes narrow as she glares at me.

"I would've apologized if I'd had the chance," I say, clenching my teeth. "I was prepared to grovel, to do whatever it took, but you didn't even let me explain."

"What the hell was there to explain?!" she shouts, almost spilling her coffee. "I caught you red-handed! That bitch was bouncing up and down on your cock when I walked into the bedroom!" A sob rips from her throat, and it kills me. She slams her cup down on the table, and coffee sloshes over the edge. She stands. "This was a mistake. I can't do this." She hurries toward the hall with me hot on her tail.

"Cheryl, please, don't go. Please, I'm begging you. I know what you saw, and I wish I could take it back, but I can't. However, I can give you the context. It doesn't change what happened, but maybe it will help explain what you saw because that wasn't me. That wasn't who I am. I hate that I hurt you. I hate that I destroyed the only good thing I had in my life. I live with that guilt every fucking day." I'm bleeding before her, showing her every emotion on my face. "Please, honey. Please don't go yet."

"You don't get to call me that, Kev. I don't belong to you anymore."

"You never belonged to me, Cheryl. You've always belonged to yourself, but you were mine, and I was yours, and what we had *was* real. And I'm asking you, for that, to please, please hear me out. I never got to tell you this back then because you were gone before I had the chance."

I've said please more times in the last few minutes than I've said it in the last couple years, but I'm not above begging.

I will do whatever it takes to get her to stay.

To win her affection again.

No measure of time apart has diluted the feelings I have for this woman.

Cheryl is the only woman I've ever loved. The only one I ever will.

And I'm going to take my brother's advice. I'm going to do everything in my power to fight for her. Like I should've done back in high school.

I stretch out my hand, pleading with my eyes. Her shoulders relax, and I breathe easy again. Ignoring my hand, she walks back into the living area, and I follow quietly behind her.

We are both silent for a couple beats as we drink our coffee. "Okay," she says, wrapping both hands around her cup. "Tell me."

"At the start of senior year, when I turned eighteen, my parents told me James wasn't my biological father."

"What?" She blinks excessively as she stares at me with her mouth open.

I quirk a brow. I was expecting she knew this by now. It was all over the news when that bastard sperm donor was murdered by the half-sister I didn't know I had. "Don't you watch the news?"

"Not if it involves you or your family. It hurts too much, so I never watch or read any of that stuff. The only thing I was aware of was Kaden and Eva's marriage because I had a vested interest in that."

And we're veering into dangerous territory, so I steer the conversation back around. "Okay, well, Kaden, Kyler, and me all have a different Dad. Kade found out the year before, on his eighteenth birthday, but he didn't tell me because my parents asked him not to. The news sucker-punched me. I was so angry and so hurt."

"Why didn't you tell me?"

"Because I didn't want to vent all that anger in your direction. It was stupid, I know that now. Of course, I should've confided in you, but I wasn't in a good place, and I didn't want to burden you with it."

"It wouldn't have been a burden, Kev." She places her empty cup down and leans forward, placing her hands on her knees. "We were a couple. Couples are supposed to share everything."

"I know, and I wish I'd told you because then everything would've turned out differently."

"I knew something was up. You were acting so weird, but you kept denying anything was wrong."

"I was an idiot. I didn't talk to anyone about it. I locked up all my feelings, which is never a good thing. I was furious with Kade too. He'd known for ages, and he hadn't told me. I know my parents asked him to keep the secret, but I was his brother. We were closest to each other, and it felt like a double betrayal, so I shut him out as well. Instead of leaning on him and talking to you, I turned to drugs."

"What?" she shrieks, her eyes darting wildly about. "That's why you were all over the place? Because you were doing drugs?"

I nod, and I'm so ashamed. Reliving my senior year is not a pleasant experience because I made so many bad mistakes. Mistakes that altered the course of my future. "It was only weed to start with, but then I started snorting coke, and I loved how it numbed everything. How it helped me forget." The thing I didn't realize at the time was that it was also enabling me to forget the only girl who had ever mattered. "I let you down so much, and I'm really sorry for that."

She flops back on the couch, staring absently into space. "I was so fucking naïve back then." She shakes her head. "It's obvious now you say it. I should have realized. I should've made you stop or got you help."

I get up and walk over to her, sitting down beside her. "Don't do that. Don't take any of the blame. The blame is squarely on my shoulders. None of it was your fault."

When she looks at me, there are tears glistening in her eyes, and I'd give anything, *anything*, to take them away. "You were high at the party," she deduces.

I nod. "Like I said, I'm an idiot. Channing Montgomery took me aside when I first arrived and gave me this tab. Said it'd blow my mind. Well, he was right. It fucking did. Found out afterward it was LSD. Man, was I tripping. The whole world was distorted, and I was big-time hallucinating. Sandra Montgomery had been hitting on me for months. You knew that. I'd told you."

Her head bobs. "Which is why it hurt so much when I saw you with her. She turned around, you know. While she was naked, bouncing on your cock, she turned to me and said 'He's mine now. You should be grateful you got the time you did because a girl like you could never hold a guy like Keven. Now run along. I'm a little busy.'" Tears prick her eyes, and I wrap my arm around her waist, needing to comfort her.

She jumps up, knocking into the table, and the empty cup takes a tumble, shattering into pieces on the floor. "Don't touch me! You don't have the right anymore."

I stand. "I'm sorry. It won't happen again. Don't go."

She moves away, sitting down on the recliner chair, looking up at the ceiling with her eyes closed. I sweep up the broken ceramic, and while she's not looking, I swipe her cell and install the tiny chip. Carefully, I set it down on the table and reclaim my seat, giving her my full attention as I finish my sorry tale. "Sandra was a bitch and I never wanted her." Cheryl lowers her chin and opens her eyes, watching me as I speak. "She set the whole thing up. Got her brother to give me LSD knowing it would make me horny and delusional."

I sit up straighter, straining toward the girl of my dreams. "I thought she was you, babe. I swear, the whole time, when I looked at her, I saw your face. I know it sounds like an excuse, but I promise I'm not lying. I even called her Cheryl, and she went along with it. When you showed up, at first, I thought I was seeing double. Then you started shouting, but I couldn't hear the words. After you left, Sandra turned back around, and I saw who it was. I threw her off me as fast as I could manage. Somehow got my clothes on and ran out of the house after you. I was still confused. Still out of it, but I was scared. I was trying to rationalize it in my fucked-up head by telling myself you being there was just my imagination, but in case it wasn't, I had to get to you. I went after you, but I crashed a couple miles up the road. Drove straight into a ditch. My head slammed into the steering wheel, and I passed out. When I woke up, I was in the hospital. My parents were furious because the doctor had informed them of the drugs and alcohol in my system. It all came back to me, and I begged them to call you, but they refused. It was part of my punishment."

"No one told me you were in the hospital," she says, frowning. "Not even when you weren't at school that week."

I scrub a hand over my unshaven jaw. "That's because my parents didn't want it getting out. While I had no serious injuries, my face was all busted up, so they hid me until I'd healed. My brothers were forbidden from talking about it to anyone, and they made a massive donation to the hospital to ensure no one leaked it. Dad took me to the house in Nantucket, and he confiscated my cell and deactivated the house phone and Wi-Fi. I might as well have been in prison. I couldn't even get through to my brothers to ask one of them to contact you. It was a fucking nightmare, and I was going out of my mind with worry."

"Sandra told the whole school you two were official. I thought you didn't come back that week because you weren't brave enough to face me yet."

"I heard that shit when I returned the following week, and I made sure everyone knew what she'd done. I didn't care if the media got wind of it. Getting to you was my sole priority, but you wouldn't return any of my texts or calls, and you weren't at school. I was sick with worry that Monday."

"I walked in on you screwing someone else, and you didn't come after me, Kev. You didn't show up to school, and you hadn't bothered contacting me. Then that bitch was bragging about being your new girlfriend. I didn't want to believe her, but what else was I supposed to think?" Pure anguish is etched across her face, and I hate that I'm responsible for it.

"I can understand it to a point, but I don't know how you could so easily forget how much you meant to me. Didn't you understand my feelings for you? Didn't everything I said and did convey how much I loved you? That's the part I couldn't wrap my head around. How easily you dismissed us. How quickly you made up your mind."

"You had sex with that bitch, and it fucking killed me, Keven! Then there was blanket silence. No contact. No apology. No indication that any of what we shared was real." She buries her head in her hands. "I can't." She shakes her head. "I can't do this. It still fucking hurts so much."

"It's okay." I drop to my knees on the floor in front of her. "I know how it must've looked, and if I'd walked in on you with another guy, I'd be in jail for murder. I get it, and I don't blame you, but I couldn't believe you were gone when I got back to school. That I'd lost the chance to explain."

"I couldn't stay there and watch you with her," she continues, lifting her head up. "Perhaps it was rash to leave so quickly, but it was the only option I could think of back then. I called my mom up and told her what happened. She enrolled me in the local high school in Delaware with no issue, and I left Wellesley that weekend with a broken heart, determined I was never talking to you again."

"I called and texted hundreds of times until they started bouncing back."

"I changed my number," she sheepishly admits. "I couldn't deal with it, and I just wanted to forget."

"I went to your new house."

"What? What do you mean?" Her brow creases.

"I got on a plane to Delaware, hired a car, and drove to your house. Your mom answered the door and told me, in no uncertain terms, to stay the hell away from you."

"When?" she whispers.

"It was about a month after you left. I was supposed to be on an away trip with the basketball team, but I took the opportunity to fly to you instead because I knew it was the only chance I'd get."

"Coach must've busted your balls for that." Her lips kick up a little.

"He tried, but I quit."

Her beautiful, big, blue eyes pop wide. "But you loved basketball."

"Not anymore. I fell apart after I lost you. I lost myself for a good while. Made some shitty decisions. Spiraled into a dark place." I channel Kade and Kyler, trying not to inwardly cringe as I speak from my heart, because she needs to hear this. "You were the light in my life, Cheryl, and when I lost you, that light extinguished. But I need you to know that I've never forgotten you. You're in my thoughts and in my heart every day. You were ripped out of my life, but I've never stopped loving you, and I never will. You're the only girl I've ever loved, and that won't ever change."

Chapter 9

Cheryl

My heart is breaking apart all over again. I needed to hear those words so badly back in senior year, but I doubt it would've made any difference to the outcome. The visual of Sandra riding Kev is forever imprinted in my brain, and I was in so much pain I doubt I would've been able to forgive him even though I now know he didn't set out to cheat.

Doesn't change the fact he still did.

Or that he enabled himself to be manipulated through his drug use—which he hid from me.

Ugh. My emotions are veering in every direction.

Not that it matters.

We can't alter our history, and I'm on a different path now.

"It's too late, Kev. Surely, you know that. You need to move on like I have."

"Answer me one thing, Cheryl." His eyes drill into me, and I'm ensnared by the intensity of his gaze. "Do you love him like you loved me?"

No.

The word pops into my mind instantaneously, but I shove it aside, like I do every time niggling doubts arise.

"I'm not answering that."

"You already have."

His face gives nothing away, but I know him well enough to know he knows. Being this close to him again is torturous. He's even more beautiful than I remember. Up close, I can see the tiny flecks in his eyes and the very light smattering of freckles brushing over his nose and cheeks. His eyes hold hidden depths I've already explored.

My fingers twitch with the longing to touch him. I want to run my fingers along the stubble on his cheeks and chin, to know if it's soft or prickly.

My lips beg to glide against his. To remember how incredible it felt to be kissed by him.

I want to know if the sensations would be heightened now that he's all man.

"I've got to go." Grabbing my stuff, I hop up, climbing over him, before I do or say something I regret.

"I want you back in my life, Cheryl," he says, rising to his feet.

"That's not possible. I'm marrying someone else, Keven."

"Don't marry him. He's not the one for you."

I snort out a laugh. "And I suppose you are?"

"You know I am."

"Your arrogance is showing again, and it's not attractive." I stomp toward the hallway, hearing the thud of his footsteps following me.

"I'm just telling it like it is," he argues, ratcheting my anger up another notch.

I grab my coat and scarf from his closet, hurriedly throwing them on. "You don't get to show up in my life again, give me an explanation, proclaim you still love me, and expect me to fall back into my arms. This isn't the movies, buddy." I prod my finger in his chest, trying to push him back out of my space.

"I know it isn't." He takes a step toward me, and I stumble back, my spine hitting against the closet door. "This is real." He cages me in with his arms, one on either side, before pressing his body flush against mine. My knees almost buckle underneath me, and I flatten my palms to the closet door, needing to touch anything but him.

His face lowers toward mine, and I stop breathing. My heart is racing so fast it threatens to explode from my chest. There isn't a millimeter of my body that isn't aware of how close Keven Kennedy is to me. Even though we're clothed, I can still feel how rock solid his body is against mine, and my core aches in a way it hasn't ached in years.

I gulp back my rising hysteria over my errant thoughts. My head is a hot mess right now, and I don't understand why I'm not pushing him away.

Why I'm letting him line our mouths up.

Why my eyes are pleading with his.

Why my nails are breaking as I attempt to dig them into the wooden door when all I want is to dig them into Keven's hips, to pull his pelvis to mine, to feel the evidence of his arousal in the place where I throb for him.

His eyes hold me in place, and his mouth is so close to mine his warm breath fans across my face, hypnotizing me. He angles his head, moving his mouth to my ear, and I almost collapse. "I could kiss you right now, and you'd let me," he whispers. I clamp my lips tight, to hold back my moan. "But I won't do that to you." He pulls away from me, and I want to cry out at the loss of his body heat, which is wrong on so many levels. "I'll kiss you again when you're mine and only mine."

"Then you'll be waiting a long time," I rasp. "Like forever."

His eyes drop to my heaving chest, and he takes a long, slow perusal of my body. I bite the inside of my cheek this time to stop from crying out.

"That's not what your body's telling me." His eyes come back up to meet mine. "Does he worship your body in the way you deserve because it looks to me like you've been neglected. Does he make you come over and over like I used to? Does he get you really wet before sinking inside you? Do you scream his name when you succumb? Do you—"

"Enough!" I shriek, finally gaining control of myself. I need to get out of here before I orgasm just from his words. "This isn't ever happening, so forget it." I brush past him, racing toward the door.

"I'm not giving up, Cheryl. I gave up last time when your mom sent me packing, but I'm not backing down now. Not when I know you still have feelings for me."

"You're crazy," I toss out over my shoulder as my hand curls around the door handle.

"Keep deluding yourself, sweetheart," he says, slamming his palm against the door. He presses into me from behind, and the hard length of his erection pushes against my ass. A whimper escapes my lips before

I can stop it. "You and me both know the truth. This isn't over between us. Not by a long shot."

He carefully positions me off to the side and opens the door. "So, go home to your fiancé." He spits the word out like it's poison. "But I'm here for you when you come to your senses. You have my number. Use it. Any time of the day or night. You need me, I'm there."

"You are so full of yourself," I bluster, trying to gain some semblance of superiority before I leave. "And completely wrong. You and me are so over. And if you keep pretending otherwise, then the only one who's delusional is you."

I take a detour to Lin's apartment on the way back. Dan's already texted to say he's home a day early, but I can't return in my current state. He'll take one look at me, see I'm a mess, and want to know why.

"Where's the fire?" Lin asks as I push my way into her apartment twenty minutes later.

"In my panties, and in my heart, and in my head, and a million other places," I admit, pacing the length of her small living room.

"Woah, girl. You've got to give me more than that."

"I'm screwed, Lin. Oh, God." I slump to the floor on the spot. "I'm so screwed."

She drops down in front of me, sitting cross-legged. "You've just realized you're still in love with Keven Kennedy."

"Yes, and I don't know what to do." I bury my head in my hands and then I tip my head up. "Wait, how the hell did you know that before I did?"

"It was written all over your face last night when you were telling me about him. Don't get mad when I say this, but I've never seen your face glow, or your eyes shine, like that when you're talking about Dan."

"I do love Dan. I do." I'm not sure if I'm trying to convince Lin or myself.

"But you're not *in* love with him, Cher. You don't love him the way you love Keven. I can see it in your eyes."

"It was like that at the start for Dan and me," I explain, because I remember those heady sensations. The feeling like I was falling, and he was the one to catch me in his strong arms. "But it hasn't felt like that for a while." I blow air out of my mouth. "I've been so afraid to admit that. Even to myself."

"I was going to say something because you're the least enthusiastic bride I've encountered. Have you even made much progress with your wedding plans?"

I shake my head. "Apart from the venue, but Dan booked that." I pull my knees into my chest. "Jesus, Lin. What am I doing? I don't have a clue what to do. Tell me what I should do?"

"I wish I could, babe." She squeezes my hand. "But only you can make that decision. All I'll say is don't make any hasty decisions. Think it all through and search your heart. The answers are in there, but before you make any life-altering decisions, make sure you know your own heart and mind. That you're making the right choices for you."

I'm still mulling over Lin's words an hour later when I pull my Audi into our driveway alongside Dan's Merc. I'm more composed than I was when I showed up at Lin's, but I'm terrified he'll see the truth written all over my face—that I'm still in love with my first love, the guy who broke my heart, the same guy who now wants a chance to mend it.

"I'm home," I call out, shutting the front door behind me. I hang up my coat and slip off my heels, toeing on my slippers. "Dan?" I shout.

"In the living room," he hollers. I walk toward him and attempt to compose my face appropriately. He has the Patriots' game on full volume, and my ears silently protest. "That rookie quarterback is fucking deci-mating the opposition," he says as I come up alongside him. He doesn't take his eyes off the screen as he slings an arm around my waist. "Heath Gilchrist is going to win us the Super Bowl." Finally, he turns to me. "Mark my words. That man is a fucking legend." He yanks me to him, crashing his mouth down on mine. He tastes like whiskey and regret, and for the first time ever, I don't want to be kissing him. Rubbing his erection against my stomach, he slides his hands under my blouse, roughly cupping my tits through my bra. "Missed you bad, babe. I'm so fucking horny."

"Missed you too," I lie on autopilot.

"I need to fuck you now." He has my jeans and panties off so fast I barely have time to respond. Pushing me down over the arm of the couch, he shoves two fingers inside me. "Always so wet for me, baby."

I fight back tears as I think of the man I'm really wet for. My head is spinning a hundred miles a minute as Dan thrusts into me from behind. He pounds into me hard, over and over, but I don't feel it. My head and my heart are in so much pain I'm immune to everything else.

I'm grateful when he comes first and immediately pulls out. Kissing my neck, he smacks my ass before whispering he loves me. Then he walks away to get another whiskey. As I pull my clothes back on, I'm glad I didn't come. I don't deserve to when I let my fiancé fuck me while my mind was consumed with thoughts of another man.

"What kind of stuff are you storing in the barn?" I ask him later that night when we're reading in bed.

"It's nothing to worry your pretty little head about." He messes up my hair, smiling at me, while he insults my intelligence.

"Don't patronize me, Dan. What kind of stuff does a lawyer need to store in a place that big?"

He puts his book down and narrows his eyes to slits. "Who the fuck are you to question me?" He doesn't raise his voice, but he doesn't need to with that tone.

"This is my house too, and I've a right to know what's going on with that barn."

"What exactly are you accusing me of?"

"I'm not accusing you of anything. I just want to know what's in the barn."

"It's none of your business," he snaps. "Don't challenge me on this, Cheryl," he warns, and the menacing tone of his voice sends shivers up my spine.

I can tell there's no point continuing to press the issue. He's not going to fess up. And I don't want to argue with him. Not when I've got much bigger concerns.

Like whether I postpone or completely cancel my wedding.

I soften my tone and appeal to him with my smile. "It was just a bit weird that you never mentioned it to me, but it's not a big deal, so forget I said anything."

He stares at me like he's gauging how genuine my response is. "Okay." Some of the tension leaves his body. "Sorry for snapping."

I rest my head on his shoulder. "Sorry for upsetting you."

He slides his arm behind my back, tucking me into his side. "No problem." He tips my face up with one finger. "But I meant what I said. I don't want you going back there, and it's not safe to be walking over that side of the woods. It's very overgrown, and I don't want you tripping and getting hurt."

"Oh, that reminds me. I put a note up in the local store. I thought we could hire a couple of students to clear the overgrowth."

"You did what?"

I flinch back from his dark growl. "What did I do wrong?"

"I don't want anyone going near that barn! You had no right to do something like that without consulting me first."

"Consulting you? I'm your fiancée, Dan, and this is supposed to be my house too." He flips off the covers and gets up. "What are you doing?"

"I'm going to the store to remove that note."

"Don't be ridiculous. It'll be closed now," I say, glancing at the clock.

He ignores me, stalking into his walk-in closet, coming out a couple minutes later dressed in a black sweater and black sweatpants. "Don't wait up." He snatches his keys and wallet from the bedside table.

"Dan, please. You're overreacting."

"Go to sleep, Cheryl. I'll talk to you in the morning." With those parting words, he storms out of the bedroom.

I try to sleep, but I can't. Niggling worries are becoming more large scale in my mind, and I'm wondering what the hell he's storing in that barn that he wants to keep hidden. The rest of my thoughts are preoccupied with Keven and what he told me earlier today, and no matter how hard I try, I can't shut my brain down.

So, I'm still awake when Dan slips into our bedroom at four a.m. I pretend to be asleep as he crawls under the covers. He lies on his side, facing away from me, and two minutes later, he's snoring like a foghorn.

This isn't the first time Dan's gone out and not come back until the early hours. Add that to his frequent business trips, deflection any time I ask him how his business is doing, his odd reaction over the barn, and his dwindling attention, and I've come to one of two conclusions.

Either Dan is mixed up in whatever Garcia was involved in or he's cheating on me.

Chapter 10

Keven

It's been three days since Cheryl came to my place, and I'm concerned I pushed too hard. I wasn't supposed to say any of that shit. Had planned on going the whole "let's be friends" route, but when I saw how she reacted, I improvised. Now, I'm worried all I've done is scare her away.

And I feel guilty as hell about planting that listening tracker on her cell while I was cleaning up the broken cup. She never noticed because she was so busy mulling over everything I'd told her. It's the latest software, so it enables me to listen in to her conversations and to hear everything going on around her while it's powered on, as well as keeping tabs on her location. I'm recording everything, per the SSA's instruction, but I wiped the incident in her living room from the memory log. It was bad enough I had to listen to that scumbag grunting and groaning as he fucked her, but I'm damned if I'm letting the whole team have access to it.

I want to rip the guy from limb to limb. I hate him even more after listening to that. Cheryl didn't make a sound the whole time, and that's how I know, for a fact, he's a selfish asshole who doesn't give a shit about her needs. When Cheryl and I fucked, she used to scream the house down.

Why is she with this guy?

I never thought she'd be the type to settle, but that's what it seems like. And he's hardly ever there. She may as well be living in that place all by herself.

I did pick up some interesting intel though. As soon as Cheryl mentioned a barn, Stanten lost his cool. Clearly, he's hiding something.

"Kennedy." The SSA pops his head into my pod. "I need to see you in my office, now."

I trudge after him, and it's a bit like being summoned to the principal's office. "I need you to get into that house and onto that property," he says before I've even taken a seat. "Where are things with Ms. Keeland?"

"She hasn't contacted me yet, but she will."

"We don't have time to wait. The sting we set up at the border was a bust. Seems someone must be onto our undercover guys, and the intel was bogus. One of our agents confirmed an assignment of weapons, drugs, and underage females have been smuggled into the U.S. in the last twenty-four hours, destined for our Boston streets. We don't know how they got in or where they're holed up, but Stanten's all over this." He hands me a file. "Agent Wentward tracked him to Mexico last weekend. See for yourself."

I open the file, and bile floods my mouth as I flick through the pictures. The first few are of Stanten shaking hands with various men. All of them are wearing suits, looking like their shit doesn't stink. They are standing beside a couple of articulated trucks while crateloads of boxes are being uploaded.

The next few shots are a bit grainy, but it shows a room with a row of dirty mattresses on the floor. A handful of guys is defiling naked, young girls while Stanten and a couple of his buddies in suits watch from the top of the room. One of the guys has a camera out, filming proceedings.

Other photos show Stanten buried balls deep in a girl who looks no older than fifteen. I slam the file shut, raising angry eyes to the boss man. "I'll move things along."

He nods. "See that you do, and be careful. Wentward said Stanten got a whole new security system fitted at his house and on the grounds of his property on Monday. It seems Cheryl stumbling onto the barn has legitimately worried him. I need to know if that's where he's hiding the shipments."

"Seems unlikely. Cheryl's been home the whole time. There's only one way onto the property, and she would've noticed trucks pulling up."

"I agree, but he's hiding something in that barn, and we need to get into it. Right now, I don't have enough to get a warrant, so find something, anything, I can use to move this along."

I stand. "Trust me, I'm all over this."

I'm at the door when he calls out to me. "Keep me posted, and no crazy heroics." He pins me with a sober look. "I know you care for her, but you can't let your feelings get in the way of the investigation. There's too much riding on this."

It didn't take long for a plan to form in my head, and it took even less time to set it in motion. After seeing those pictures, I need to get Cheryl the hell away from that asshole, and I don't have the luxury of time anymore. There's no greater incentive.

I'm following Cheryl from a distance as she drives out of the city toward Walpole. The slow puncture I inflicted on her front tire should become obvious in the next ten minutes, and then I'll ride to the rescue, and she won't be able to say no. Not if she wants to get to the residential home in time.

Part of me hopes she'll call me, but I switch the screen on my laptop on, as I'm parked at a rest area a couple miles back, scowling while I watch her place the call to Stanten. Predictably, he doesn't answer. When her next call is to Triple A, I start the engine of my X5 and maneuver back out onto the road, slowly heading in her direction.

I act surprised as I roll down my window. "Cheryl? You need help?"

She blinks repeatedly as if she can't believe her eyes. I pull in in front of her car on the road and cut the engine. Shutting down the feed on my laptop, I close the lid and shove it on the back seat before hopping out.

"What are you doing here?" she asks, suspicion underscoring her tone as she ends her call, slipping her cell in her pocket.

I hold up my hands. "Calm the fuck down. I was on my way to a client's house, and I spotted you. What's the problem?" I lower my head, inspecting my earlier handiwork.

"I've got a flat," she says, frustration washing over her face as she sighs.

"You need me to change that for you?"

"How long will it take?"

"About thirty minutes," I lie. I can change a flat in less than twenty, but I'm not admitting that. My plan hinges on her leaving her car here and coming with me.

"Shit." She huffs, stomping her booted foot.

My lips tug up. "Did you just stomp your foot?"

"Yes. Trust me, it's a stomp-worthy moment."

"You in a rush somewhere?"

She looks behind her at my SUV. "Yeah, and I wouldn't ask this if it wasn't important, but is there any chance you could give me a ride to Walpole?"

"No problem. Just grab your stuff, lock up, and follow me."

"Thank you for this," she says, a couple minutes later, when she's securely settled into the passenger seat of my X5. "You've gotten me out of a jam."

"I'm glad to be able to help," I say, moving back out onto the road. "Where we heading to anyway?" I ask, even though I already know.

"To a residential home for kids. I volunteer there; teach a photography class every Wednesday evening. I'll direct you when we hit Walpole."

My proud smile is genuine. "You always loved helping others."

She shrugs it off. "It's not a chore. I love photography, and I get as much of a kick out of it as the kids do."

"Tell me about the place." It's difficult to keep my eyes on the road when the woman I love is sitting beside me. I just want to drive away with her and keep her safe. Now, more than any other time, I can relate to how Kaden felt when he was in my shoes. I would willingly sacrifice everything to protect Cheryl, no question about it.

"The home provides a variety of different programs for kids who have nowhere else to stay. They arrive for all kinds of reasons. Some have behavioral issues; others have been neglected or abused. The program gives them structure and focus while they work through their issues." I can feel her looking at me, and I take my eyes off the road for a second. "Meeting these kids makes me realize how lucky we were to have come from loving families who had the means to take care of us."

"We were fortunate," I agree, "but it's difficult to see it like that when you're a kid. When every little thing seems like a big thing and stuff seems impossible to overcome. I was too focused on my problems and blaming my parents for them to properly see all the ways in which I had it good."

"True. It's easy, with hindsight, to look at it objectively. But these kids are different. They've seen the ugly side of life at far too young an age. Some self-destruct, and no amount of help can pull them back from the path they're on. But a lot of them are the opposite. They fight so hard because they want to have a better life, and they grasp the opportunities given to them with both hands. It's both humbling and awe-inspiring."

She's humbling and awe-inspiring, and I'm more determined than ever to worm my way back into her heart.

"Thanks so much for the ride," she says when we reach the home twenty minutes later. "And sorry for derailing your meeting. I hope you aren't too late."

"I canceled it."

Her brows knit together. "Why did you do that?"

"You need a ride back to your car." I shrug like it's no biggie.

"You didn't have to do that. I'm sure one of the other volunteers would've dropped me off."

"Well, it's done now, and I've got some spare time on my hands."

Her eyes light up. "You want to come in?"

"Thought you'd never ask," I say, smiling as I pocket my keys and get out of the car.

She introduces me to a bunch of men and women who work in the place before bringing me over to the room she uses for her class. There's about twenty teenage boys and girls, of varying ages, in the room. All their heads swivel in my direction when I step into the room with Cheryl.

"Who's your boyfriend, Cheryl?" a girl at the front asks, blatantly checking me out. I wink at her, and she shoves one of her fingers in her mouth, moving it in and out as she licks it in a provocative manner. Holy shit. I smother my laugh, schooling my lips into a neutral line when Cheryl sends me a warning look.

"Keven is my friend, and he's going to help out today." She shoots me a smug look, and I wonder what I've gotten myself into.

"Yo, girl, why you not tapping that?" a girl at the back speaks up. "He sure is pretty to look at." Peals of laughter ring throughout the room, and I cough this time to disguise my laughter.

"Wanda. Behave or I'll have to ask you to leave."

"Aw, you're no fun anymore, Ms. Cheryl."

"Hey, what you bench, man?" a dude with dreads and tats at the front asks me.

"Two twenty."

"Get the fuck out," he replies, lifting his fist for a knuckle touch. "You the man."

Cheryl is fighting a smile as she sets up the lesson.

"Are you one of those Kennedy dudes?" a skinny guy with glasses asks. "'Cause I saw a picture online, and you really look like one of them."

"Hey, leave Keven alone, or he'll never agree to help again." Cheryl pushes me toward the back of the room. "Sit there and try to look invisible. I'll call you when I need you." She turns around but not before I spot the wicked glint in her eye.

Propping my butt on the edge of the desk, I watch her teach the class. I'm fucking mesmerized by her. She's clearly in her element. Her face comes alive, and she gestures wildly with her hands, as she flicks through photos on the screen. The class discusses color and aesthetics, entering into healthy debate. After a half hour, she gestures me forward with a nod.

"Next week, we're going to study portraiture and capturing the human form. I thought we could have a little introduction to it today seeing as we have a helper." A few hoots and hollers ring out in the room, and I stop my forward trajectory, suddenly very, very afraid. "Come here, big guy," Cheryl taunts, struggling to contain her mirth. "You're not afraid of getting your picture taken, are you?"

"When you say human form, please tell me you mean naked human form," the girl who did the fucked-up finger licking thing pipes up.

"Hell to the no." I drill a serious look at Cheryl, and she convulses into fits of laughter. Half the class joins in.

"Spoilsport," she whispers when I reach her side.

I press my mouth to her ear. "If you want to see me naked, you only have to ask. I'll strip for you anytime, babe—once it's a private show." I lick my lips and discreetly roll my hips.

Her cheeks enflame and, oh yeah, I think I won this round.

"Can he at least take his shirt off?" another girl asks, and that starts up a chorus of chants. Even I'm laughing now.

"Tell me what you're comfortable with," Cheryl says with a soft smile. Her entire face is glowing, and she looks so beautiful that I'd happily strip naked in front of the class for her.

"Tell me what you want, and I'll do it."

Ten minutes later, I'm standing in front of a white screen in only my jeans while a bunch of teenagers pretend to listen to Cheryl's instruction instead of drooling.

Two cameras are passed around the room, and each student is given the opportunity to pose me to their liking and take a couple shots. I don't know how professional models handle this shit day in, day out.

Cheryl was constantly taking my picture in high school, and I let her use me as her guinea pig, but that was fun because I loved every second in her company, and it was never a chore. I've also done a few shoots for sports magazines before, but they've been active stuff, shots of me in the gym or outside jogging, and I didn't mind that, but standing around primping and preening bores me to tears. Still, I don't mind too much because I'm helping Cheryl out, and the kids seem to be enjoying it.

After, Cheryl takes a photo of me—with my shirt back on—and all the kids, and then class is over.

"Thanks for being a good sport," she says, as she gathers up her things.

"No problem. It was fun. They're a lively bunch."

"I love this group of kids. They're enthusiastic."

"A few of them seem like naturals too," I say although I'm probably talking out my ass. I used to take off on long afternoons with Cheryl when she wanted to photograph stuff. I'd drive her everywhere and anywhere so she could capture a multitude of settings. She was always so passionate about it, and bits and pieces rubbed off on me. I remember when I got her this Nikon camera she'd been saving for, as a surprise, our

85

last summer together, and she was so excited I got laid three times that night. Those were some of the best times of my life.

"They are, and I wish we had more funding, so I could encourage them, but the budget's always tight," she says, dragging me out of my head.

"That's why you were sharing two cameras around."

"Yep," she says, hefting her bag over her shoulder. "I'm all packed up. Let's go."

I take the bag off her shoulder, ignoring her feeble protest, and place my hand on her lower back as I guide her forward. I expect her to argue or slip out of my grasp, but she doesn't.

My hand begs to explore. To slip under her shirt and feel her soft skin. To wander over her body, examining all her new curves. But I hold myself back, because I meant what I said to her on Sunday.

When I touch Cheryl again—and I'm determined I will get to touch her again—it will only be when she's broken all ties with Stanten and acknowledged her feelings for me.

Until then, cold showers and wet dreams will have to suffice.

Chapter 11

Cheryl

Rob—the manager in charge today—waylays me before we leave, asking if I've time to help out in the kitchen. "I normally stick around for a while to help with dinner, but I don't want to delay you any longer," I explain to Keven.

"I'm in no rush." He extends his hand to Rob. "I'm Keven, and whatever you need us to do is fine by me. Lead the way."

"Nice to meet you," Rob says, shaking his hand. "And thanks. We never turn down an extra pair of hands."

Rob puts us to work chopping vegetables alongside Mira and Freya and the five of us maintain a steady banter as we work. Kev is chatting away to Rob, learning all he can about the home. My heart soars as I watch him listening avidly to everything Rob says.

"He's definitely a keeper," Freya whispers, nudging me in the ribs.

"Charming, caring, and so damn hot," Mira adds. "I fucking hate you, girl."

I laugh, but I don't correct them. I let them believe Kev's my fiancé, and the thought excites me so much.

Which in turn makes me feel guilty.

The longer I'm in Keven's presence again, the more I'm remembering of our past. All the little ways he showed me he cared. How compatible we were. How we used to get one another with just one look or one word.

When we broke up, I subconsciously let all those good memories disappear, choosing to remember only the ugly ending, and I wish I hadn't done that, because if I'd remembered what it was like to be crazy in love with a guy who made you the center of his world, I'd have realized that Dan was never that for me.

My dating experiences in college only added to the poor perception I've garnered of guys in my head. I didn't date at all my first year at UD, and last year, I went out with a guy for six months, but he ended up cheating on me too. Dating wasn't even on my radar when I arrived back in Massachusetts, but Dan swooped in and swept me off my feet.

Now, I'm wondering if I didn't have blinders on. If I wasn't so dejected and disheartened after my last relationship ended badly that I failed to see what was in front of my nose.

Dan doesn't treat me the way I want to be treated. And he doesn't love me the way a man intending to marry a woman should. Irrespective of whether anything happens with Kev or not, I have to end things with Dan. Deep inside, I've known things weren't right for some time, and I can't live in denial anymore. It's time to confront my feelings once and for all and have a serious conversation with him.

Rob ropes Kev into looking at some problem on his laptop, and they disappear into his office while I help the girls serve dinner. The noise levels in the cafeteria are almost deafening, but it's great to see the kids chatting and laughing and enjoying each other's company.

Rob and Kev return, and we take a seat at the staff table, tucking into the delicious food we've just prepared. Kev fits right in, chatting as if he's known my colleagues his entire life.

"Don't be a stranger," Rob tells Kev as we make our way outside a couple hours later. "And you're welcome anytime. Thank you so much for everything today."

Kev shrugs, shoving his hands in his pockets. "It was my pleasure, and I'd be delighted to help out again, provided Cheryl doesn't mind."

He looks at me with so much vulnerability and longing that my breath hitches in my throat. "I don't mind," I half-whisper.

"Then I guess we'll be seeing you again." Rob waves us off, and we are both quiet as we climb into Kev's SUV.

The engine purrs to life, and Kev glides out onto the road. The air is heavy with unspoken words, and I'm confused all over again.

"Thank you for letting me share that with you today," he quietly says, a few minutes later. "I see what you mean now." His eyes flick to mine briefly. "And I hope you don't mind that I'd like to get more involved. I don't want to encroach on your—"

"It's okay. I like that you want to help out."

The biggest smile spreads across his mouth, and it's like being sucker-punched in the ovaries.

"Yeah?"

"Yeah." I return his smile.

"I enjoyed spending time with you today. It reminded me so much of hanging out with you in high school."

My stomach tightens, and I don't know how to respond to that. I want to tell him I felt the same, but I don't want to give him false hope either. I need to figure things out with Dan before I even contemplate what to do about Kev. So, I end up shooting him a timid smile and keeping my mouth closed.

"Oh no!" I exclaim, sitting upright in the chair as we pull up alongside my Audi. I jump out the instant Kev kills the engine, surveying the damage to my car with a sigh. Someone has stolen the three non-punctured tires, and my car is completely undriveable.

"Little shits," Kev says, shaking his head and pulling out his cell. "I'll drive you home, and I know a guy who can tow your car. Get whatever else you need while I make a call."

I open my mouth to protest, but he silences me with a deadly look, so I do as I'm told, grabbing my book bag from the back seat and my laptop from the trunk. Then I lock the car and text Dan to see where he is. He replies instantly letting me know he'll be late, and I scowl as I toss my cell in my bag and climb back into Kev's car.

"Everything okay?" he asks, frowning a little.

"Peachy," I lie, while punching the coordinates to my house into the GPS system.

We start moving again. "My guy will tow your car to his garage and fix the tires. I said I'd drop the keys into him later, and he'll drop the car back to your place sometime tomorrow. I can come pick you up in the morning if you need a ride to school?"

"Thanks for organizing that, and I'm sure Dan can drop me at school in the morning."

"Of course." A muscle clenches in his jaw, and an uneasy atmosphere descends again. After a few minutes, he clears his throat. "I was wondering ... what'd you ever do with all those photos you took of me?"

"I still have them," I truthfully admit. "Along with other stuff of yours. I tried to throw them away, countless times, but I couldn't do it." Subconsciously, I think I've always been holding onto the notion of Keven and me. I can't believe that we're back in each other's lives. Maybe my belief in fate isn't as misplaced as I've come to accept.

"I have that picture of us at junior prom by my bed," he admits. "It was always my favorite."

"You do?" I arch a brow. "I'm betting that goes down well when you bring a girl home."

"I don't bring girls home."

I snort. "You seriously expect me to believe there haven't been other girls?"

"I didn't say that," he says. "I'm a horny bastard, and I love sex. I'm sure you haven't forgotten." He drills me with a look so darkly seductive my panties are instantly soaked. "There have been hookups but always at their place or in a hotel."

"What about girlfriends?" I ask.

"I haven't had a girlfriend since you."

My mouth drops to the floor. "You're lying."

"I'm really not." He reaches over, taking my hand and raising it to his mouth. He plants a light kiss on my knuckles, and I feel the effects all the way to the tips of my toes. "No one else ever measured up to you, and even if I had found someone worthy, how could I be with her when I'm still madly in love with you?"

I can count on one hand the number of times Kev told me he loved me back in high school. Kev was hugely romantic when it came to doing things for me and showing me all the ways in which he cared. But he always struggled to articulate those feelings. It never bothered me, because I knew he loved me anyway. I didn't need to hear him say it a million times to know. Which is why I understand how big a deal it is that he's said that to me now.

"Keven." Tears prick my eyes as I look at the adoring expression on his face. Reluctantly, he drops my hand to maneuver the car around the next bend.

Silence engulfs us again as we pull up to the gate to my house. I input the code on the keypad, and the gates slowly open. When we reach the top of the driveway, he cuts the engine and swivels in his seat so he's facing me. "Tell me you feel nothing for me, Cheryl. Tell me it's all in my head, and I *will* leave you alone. I promise."

"I'm a hot mess right now, Kev. I'm feeling so many things."

"Can we go inside and talk?" He glances around. "I don't see your fiancé's car, so I'm guessing he's not here?"

"He's not, but—"

"Please, Cheryl." He pins me with puppy dog eyes, and I'm powerless to resist.

"Okay, but just for one coffee."

He smiles before tentatively reaching out to brush some loose strands of hair behind my ears. His fingers leave a fiery trail on my skin, and the urge to fling myself at him is riding me hard, but I sit on my hands to harness the craving. "You're so incredibly beautiful, Cheryl. I hope you know that. I think it's because you're so good, so pure, on the inside, and it just radiates all over you."

Tears roll down my face. "Keven. Please stop. I can't ..." A choked sob rips from the very essence of my soul.

"I'm sorry. Please don't cry. I don't want to upset you. I just want you to know how much I love you because I didn't tell you enough in high school. I was an idiot. Thought saying it out loud would make me sound like a pussy. After we broke up, I kicked myself in the ass so many times over all those wasted opportunities. And I know I'm not good at this romantic stuff, but—"

I put my hand over his mouth. "You're the most romantic man I've ever met, and I never doubted how much you loved me. At least, not until the end. You never needed to say those words, Kev. I felt your love every second of every day because you were always there for me and we just got each other. So, don't beat yourself up about that." I remove my hand and open the door. "C'mon. Let me make you that coffee."

Thankfully, he doesn't mention anything else about us once we head into the house. He insists I give him a full tour, and I do my best to summon enthusiasm as I show him around, but I can tell he's picked up on my lethargy. The only room I don't show him is the master bedroom because that would just be way too awkward.

After I make coffees, I suggest we take them into the living room, but a dark look washes over his face as he maintains he's fine to stay in the kitchen. "How are your parents?" he asks. "And Bryan and Violet."

"They're all good," I reply, sipping my coffee. "Dad's still working for the same pharmaceutical company, and he's in charge of the whole finance operation now. Mom volunteers for a few local charities when she's not moonlighting as Violet's personal taxi service." I grin as I think of my little sister.

"Violet was close in age to the triplets, wasn't she?" Kev says, propping his chin in his hands and leaning his elbows on the marble countertop. I work hard to ignore the way his massive biceps flex and roll under his shirt with the movement.

I nod. "She'll be eighteen in a few months, and she's a senior now. Bryan's a freshman at UD. He's studying business and finance like my dad did."

"Tell them I said hi," he says before his face contorts. "Or maybe not. I'm not sure your mother would be happy to know we're on speaking terms again."

"Mom always loved you. I think she was as disappointed as me when we broke up."

"I loved your family. Loved going to your house. My mom was hardly ever home, and I resented her for that. Going to your house was bittersweet because I loved how your mom fussed over me, but it also highlighted how little my mom was involved in my life."

"That didn't mean she didn't love you," I say, feeling the need to defend Alex. "She was trying to provide for all of you, and your dad didn't work, so he was home to take care of you."

"I know, and I'm not as resentful now. When I discovered James wasn't my bio dad, I hated him and Mom for ages for concealing the truth, but then I started to look at it differently. He took Kade and me on knowing we weren't his biological children, but he never treated us any differently, and I always felt his love. Over time, it was easier to forgive him, and to forgive Mom. Sometimes, it's easy to forget that our parents are fallible too. They fuck up on occasion, but it doesn't mean they love you any less."

I subconsciously lean toward him. Everything about him draws me in. From his heartfelt words to his dark, sultry voice, his sexy face, and the hypnotic way he's staring at me. It's as if someone took my dream of my ideal man and packaged him as Keven Kennedy. How I ever thought I could leave him in the past is beyond me.

He's right—I'm clearly delusional.

"Cheryl, honey." He leans across the counter until our faces are only centimeters apart. "Unless you want me to spread you out across this island unit and impale you with my cock, you've got to stop looking at me like that."

"Holy fuck." I straighten up, jerking back out of his space, exhaling deeply. "You can't say things like that to me either." My heart is beating so fast, and my body throbs with need. I want to pull him close and lose myself in him, and I'm not sure I'm strong enough to resist. "I think you should go."

"Rain check then," he says, smirking, and I send him a cautionary look. "Mind if I take a piss before I go?"

"Of course not. You know where the bathroom is."

I watch him walking out of the kitchen, using the opportunity to fully check him out. His designer jeans hug his shapely ass and muscular thighs causing saliva to pool in my mouth. His back is a solid block of muscle, rolling and stretching under his tight shirt. He runs one hand through his hair, and I'm envious.

I want to be the one to do that.

Happy memories resurface in my mind, and this time, I don't resist. I let them replay, reliving each moment as if it's the first time, and with each memory, I fall all over again.

I realize I'm staring at an empty doorway, daydreaming, about ten minutes later, and I snap out of it, glancing at the clock on the wall with a frown.

Where on Earth is Keven?

Chapter 12

Cheryl

"What the hell are you doing in Dan's office? And how did you even get in here?" I demand, planting my hands on my hips and glaring at him. I know for a fact that Dan keeps this office locked. It was something else I've become wary of, especially after he got that new security system installed on Monday.

"I picked the lock, and you need to see this." Kev is completely unapologetic as he gets up from Dan's desk, coming toward me.

"Get out!" I shout, pointing my finger into the hallway. I know Kev wants me back, but snooping in Dan's office is a low blow and not the way to win me over.

He stalks toward me, picking me up and throwing me over his shoulder before I've had time to even contemplate the move. My head dangles just above his ass.

Not a bad view, my cheeky inner devil whispers in my ear.

Before I can demand he let me down, he's placing my feet on the floor, his hands on my shoulders holding me in place. We're positioned in front of Dan's large mahogany TV unit. The doors are pushed to either side, revealing a row of hidden screens. "Were you aware your fiancé has cameras all over this house?"

My eyes almost bug out of my head as I skim over the rotating images of the inside and outside of the house.

What the fuck?

"Dan said the only cameras were outside, mainly around the perimeter," I mumble.

"And did he tell you he has armed men guarding that barn in the woods?" He jabs his finger at a screen on the top left. I squint as I struggle to make out the shadowy forms in the dark. A sensor light flicks on at that exact moment, illuminating two men standing in front of the entrance doors to the barn, lighting up cigarettes. Both have rifles strapped around their torso and they look like the type not to be messed with. Bile floods my mouth, and fear spikes my blood pressure to coronary-inducing levels. My legs buckle, threatening to go out from under me, but Kev is there to catch me. He scoops me up into his arms and walks over to Dan's desk, dropping into the chair with me in his lap.

"I knew there was something fishy about that barn," I murmur, as Kev's fingers race across the keyboard.

"You need to get out of here, Cheryl. Tonight. It's not safe for you," he says, his fingers click-clicking as he speaks.

"What are you doing?" I ask, watching lines of code race across Dan's desktop screen.

"I'm implanting a virus into the security system. It's the only way to erase the images of me here tonight."

I can't argue with that. If Dan knew I had another man in our house, he'd freak out. Not that it matters anymore.

Our relationship is over.

This has cemented the decision in my mind, and now I know I'm right in ending things with him. "He lied to me. He's mixed up in the same shit Garcia was involved in, isn't he?" I don't actually direct the question to Keven, I just kind of throw it out there into thin air, but he answers all the same.

"Yes, and he's dangerous, Cheryl. I don't want you spending another second in his company. Go pack a bag. You can stay in my guest room tonight. Hell, you can stay as long as you like. Or I'll help you move into your friend Lin's place or help you find a place of your own, but you can't stay here."

I'm only half paying attention to him as I watch the camera feeds alternating from room to room. My stomach churns as I spot the feed in our bedroom. I wonder how long these cameras have been there. *Were they all installed on Monday while I was attending classes at MassArt, completely ignorant of what was going on in my own home, or have they been here all along?*

I wonder if I ever knew Daniel at all?

Has everything been a lie?

And how stupid am I not to have seen the signs?

I knew he couldn't be making this kind of money as a new attorney, yet I accepted the bullshit he fed me without truly stopping to question it.

What the hell is wrong with me?

Why am I so fucking naïve all the time?

Why do I keep trying to see the good in people when all they do is let me down?

"Honey." Kev tilts my face to his worried one. "It's going to be okay. I'll protect you. I'm not going to let him hurt you. I promise."

"He won't hurt me."

"Cheryl." He sighs, shaking his head. "That's what guys like Daniel do. They have no empathy. No remorse. He'd hurt you like that." He clicks his fingers, standing with me still enveloped in his arms.

The images on the screens flicker before fading away, replaced with cloudy static. Kev's still got the magic touch.

"Let me down, please." I shuffle out of his hold, crossing my arms over my chest. "I appreciate your offer of help but I'm not going anywhere tonight."

His jaw tenses and his eyes narrow. "What the fuck, Cheryl? Please don't tell me you're staying with him. Please don't tell me you're that stupid?"

That is like a red flag to a bull, and I shove at his chest, channeling my anger in the totally wrong direction. "Who the hell are you to call me stupid? After all the stupid shit you did back in high school? And, not that it's any of your business but I'm breaking off the engagement and leaving Daniel; however, I'm confronting him first. I want him to look me in the eye and tell me he's been lying this whole time."

Kev is violently shaking his head. "No! No way! You can't stay here! He could fucking kill you! Or worse, sell you to those perverts he's in business with!" He grabs hold of my arm, dragging me out of the room. "I'm not taking no for an answer. Go pack a bag, and we're leaving."

"No, we're not." I wrestle out of his hold, trying to calm myself down. It's not Keven I'm angry at. "Look, I don't want to argue with you. I'm going to end things officially with him tonight, and I'll come to your place then. I know you want to protect me, but he won't hurt me, no matter what you think of him, he wouldn't do that."

"Fuck!" He lashes out, kicking the wall in frustration. "How can you be this naïve?" he shouts. "Eva was married to Jeremy for years, and he kidnapped her and was going to let his men gang rape her before handing her over to his network of pimps. Wake the fuck up, Cheryl! Stanten is no different. If Jeremy could do that to his wife, what do you think Stanten would do to his fiancée of a few months?"

"I'm not walking out without an explanation," I calmly reply, although I'm shaking all over at his words.

He claws his hands through his hair, growling in frustration. "Have you any idea the things he's been doing? He's been fucking underage girls behind your back, and he's involved in all kinds of illegal shit."

"What? No! How could you even know that?"

He grips my shoulders, pushing his face into mine. "I can't tell you that, but please trust me when I tell you it's the truth."

I snort. "Trust you? You've been back in my life a hot minute and you want me to trust you?" I push him away. "I trust you about as much as I trust Dan right now."

It's a low blow, and I know it, but I'm done with men manipulating me. I'm going to end things with Dan on my terms. I'm going to get closure this time. I'm not being naïve. I know it's risky, but I'm taking control this time. I'm ending this on my terms and walking away with my head held high.

Hurt lances across his face, and I'm instantly remorseful. "Kev, I—"

"I got it," he barks. "You still hate me."

I step in closer to him, planting my hands on his impressive chest. "Kev, I've never hated you. I wanted to, believe me, but I just couldn't. I love you too much to hate you. I know you're worried, but you've got to let me do this my way." I stretch up on tiptoes and kiss his cheek. "I'm sorry I said that, and I take it back. I trust you more than I trust him, but trust works both ways. You've got to trust me to know how to handle this. I need to do this my way."

"I don't want anything to happen to you." His eyes fill up, and my heart melts.

I wrap my arms around him, closing my eyes as I lay my head on his chest. His arms automatically go around my waist. "Nothing will happen to me, but if it makes you feel better, put one of those tracker things on my cell."

"Is there anything I can say to convince you to leave with me now?" he asks, running his hand up and down my spine.

I look up at him. "No," I truthfully admit, and he lets loose a string of expletives. I pull my cell out of my pocket. "Put the tracker on it, and then you better go. He could be home any second."

"I really don't like this," Kev says as I walk him to the door ten minutes later. He put some tracking software on my cell and insisted on adding these little chip trackers to my shoes. I'd teased him that he was like James Bond, always carrying useful gadgets, but it didn't go down well as he pinned me with a dark look and growled low under his breath.

"But you're trusting me, and I promise I'll text you as soon as he comes home and the minute I'm out of here. I'll call a taxi, and I'll come straight to your place. I promise. Now, go." I gently nudge him toward the door. "I've got to pack."

He goes to open the door, but then he swings around, reeling me into his strong arms. His body trembles against mine. "I love you, Cheryl Ann Keeland, and if anything happens to you, I'm holding you responsible."

I hold him tight, closing my eyes and enjoying his warmth and his comforting strength. "Nothing is going to happen to me. I'll talk to you later or tomorrow."

I have to almost physically force him out the door, but eventually, he leaves, and I hurry around the house, gathering my personal possessions and boxing them up. It's after midnight by the time I've packed up all my stuff, and there's still no sign of Dan.

My cell pings, and I check my messages. I've one from Dan telling me he'll be late and another from Keven telling me to open the front gate to let his friend drop my Audi off. The buzzer for the main gate goes, and

I let the man in, hurrying out to meet him so I can thank him in person for getting my car back to me so fast. I'm guessing Kev called him the minute he left and offered him some ridiculous amount of money to get my car back to me tonight.

His thoughtfulness and protectiveness cause my chest to swell with so much emotion. This is the Keven I know. The guy who goes out of his way to take care of me. I'd almost forgotten how incredible it feels to be cared for like this.

As I wait for Dan, I think over everything Keven said, and I can't believe I was so blind. So naïve to believe Dan when he said he had all these late meetings. It's obvious he's cheating on me, but the thought of him sleeping with underage girls sickens me. I don't know what Keven knows, or how he knows it, but I'm really hoping he's wrong about that fact. And don't get me started on the armed men out in the woods. I don't think they mean me any harm, but who knows what their instructions are. I try not to think about them as I wait for my soon-to-be ex-fiancé to come home.

By two a.m., my eyelids are drooping, and I'm yawning profusely. I text Keven to tell him I'm going to sleep and I'll talk to Dan in the morning. I'm asleep before his reply arrives.

My alarm goes off at six a.m., and I roll over in the empty bed. Dan didn't even come home last night. I shower and get changed, skipping breakfast because I've no appetite, and then I load up my car with my stuff. I message Keven and Lin and take a last look around the house for anything I might have missed before grabbing a coffee and phoning my mom. She's an early riser, like me, and I know she'll be awake.

"Sweetheart, it's so good to hear from you," she says, sounding all sunny and cheery on the other end of the line.

"It's good to hear your voice too."

"Oh no. I know that voice. What's happened?"

I proceed to tell her everything about Dan and Kev and what Kev said about Dan. "I'm going to have to side with Keven on this one. Please get the hell out of that house."

"I'm going Mom as soon as we finish this call. My car's already packed."

"I knew there was something off about that man," she mumbles.

"I should have listened to you." I'd brought Dan home a couple times since we got engaged, and my parents never really warmed to him. Mom took me aside on the second visit to ask me if I was sure and to share her concerns. I brushed them aside without giving them too much attention which was a big mistake.

"There's just something so ... cold and unnatural ... about that man. Sure, he looked like the doting fiancé, he played the role well, but he didn't look at you the way Keven Kennedy used to."

"What way did Kev look at me?" I ask, chewing on the inside of my cheek.

"Like you were the only girl in existence. Like his world started and ended with you." I can hear her smiling down the line. "I'd watch you both when you were at the kitchen table doing your homework, and sometimes, I'd catch him watching you when you weren't aware. Your head would be stuck in a book and he'd just look at you with so much love in his eyes. It astounded me. You were both so young, but the love between you wasn't. Which is why I was so disappointed in him."

There's a telling pregnant pause. "I know how strongly you felt about him, and I'm glad he's explained what happened back then, but I don't want to see you hurt all over again."

"He's made some foolish mistakes, and while it was still a betrayal, it wasn't a betrayal of the heart," I quietly say before adding, "Do you think I should take him back?"

"Only you can answer that, but don't rush into anything until you're sure. You're ending your engagement, and your childhood sweetheart might seem like the answer to all your prayers, but you won't know how you feel until you can separate your emotions. If it's meant to be, you two will find your way back to one another."

Silence engulfs us for a few beats until her concerned voice filters down the line. "Don't worry about that now, Cheryl. What's most important is that you get the hell out of that house and sever all ties with Dan. So, go, baby girl. Go and get to safety. You'll figure out the rest after that."

"Thanks, Mom. I love you."

"I love you too. Now leave! And text me when you're safe."

Hayley drops into the seat beside me in the auditorium while we wait for the prof to show up. I'm surprised to see her. Lately, she's been missing a lot of morning classes. "Hey," I say, turning to face her. "Oh my God. Are you okay?" I ask the instant I spot the raw red markings around her neck. She's attempted to hide them with an expensive, new Hermes silk scarf, but she's done a piss poor job of it.

"Why wouldn't I be okay?" she smirks, sipping from a paper cup.

"What happened to your neck?" I whisper, leaning in close to inspect the raised, angry welts.

"Kinky sex." She waggles her brows, and my face contorts. I try to be open-minded, each to their own and all that, but those marks look nasty and painful. "Christ, you're such a fucking prude." Her eyes glint maliciously as she pins me with a smug look. "No wonder Dan has to seek his pleasure elsewhere."

Pressure settles on my chest, and bile travels up my throat. "What did you just say?"

"You heard me." She can't contain her grin. "I've been fucking Dan for the past three months. Where else do you think he is late at night or when he doesn't come home? I was blowing him when he sent you that text last night, and he only left my bed an hour ago."

"He doesn't even like you."

She bursts out laughing, drawing attention from some students in the rows in front. "You're so fucking gullible, which makes this easy. You deserve to be cheated on if you're that naïve. I've grown tired of waiting for him to tell you, so I'll do it. He's leaving you for me. I guess I'll be the one driving around in the fancy Audi and living in the mansion." She winks, grinning like the cat that got the cream.

I stand, feeling ill to the pit of my stomach. "You're welcome to all of it, and I hope you get what's coming to you. Now that I think about it, you two make such a lovely couple. Let's hope you have what it takes to hold him, or one day, you could find yourself in my place." I hold my head up high as I leave my former best friend, and the auditorium, behind.

As I walk through the parking lot toward my car, a massive sense of relief washes over me. Hayley may believe she's screwed me over, but she's just done me a huge favor.

I get to end this now without admitting I know anything about cameras or the armed men or the underage girls which I one hundred percent believe now. I know Keven was worried that I'd blurt too much out in the heat of the moment, and he'd cautioned me to be very careful what I said to him. Now, I can let Daniel believe he is the reason our engagement is ending. His cheating has broken us up and it ties it all up nice and cleanly. I can walk away with him believing I know nothing of his shady operation and live my life without fear of retaliation.

Most of all though, this has proven that I never really loved him, not enough to have ever consented to marry him. Because the devastation I felt when I thought Keven had betrayed me was heartbreaking, and I was inconsolable. Hearing Dan has been cheating with Hayley, and God knows how many others, has left me feeling nothing but sheer relief. Yes, I feel stupid and naïve for not realizing but I've found out the truth in time.

I've dodged a bullet, avoiding making the worst mistake of my life.

Right now, that's all that matters.

Chapter 13

Keven

"This is excellent work, Keven. I'm very impressed." I should be happy the SSA is singing my praises, but I'm anxious for this fucking briefing to end so I can get home to Cheryl. I was too worried to leave her at my place all alone, so Eva and Kade are with her, and my brother has promised he won't leave until I arrive home.

I managed to install a hidden feed linking from all the cameras in Stanten's house to a secure private video network where we can watch the comings and goings at will, so the boss man wants everyone working overtime to try and nail these bastards.

I tilt my head from side to side, attempting to loosen the kink in my neck and stiff shoulders. I spent all night in my car, tucked into the shadows about a half a mile from Stanten's place. There was no way in hell I was leaving Cheryl in that house by herself waiting for that monster to come home. I wanted to be close by so I could be there in a flash if she needed me. And, only for the fact I had to complete a routine physical this morning, I would've been shadowing Cheryl when she confronted Stanten at his office and broke things off with him.

I can't keep the smug grin off my face as we watch the fallout from that meeting on the screen. I knew Stanten would get his security people in to fix the system immediately. I've crossed paths with this company before, and they're notorious for using outdated systems so they can skim extra profit off the top. Lucky for us, they aren't using the latest tech, or I'd never have been able to install the hidden program which gives us access to the feed.

I've hacked in now, focusing on the living room where Stanten is presently wearing a line in the carpet. He paces back and forth, screaming and shouting at his three associates. The room is a mess, because when he first arrived home, he trashed it in a scary display of uncontrollable rage. I'm not a behavioral analyst, but the guy looks psychopathic to me.

"How the fuck did this happen?!" he roars, prodding his finger in Jesse Robert's chest. "You were supposed to keep that bitch Hayley on a leash."

"Don't fucking blame me for this, man. You're the one who started spending more time with her. Staying over and leading her to believe you loved her."

"The only thing I loved about that whore was choking her while I was fucking her in the ass."

Jesse snorts. "She's a dirty bitch, but she has zero limits. She let me do all manner of shit that most girls would balk at. You sure you want to get rid of her?"

"I can't get Cheryl back unless she's out of the picture."

All the blood drains from my face. I'd hoped Stanten would let Cheryl go without a fight, but that was clearly wishful thinking.

Jesse leans against the wall. "I don't get it, man. Why her? She's too vanilla. Too honest. Too sweet. If you ask me, Hayley did you a solid. Cheryl doesn't belong in this world."

Stanten flies across the room, grabbing Jesse around the throat and slamming him into the wall. "Don't you ever fucking talk about Cheryl like that again." His eyes glisten with murderous intent. "My father told me to find a nice, pretty girl to raise a family with. Someone with good genes and from a wholesome family. Someone bright but not too bright who wouldn't pry into my business affairs. Cheryl has big plans for her own career, so she won't be bothered with mine. She looks good on my arm, and she has a tight little cunt I happen to love fucking."

My hands ball into fists under the table, and I bite back the primitive roar dying to burst free of my chest. I glare at Agent Wentward as he sends me a knowing look.

"Cheryl ticks all the boxes. That slut Hayley was never in contention for the role. She's a hole to fuck when I'm bored and need the distraction. Now she's a pain in my ass because she's messed things up with Cheryl, but I'll get her back. There's no other choice. I don't have time to look for a suitable replacement."

That asshole better hope I never get my hands on him because I will squeeze every last breath out of his body for disrespecting the girl I love.

"Boss." The short, stocky dude steps up. "He's turning blue."

"Do I look like I fucking care?" Stanten roars.

"We need him to lure Hayley out unless you plan on doing that yourself?"

It's like a light goes off in his head. Stanten drops Jesse and steps back, his face smoothing out into a calm mask. He dusts down the sleeves of his suit jacket and stares at his so-called friend with an emotionless expression. It's scary as shit. Jesse slumps to the floor and instantly pukes all over his legs. It couldn't happen to a nicer dude.

"Get yourself cleaned up." Stanten kicks at Jesse's feet. "Borrow one of my suits. Grab Hayley, and take her to the meeting point. Gonzalez will be waiting, and he'll take it from there."

Jesse nods, scrambling to his feet and running out of the room like a scared little pussy.

A few minutes later, they all leave the house and the SSA starts barking out orders. "Wentward, keep tabs on Stanten. Cunningham, I want eyes on those feeds twenty-four seven. Organized crime is loaning us a few bodies for surveillance, but I want you supervising. Higgins and Mead, you're with me and the task force. We'll go to Hayley's apartment and wait for Roberts to show up. Kennedy, walk with me." He snaps his fingers as the meeting is disbanded, and everyone scurries away. The sense of urgency is palpable in the air, but it finally feels like we're getting somewhere.

I keep stride with SSA Clement as he heads toward his office. "Continue to trawl online for any evidence we might use against Stanten. Keep Cheryl at your place for the moment. However, I want to talk to her. I want to see how she might aid the investigation."

"No," I snap. "Leave her out of it."

He slams to a halt in the corridor. "That is not your decision to make." He scrutinizes my face. "I warned you not to make this personal. Are you too emotionally involved? Do I need to remove you from this case?"

My jaw is locked so tight it's a wonder it doesn't break. "That won't be necessary." I want to punch something. Preferably his face.

"Good." He resumes walking and I keep pace with him. "You have twenty-four hours to tell her you're an FBI analyst and explain about the case. I understand this has been a lot for her to process, but we don't have the luxury of time. I want her in here on Saturday, at the latest. Understood?"

I nod, while the whole time I'm trying to think of a way of getting her out of this. And while part of me wants to come clean about everything, now isn't the right time.

I'm only starting to win her trust again, and this will set us back. She'll be furious when she finds out I've been lying to her even if it was in the interests of protecting her. I can't risk losing her. Especially when she needs me to keep her safe. That asshole is not getting near her again. I don't care if I have to fucking kill him with my bare hands to ensure it.

"Thanks so much for keeping her company," I tell my brother as Eva hugs Cheryl goodbye.

"Anytime. It was good to catch up with her. You know I always liked Cheryl."

"How is she?" I quietly ask, tossing my jacket on the back of the chair.

"She's doing good. She's angry, and she feels foolish, but she doesn't seem scared."

"That's what I'm worried about." I rub a tense spot between my brows.

Kade bores a hole in my skull. "Out with it."

I glance over my shoulder, making sure the girls aren't listening. "He's not going to let her go, and he thinks making her friend disappear is the solution. The guy's a fucking psycho Kade, and I'm terrified."

Kade's large hand clamps down on my shoulder. "We'll keep her safe, but you can't shut us out."

"This is fucking dangerous, Kade. As bad as the situation with Garcia. I don't want my family anywhere near this, so you're to butt out, just like you told me to butt out when it was you in this position."

"And you didn't listen to me." He sends me a smug, challenging look. "I'm helping. Get over it."

"*We're* helping," Eva says, coming up behind her husband.

Kade tucks her into the nook of his arm, pressing a kiss to her cheek. "Not happening, love."

She punches him in the stomach and he groans, hunching over. Cheryl and I exchange amused smiles. "We're a team, and whatever you're cooking up will involve me," Eva coolly replies.

"We're not cooking up anything," I say. "I want him to stay out of it. I want *both of you* to stay out of it."

"You want me to punch you too?" she threatens, planting her hands on her shapely hips.

"No, ma'am." I hold up my hands.

"Good. Then what's the plan?"

It's pointless to keep arguing, and maybe I can use this to my advantage without putting Eva or Kade in danger. I turn to Cheryl. "Have you ever learned to shoot?" She shakes her head. "Any objection to learning now?"

"Not a bit. I want to know how to protect myself."

I nod. "Okay." I look at Kade. "We'll meet Tuesdays, Thursdays, and Saturdays at the firing range. Alternate days we'll meet in the gym for self-defense lessons." I know Kade has been teaching Eva self-defense for months, and after the warehouse shooting, she finally agreed to learn how to use a firearm, so she has a head start on Cheryl, but I figure the moral support can't hurt. Plus, they'll be helping in a way that keeps all of them safe.

"Agreed."

"I'll need to talk to everyone in the family," I add. "I want to upgrade the tracking software on everyone's cells, and I have a few other items I want people to take." I can see Cheryl smiling out of the corner of my eye. I pin her with a sharp look. "This is a James Bond and Jason Bourne comment-free zone."

She smiles even wider, and I can't hold onto my sharp look in the face of such devastating beauty. I return her smile, and so much passes between us as we stare at one another.

"We can talk to everyone when we're in Nantucket," Kade suggests, breaking me free of the spell.

I walk right up to Cheryl. "Do you have set plans for Easter, or can you come with because I'm not leaving you here unprotected."

"Kev, I appreciate all you're doing for me, but it's not your job to keep me protected."

I glare at her. "The hell it isn't. And I'd like to see you try stopping me."

Her chest heaves, and tears glisten in her eyes. "I don't want to burden your whole family. And I don't want to bring danger to your door. It's not right."

"You're our family, Cheryl," Kade says, helpfully stepping in. "You always have been, so don't even try to deny it. And we protect our family. As for the danger, it's been on our doorstep for some time. You're not bringing anything that doesn't already exist."

"It's true. We're already entangled in this." I cup her face. "Any other objections, or can I text Mom to set an extra place for you?"

"Kev," she whispers, peering deep into my eyes. "Are you really sure about this?"

I silence her by pressing my lips to hers. I don't know any other way to convey how serious I am about her and wanting to keep her safe, and I've been longing to kiss her again for years.

She melts against me, and I mentally fist pump the air. It feels like I've waited for eternity to hold her in my arms again, to feel her mouth moving against mine. I angle my head, deepening the kiss, while I haul her close to my chest, snaking my arms around her waist. My head is drowning in so many thoughts, my heart swollen with so many emotions. I hear the soft tread of retreating footsteps as Kade and Eva slip out of the room, granting us privacy. Cheryl sighs into my mouth, and I wind my hands through her hair, kissing her with every ounce of love swirling inside me.

For years, I believed I'd never get to experience this again. Now I've got her back in my arms, I'm never letting her go.

She might not have accepted it yet, but Cheryl Keeland is the only woman for me. When I look at my future, she is all I see. I'm not backing down, and I'm not giving up. I'm going to bend over backward until I prove it to her.

Chapter 14

Cheryl

Keven kisses me like he never thought he'd get to do it again. I know I didn't. His love wraps around me, blanketing me in a safety net I so desperately need right now. Despite my earlier bravado, I'm scared about Dan's next move.

The meeting in his office was terrifying. I've never seen someone so enraged. Part of it was directed at Hayley, and part of it was directed at me. He swears it was only sex, as if that excuses it. He knows how I feel about cheating, so me hurling my engagement ring in his face shouldn't have come as any surprise. The scariest part was how quickly he switched emotions. In the blink of an eye, he transformed from anger-driven rage to pleading with me to forgive him and begging for a second chance. I didn't entertain it for even a second. I told him there's no going back, and I walked away.

But I don't think he's going to go that quietly. And, quite frankly, the thought frightens me.

"Hey." Kev breaks our kiss, peering into my eyes with concern. "Are you okay?" He grips the nape of my neck, flooding my body with warmth.

"Everything's changing so fast, and I feel like I'm on a rollercoaster, and it's going a hundred miles an hour, and I don't know how to get off." Hurt briefly flashes in his eyes, and he slides his hand off my neck, but I grip his wrist, holding it in place. "I don't mean that in a bad way.

Just that I need time to process. If we're going to do this again, I need to be sure I can let go of the past and start with a clean slate."

He pulls my head to his, pressing a delicate kiss to my lips. "I completely understand, and I don't want to pressure you, but I can't lose you again, Cheryl. I won't survive it a second time."

I blink back tears. "Neither would I," I whisper.

He lifts his head, spearing me with an intense look. "Did you mean it? Last night, when you said you loved me?"

I cup his face, brushing my mouth against his in a feather-soft kiss. "Yes. I don't think I've ever stopped loving you, but I've been in denial. And I've only just broken off my engagement, and you've recently come back into my life, and I just need some time."

He pulls me into a hug, pressing a fierce kiss to the top of my head. "Take all the time you need, but don't shut me out. And I want you to stay here where I can protect you. I don't trust Stanten."

I sigh. "Neither do I, and that scares me," I honestly admit.

"Don't be scared, babe. I'll kill him before he lays a hand on you."

Hayley is a no-show on Friday morning, and I fleetingly wonder if that's because she's shacked up in bed with my ex-fiancé. I don't actually care. I'm just glad she isn't here because it makes things less awkward.

I meet Kev, Kade, and Eva at the gym later that night for our first self-defense lesson.

I'm a terrible student.

In my defense, every time Kev puts his hands on me, I zone out, lost in the sensation of his touch. Kev figures out I'm distracted, and why, shooting me a cocky grin as he asks Kade to switch places. With Kade working with me, and Kev working with Eva, we actually manage to get something done. Then we all head out for dinner, and it's one of the best nights I've had in ages.

We're back at Kev's place now, enjoying a glass of wine before bed. "I heard something interesting today," I say, sipping the cool, crisp wine. "A little birdy tells me an anonymous donor made a sizable donation to the residential home with strict instructions that at least half the funds were to be used to purchase new cameras for the photography class."

His brows climb to his hairline and he avoids looking at me as she speaks. "Yeah? That's awesome."

I get up and move over beside him. Taking hold of his face, I force his gaze to mine. "I know you did that." My eyes probe his, and I see the truth. "And I think I fell a little bit more in love with you for it." I lean in and kiss him slowly. "Thank you," I whisper over his lips, as he pulls me into his warm body.

"I was happy to help, and you know I can afford it. If you need more, you only have to ask." He hauls me into his lap, and my legs go on either side of his hips. My core aches deliciously, but I try to ignore my libido. "I have more money than I need, so if I can do some good with it, I want to help."

"Your altruism is one of the many things I love about you."

"It's one of the things I love most about you too." His hands slip under the back of my blouse, and I shiver all over from his touch.

"Wow, you're really embracing the 'l' word," I pant, my hips grinding involuntarily against his growing hard-on.

"I'm trying. I never want you to doubt what I feel for you." His hand moves around to my belly and starts inching up.

"I don't. Not anymore." A tiny whimper escapes my lips as his fingers brush the underside of my breasts.

"Can I touch you? I really want to make you feel good," he whispers against my lips.

"You already are, and yes, please touch me. I need your hands on me."

He fuses our mouths together in a searing-hot kiss as his hand moves up, cupping one of my tits through my bra. I gyrate against him, and he thrusts his erection up against the softest part of me. I moan, unashamedly, into his mouth when he yanks one side of my bra down, exposing my bare flesh to his hand. He rolls my hard nipple between his thumb and forefinger, and I gasp as my body floods with heat. "More," I mumble as his lips devour mine. He breaks the kiss momentarily to remove my blouse, and then he slowly drags the straps of my bra down my arms, his greedy eyes following the movement.

115

"Fuck, Cheryl. You're gorgeous." He cups first one, then the other, breast, weighing it in his hands. My chest heaves, and a shot of liquid lust whizzes straight to my core. "These are bigger than I remember."

"I hadn't finished developing when I was last with you," I groan, as he starts kneading my sensitive flesh.

"I'm going to fuck these," he says, smushing my breasts together. "Someday soon." I don't have a chance to respond because he leans in, flicking my nipple with his wicked tongue, and I cry out, overcome with pleasure. He lavishes my breasts with attention, nipping, licking, and sucking, and I'm writhing on his lap, my panties completely soaked. I palm his erection through the denim, biting my lower lip when I feel how hard he is for me. I fumble with the button on his jeans, but he stops me, pulling my hand away. "Not tonight. Tonight is all about you."

"But—"

He places his hand over my mouth. "No buts." He pierces me with a warning look. "Now lie back so I can remove your jeans." I lie down on the couch without hesitation. It's been so long since I've had an earth-shattering orgasm, and I'm starving for it. Hell will freeze before I refuse him. Kev's the only man to elicit screams of pleasure from me, and I need that so badly right now.

Slowly, he peels my jeans down my legs. When I lift my hips to shimmy my panties off, he pushes down on my stomach. "Not yet." Flinging my jeans aside, he starts a slow perusal of my leg, licking his way up from my ankle to my calf and on to my thigh. I think I might come before he's even touched my clit; I'm that turned on. Burying his nose in my panties, he inhales deeply, and a loud groan flies from his lips. "Fuck, you smell so good, babe." He presses his nose in farther, and I squirm on the couch.

"Kev, please."

Grabbing the lace material of my panties and pulling it into a tight line, he slides the material up and down my slit, teasing me with slow gliding motions. I need to come so badly that I cry out in sheer frustration, bucking my hips and pleading with my body. He doesn't torture me anymore, instantly ripping the panties off and diving between the apex of my thighs with his mouth. His tongue licks up and down my slit before he slides two fingers inside me.

I'm so wet I can barely feel it until he adds a third digit and curls his fingers in the right spot. Pressure is building and building inside me, and when he sucks hard on my clit, while his fingers pump furiously in and out, I explode, climaxing hard, seeing stars as I buck and thrust while Kev keeps his fingers and his mouth on me.

When I'm sated, like a boneless jellyfish on the couch, he extracts his fingers from my pussy and puts them into his mouth. He pins me with dark lustful eyes as he licks my essence off his skin, and I watch as he sucks his fingers dry, my arousal spiking again. Then he leans down and kisses me tenderly. I taste myself on his lips, further igniting my desire.

No man has ever aroused me as much as Keven, and I can't believe I forgot how much we turned each other on. I was so wet for him back in high school, and from the moment we slept together for the first time, we were insatiable for one another. I reach out for the bulge in his pants, but he stops me a second time. "Not tonight, babe. You need time, and I can wait."

"I've changed my mind," I hiss, making a grab for him again. "I want you inside me, Kev. I want to feel you moving in me, with me. I want to remember how incredible we are together."

Grabbing a blanket off the back of the couch, he lays it over me, leaning in to kiss me again. "I want that too, Cheryl. I want it so badly I could cry. But we're not going to rush this. When I'm inside you again, it will be when you're one hundred percent sure about us." He takes my hand, pressing a delicate kiss to my wrist. "We don't have to rush. We have the rest of our lives to figure this out."

Lin is swooning the next day when I fill her in on everything over lunch. The studio is busy, so we've just grabbed a sandwich at the local deli. "Oh my God. He's so romantic and so sweet yet fucking sexy at the same time," she says in a dreamy voice.

"I know. Believe me, I know." I'm grinning like a loon, which is a miraculous thing because the Dan cloud still lingers ominously. "I was crazy in love with Kev back in high school, but he's all grown up now, and I think

I have the potential to completely lose my mind over him. I'm glad he stopped things last night. I'm not sure I'm ready to handle that level of intensity yet."

"I'm really happy for you, Cher." She squeezes my hand, grinning. "You are positively glowing, and you deserve this."

"Do you think I'm right to entertain a second chance with him?" I ask, because our past still haunts me. Still worries me.

"Yes, because it isn't true love if it isn't scary as shit. I know you're worried he'll hurt you again, but you won't know unless you take that leap of faith. You could miss out on the love of a lifetime if you don't push yourself out of your comfort zone."

I hug her as we get up to leave. "Thank you for being such a good friend to me."

She loops her arm in mine as we walk back to the studio. "It works both ways. You were there for me when Summer and I broke up, and I'm glad to be able to return the favor."

"Woah." Lin's eyes pop wide when we arrive back at the studio to the sight of a massive bouquet of red roses resting on the table in the staff room.

My stomach twists into ugly knots, and I veer away from the table as if they're poisonous. I don't need anyone to tell me they're for me. And I don't need to be a rocket scientist to know who they're from. "Get rid of them," I say through gritted teeth. "Please."

She glances at the card and her lips pinch together. "Got it." Snatching them up, she leaves the room and my breathing recalibrates.

The afternoon is extremely busy, and the last client has just left when two gentleman wearing black coats, black pants, and shiny black shoes step into the studio. Alarm bells ding in my head, and my blood pressure soars. The taller of the two steps up to the desk, approaching me. Sara—the photographer and owner of the studio—hurries toward us. "Ms. Keeland." The man pulls out a badge, flashing it at me. "I'm Special Agent Higgins, and this is Special Agent Mead. We need you to come with us."

"What's this about?" I ask, my voice quaking a little.

"We need to ask you some questions about Daniel Stanten."

My stomach lurches as I nod. I should've known to expect something like this. "Okay. Just let me grab my bag and jacket."

Sara and Lin follow me to the staff room. "Do you want me to call my attorney for you?" Sara offers, but I shake my head.

"I don't think I'll need an attorney. I haven't done anything wrong, and I don't even know anything that Dan is involved in."

"Are you sure?" She pins me with worried eyes, and that's without knowing any of the background as the only one I've confided in is Lin.

"I'm sure." Besides, if I do happen to need an attorney, I'm pretty sure Keven will send the Kennedy family attorney to help me. I send him a quick text, letting him know the FBI is taking me in for questioning. He'll only worry if I don't show up at the firing range.

I walk back outside and tentatively smile at the two men. "I'm ready."

Chapter 15

Keven

I'm at the firing range where Cheryl is a half hour late, and I'm officially worried. I stupidly left my cell at home on the kitchen counter although I have her number memorized, so I've called and left a message from Kade's phone.

"There's no point in you staying here," Kade says, watching me pace back and forth. "Go to the studio. I'm betting she got caught up in work and forgot the time."

"Or he's taken her. I knew I should've gone to pick her up."

"I thought you said an agent was assigned to follow Stanten? Surely, he would've informed you if he'd gone anywhere near Cheryl?"

"He could've sent one of his lackeys. Give me your cell." I hold out my hand, and he places his cell in my palm. "I can log into the tracking software via the cloud, and that should give me a lock on her location." My fingers fly over the keypad as I log into the system, scroll through the list and call up her number. All the blood leaches from my face when I see the location. "Shit!"

"What?" Eva removes her earmuffs and glasses, looking worried as she loops her arm in Kade's.

"My fucking boss has taken her in. I've got to go." I practically throw Kade's cell at him and take off running.

I slam my X5 into reverse, tires screeching as I peel out of the parking lot. I was planning on fessing up tonight over a home-cooked meal, and I'd sent the SSA a text earlier explaining I'd bring Cheryl in tomorrow. I can't believe he's gone over my head with this. I know he's in charge, but he fucking knows who she is to me. He has totally screwed me over, and I'll be lucky if Cheryl gives me the time of day after this.

As I race up the highway toward Chelsea, I call Dad's security guy. I've worked with Paul several times over the last few years, and he's the only one I trust to help me protect Cheryl. I should've trusted my instincts and done this weeks ago, but I was afraid it would just be something else I'd have to explain. "Keven, to what do I owe the pleasure?" Paul says answering on the third ring.

"I need a bunch of your men for bodyguard duty. The best you've got available. Two for here and a couple for Delaware." I don't want to leave Cheryl's family unprotected in case Stanten attempts to use them to get to her.

"Consider it done. Send me the details, and I'll have someone on it within the hour."

"Thanks, man." I end the call and press the pedal to the metal, hoping I can get to Cheryl in time to conduct damage limitation.

I tear into the building, grinding my teeth to the molars. I feel like kicking in the door to every interrogation room until I find her, but I rein my emotions in and think about this objectively.

Heading to my desk, I pull up the internal system, quickly locating the room she's in. Agent Cunningham is assisting the SSA with the interview. I stride toward the room as fast as my legs will carry me without drawing attention. I slip into the observation room, and my heart sinks as I watch Cheryl sitting across the desk from my boss and my colleague.

"I understand you're upset, Ms. Keeland, but I'm sure Mr. Kennedy will explain later. Right now, we need to ask you some questions pertaining to Mr. Stanten and his business interests. We are also concerned about Hayley Jackson. Her roommate has officially reported her as missing, and we have reason to believe Mr. Stanten is involved in her abduction."

I don't wait to hear Cheryl's reply, bursting into the room even though it could mean I lose my job.

Three heads swivel in my direction.

None of them are happy to see me.

Cheryl wears her hurt and her upset like a weapon. The SSA narrows his eyes in disappointment, and Sinead shoots me a sympathetic look. "I was going to tell you tonight," I blurt, eyeballing Cheryl. "I swear."

"This is an official interview, Mr. Kennedy, and I need you to leave the room," the SSA says in a level tone.

"You couldn't give me a few more hours?" I bark at him, standing my ground.

"I informed you by text of my intention."

"I left my cell at home." I can't ever remember doing that, but my head's cluttered with shit right now, and I was distracted. I should've returned for it when I realized I didn't have it on me. If it was physically possible, I'd kick myself in the ass.

"Well, that's unfortunate, but it doesn't change things. I need you to wait outside. You can speak to Ms. Keeland then."

"Cheryl, I'm sorry, and I can explain," I say, as the SSA takes my arm, ushering me toward the door.

"Save it," she snaps. "I've heard it all before."

My shoulders are heavy with dejection as I let the SSA drag me out of the room. "Pull another stunt like that and you're out of here," he snaps, shoving me into a chair outside the room. "I'm warning you, Kennedy. I've pulled a lot of strings and made a lot of allowances to get you on this task force. You have the makings of a very fine agent one day. Don't blow it. And don't betray the faith I've put in you. Do not come back into that room, or you're fired. Just stay put until we're done." He stalks back into the room, closing the door firmly after him.

Because I'm a glutton for punishment—and I fucking hate anyone telling me what to do—I slip back into the observation room, only this time it's not empty. Agent Dickhead sends me a gloating look as I stand in front of the hidden window. "Real smooth, Kennedy. You fucking idiot."

"Tell me how you really feel," I snarl, focusing on Cheryl as she listens to the SSA explain about Hayley and how she slipped through our hands.

Somehow, Jesse Roberts managed to get her out right under our nose. The sting was a bust, and the SSA's been in a pissy mood since.

"Stanten's used to getting his way. He's not going to give her up without a fight."

"If it's a fight he wants, he'll get one."

"That's a surefire way to lose your job."

I glower at him. "Do I look like I give a fuck? Keeping *her* safe is the only thing that matters." I point at Cheryl.

"Well, you won't be able to do that from behind bars, and that's where you're headed if you don't take your head out of your ass and play it by the book."

"If I wanted your advice, I'd ask for it." A muscle clenches in my jaw.

He puts his face all up in mine. "Stop acting like the stereotypical poor little rich boy."

I shove at his chest. "Get the fuck out of my face."

"I was dead set against bringing you into this team," he says.

"Tell me something I don't know," I sneer.

This time, he shoves me, pinning his arm underneath my chin and backing me up against the door before I've time to deflect the move. Although Colin has at least fifteen years on me, he's in peak physical shape, and the dude's strong. I can't wrangle out of his hold, and that irritates the fuck out of me. "Shut up and listen."

Steam is practically billowing out of his ears.

"I didn't want you here. Hated how easy it was for you to get a position on this team when most of us have had to work our butts off to get a foot in the door. Knew you were only doing this for that girl." He jerks his head in Cheryl's direction. "And I hated you more for that, but you've got talent and intelligence, and if you stop acting the idiot, you'll see you can protect your woman, put that asshole away, *and* keep your job."

He lets me go, and I drag in a few lungsful of air. "Screw you."

"Lose the shitty attitude." He straightens his shoulders and eyeballs me. "I'm trying to bury the hatchet here, and if you're half as smart as you appear to be, then you'll accept my olive branch." He looks through the window into the interrogation room. "Because if you want to keep that girl safe, you're going to need all the help you can get."

"Stay away from me," Cheryl hisses as I follow her out of the FBI building.

"If you'll just let me explain."

She twirls around, jabbing her finger in my chest. Heat flares in her eyes. "I've had enough of your explanations to last a lifetime!" she screeches.

"I couldn't tell you at first, but I swear I was planning on telling you tonight. I was going to tell you last night, but I didn't want to spoil the mood, and I—"

"Don't!" She shoves my chest. "Don't you dare say it. I let you kiss and touch me, and this whole time, you've been lying to me!"

"I was protecting you." I slip my hands into the pockets of my jeans, rocking back on my heels.

"By lying to me!" She throws her hands in the air.

I rub a hand along the back of my neck. "I know you're pissed, and you've every right to be, but if you come home, I can explain everything. I'll answer anything you want to know."

"Are you crazy? I'm not going home with you."

Goose bumps sprout on my arms. "The hell you aren't! That fucking psycho is out there, and he wants you back. What the hell do you think he'll do if you don't go willingly?"

"That's not your problem anymore," she says, waving her arms at an incoming vehicle.

I grab hold of her arm. "Don't fucking do this. Be mad at me all you want. Hate me and never speak to me again, but don't risk your life like this. Even if I've ruined everything, at least let me keep you safe. Let me protect you."

"The only one I need protecting from is you!" she shrieks as a car pulls up to the curb.

"Where are you going?" I demand, keeping tight hold of her arm.

"I'm going to stay with my friend Lin. You can drop my stuff off at her place. I guess you already have the address, considering you knew who she was before I'd told you anything about her!" I forgot that I screwed up by mentioning Lin, but I thought I'd gotten away with it as Cheryl didn't seem to notice. Looks like she's been going over stuff in her head, and that's not going to end well for me.

"Cher?" A girl with long dark hair walks around the back of the car toward us, and I recognize Lin from the photos I've seen of her.

"Let me go, Kev."

"Please, Cheryl. I'm begging you. Please don't do this. Don't run away again before I've had a chance to explain."

And that was totally the wrong thing to say. A frustrated scream rips from her lips and she starts pummeling my chest with her fists. "Let me go, Kev, or I'll call Supervisory Special Agent Clement and tell him you're holding me against my will."

I let her go although it pains me to do so. "Fine. You win, but I'm not going away Cheryl. You can't run from me this time. I won't let you." I walk away, before listening to her response, with a heavy weight pressing down on my chest.

I drop a bag with some of her stuff over to Lin's apartment a couple hours later. I'm pissed and concerned, but at least the bodyguard I hired is in position now. He'll swap out with the day guy in the morning. Cheryl looks like she wants to flay the skin from my bones when she realizes I didn't bring all her stuff. Tough shit. I'll give her time to cool off, but I'm not facilitating her to move out permanently. If she wants to get all her belongings, she'll have to organize it herself. She slams the door shut in my face when I articulate that point.

With nothing better to do, I head over to the FBI building and work into the middle of the night trying to find any evidence online of what happened to Hayley Jackson. We need to pin something on Stanten in order to have enough grounds to issue a warrant. But it's like the girl vanished into thin air, and I can find no trace of her being taken out of the city.

Frustrated, I shut off my laptop after sending an email to the SSA with a status update. I'm on my way home to grab a few hours' sleep when I change course for the city.

Parking my butt in the hallway outside Lin's apartment, I cover myself with the blanket I had in the trunk of my X5 and settle in for the night.

The next thing I know, I'm being shaken awake. The distinguishable scent of coffee tickles my nostrils, and I force my eyelids open. Cheryl's friend Lin is crouched down in front of me, waving a cup of joe in my face. "Good morning, sunshine. Time to get up." A couple of people stare at me as they walk by. "I don't want the super getting on my case. Come inside and drink your coffee."

I stagger to my feet, grab my blanket, and follow her into the apartment. "Where's Cheryl?" I mumble, fighting a yawn.

"She left already," Lin confirms, gesturing for me to take a seat at the same kitchen table. "She's meeting her study group to discuss a project they're working on."

"I'm guessing she's still mad at me. Awesome," I deadpan, inhaling the coffee aroma before I bring the cup to my lips.

"She's seething," Lin confirms. "But she'll cool down. Just give her a little time and space."

"I'm terrified if I give her too much time and space she'll believe she's better off without me."

Lin grins, handing me a bacon and egg sandwich. Sitting down across from me, she blows on the steam arising from her mug. "I don't think so. Girl's crazy about you although I'm not sure if she fully realizes it."

"Why aren't *you* mad at me?" I ask, taking a big bite out of the sandwich. I groan. "Ugh. This is so good."

She grins again. "Anyone that appreciates a good bacon and egg sandwich gets the thumbs-up from me. Besides, I can be objective about this where Cheryl can't. I figure you couldn't tell her about your job because you were afraid it'd get back to that asshole she was engaged to and it would jeopardize the case."

"Got it in one. And I hated not being wholly truthful with her, but I was doing what I could to keep her safe. It's killed me these last few weeks having to stand by and watch her go home to him every night, but my hands were tied."

"I get that, and she will too, but you've got to see it from her perspective. It feels like another betrayal."

"I screwed up once, and I don't want to make the same mistake again, but I'm scared for her, Lin. Stanten isn't going to give up until he gets her back."

"Well then," she says, talking over a mouthful of food. "We'll just have to make sure that doesn't happen."

Chapter 16

Cheryl

The next week crawls by in an agonizingly slow fashion. I throw myself into my studies and my projects and do a few extra hours in the studio to keep myself distracted. I stay up studying late every night until my eyelids grow heavy and I slip into a sleep coma before I can think about the new layer of pain blanketing my heart.

I'm trying hard to ignore Keven, but my mind meanders a lot while I'm in class and at work, and he's all my lovesick brain can think about. I've probably gone through the whole gamut of emotions this week, and I'm tired of overanalyzing it.

I know he's trying to protect me.

Only a fool would deny that, but I can't get over the fact he lied to me about so many things. It makes me question every moment we've spent together recently, wondering if all of it was a lie.

I'm hurt and feeling betrayed all over again, and I just want this piercing pain in my chest to go away. It doesn't help that he refuses to sleep at home.

Every morning, I leave Lin's place and he's there—propped against the wall, softly snoring, with a light blanket covering him. It looks awkward as hell, and I'm sure it's uncomfortable, but he shows up every night, at some point, taking up residence in the hallway.

He's making it very difficult to hold onto my anger.

Not just because he's doing everything in his power to watch over me, but because he looks so Goddamned adorable when he's asleep. I have to hurry past him each morning because the craving to wrap myself around him is almost too much to control.

I love him.

I love him so much.

And this is killing me as much as it's killing him.

But how can I trust him when he keeps letting me down?

Lin's no help. She's clearly turned to the dark side. Oh, she thinks I haven't noticed, but I have. She never misses an opportunity to sing his praises. To subtly champion his cause. She's tiptoeing around me because she can see I'm an emotional maelstrom, but she's biding her time, and she's going to hit me with it any day now. I have a sneaking suspicion she's bringing him into the apartment after I leave because I swear I smelled his cologne in the living room the other day.

Sunday morning, I open the door carefully, poking my head into the corridor. Sure enough, there he is. This time, he's fallen asleep on his side on the floor, and he's shivering even under the blanket. My heart melts a little at the sight of him, and I can't leave him like that.

I'm not completely cruel.

Padding quietly to the guest bedroom, I grab my pillow and comforter and head back outside. I close the door with military precision, and only those with supersonic hearing would hear the tiny click as the door locks. Very carefully, I rest my comforter over the sleeping hulk of a man and gently slide the pillow under his head. "Cheryl," he murmurs in a sleep-drenched tone, and I freeze.

I don't want him to wake up. I'm not ready to confront him yet.

But he's not awake.

He's talking in his sleep.

And he's murmuring my name.

I press a shaky hand over my mouth, stifling a sob, staring at him for a few minutes while my heart battles my head. I know the only person I'm kidding with my cold-shoulder approach is myself. I understand it's only a matter of time before I cave, but I need to make a point. Keven can't expect to be in a relationship with me if he's going to keep secrets.

That's not how it works, and unless he's prepared to level with me, we have no future.

I'm melancholy as I walk to meet Eva at the gym. She's agreed to help me with self-defense lessons for now. I don't want to disregard Keven's warning about Dan. I've seen for myself how unhinged he was the day I broke things off with him, and he isn't showing any signs of backing down.

He's sent flowers to me every single day, and he even had the nerve to show up at the studio on Thursday evening. I got Sara to throw him out. He stood out on the sidewalk, staring at me, making it clear he intended to wait until I'd left for the evening. But Sara threatened to call the cops. The minute she mentioned a restraining order, he took off, and I could breathe again.

I know the FBI has someone following Daniel and that Keven is paying for twenty-four-hour bodyguard protection for me. Eva let that slip, but she hasn't said much else about Kev, and I appreciate that she's trying to be a good friend to me and not choosing sides.

After an hour practicing, we both hit the showers and walk together to a nearby café for breakfast. "Can we talk about the elephant in the room?" she says after the waitress has cleared our plates and refilled our coffee cups.

I sigh, leaning back in my chair, knowing exactly what she wants to discuss. "I'm hurting all over again," I admit, accepting we need to have this conversation.

"I know you are, and he hates himself for upsetting you." She takes a sip of her coffee. "Is he still sleeping outside your friend's place?"

I nod. "He's there every morning, without fail."

"He's also working around the clock, not finishing until the early hours. He is trying his best to find something, anything, that can link your ex to something illegal. He's worried sick, Cheryl, and he cares about you so much."

"I know."

"Do you?" She puts her mug down and stretches across the table, lowering her voice. "He only took that FBI job to protect you, and he's bent plenty of rules to ensure you're safe. When you refused to leave the house until speaking to Daniel, he slept outside in his car. He has also assigned bodyguards to keep watch over your family in case Daniel tries to get to you through them." She reaches out, taking my hand. "He wanted to tell you, but he couldn't."

"Because of his job."

"No." She shakes her head. "Because of you. If he told you at the very start that he was an FBI analyst and he shared all the intel he had on Daniel, would you have believed him? Or would you have pushed him away and confronted Daniel to know if it was true?"

I stay quiet, because no one needs to hear me admit it out loud.

"If he'd come clean, you might have jeopardized the entire mission. He didn't care about losing his job—only that he'd go to jail and be unable to take care of you then. But it's more than that. Truckloads of new girls are being smuggled into Boston on a daily basis. Your ex has established new contacts, and more and more young girls are being forced into prostitution. They are subjected to inhumane conditions and horrendous abuse. Some of them are as young as ten. Keven couldn't risk telling you the truth because there was far too much at stake."

I know it makes sense, and I know he's only trying to do the right thing, but I can't force that lingering doubt aside. The past continues to threaten my present and my future. "But is it real, Eva? How do I know it's real?"

She places her hand over my heart. "What do you feel in here?" She presses her palm down. "Your heart will never let you down, and you need to learn to trust in it."

Tears prick my eyes. "I'm afraid to let him back in, because if it doesn't work this time, it will kill me. I will never recover a second time."

"I understand that so well, but you have to believe in your love. Trust it to guide you along the right path." She takes her hand away, gesturing at the waitress for the check. "I don't know if this helps, but I understand the way a man looks at a woman when he loves her with every part of his being. Jeremy never looked at me like that. I was a possession, a commodity to him, but it's the complete opposite with Kade. I know how much he loves me by the way he looks at me. It's the same way Keven looks at you." She glances over my shoulder, and her eyes light up.

"Ready to go, love?" Kade asks, leaning down to kiss his wife on the lips. It's only a brief kiss, but it's wholly intimate because of the way their eyes lock on to one another and the way they both reach for each other at the same time. Kade has just proven Eva's point, and my heart hurts looking at them even though I'm happy they're happy.

"Can I give you a ride, Cheryl?" Kade asks, leaning in to kiss my cheek as Eva stands, pulling on her coat.

"It's not that far to walk. I'm good."

He pins me with a stern look. "You're coming with us, and don't attempt to argue because Keven isn't the only Kennedy with a wicked stubborn streak."

I don't fight it, letting Kade and Eva drop me off. Before I walk away, Kade calls me back. "I know you're angry at my brother, but don't let him go. Haven't you wasted enough years apart? He loves you. You love him. You two were always meant to be together. Stop fighting it. Talk to him. Work out your issues, and find a way to move forward. A love like yours is too precious to walk away from."

Eva swipes at the tears pooling in her eyes, and the look of love on her face as she stares at her husband is something I aspire to.

"Thanks, Kade."

"Anytime. Like I said, you're family, Cheryl."

I wave them off and head back to Lin's apartment with a new spring in my step.

"I'm glad you've come to your senses," Lin says a couple of hours later as I'm preparing to leave. "And even though I'm going to miss having you around, I'm glad you're going back to Keven's. I feel less panicked knowing you're with him."

I pull her into a hug. "Thank you for everything."

"Anytime, girlfriend. Anytime. Now go eat humble pie and lure that hunk of a man into your bed."

I roll my eyes, laughing, as I pick up my bag and walk away.

Butterflies are tumbling through my chest as I take the elevator to Kev's penthouse. I didn't call him in advance, wanting to surprise him. But as I step out of the elevator, the only one surprised is me.

Keven is standing in the doorway of his place with his arms wrapped around a gorgeous redhead. He's smiling down at her, and she's clinging to him in a way that screams familiarity. My stomach lurches violently, and nausea swims up my throat. The pain in my chest is so intense it feels like I'm having a coronary. I repeatedly stab the down arrow on the elevator, willing the doors to shut before he sees me.

I'm fighting tears, swallowing over the lump in my throat as the doors start closing. At the last second, Keven looks over and sees me, and his face drops. Then the doors shut, and I collapse against the wall, sobbing, while my heart breaks all over again.

Chapter 17

Keven

"Shit!" I release Rachel and race after the elevator, but it's too late. It's already on the descent again.

"What the fuck, Kev?" Rachel comes up alongside me, frowning.

I grip her shoulders. "Do me a favor. Ask Brad to park and come back up. Cheryl just saw us hugging, and she's jumped to conclusions. I'm going after her, but I'll need you to explain it because she won't believe me." I thrust my keycard at her. "Go back inside and call Brad. Then wait for me."

"Okay, fine. But who's Cheryl?" she asks, looking confused.

"She's the love of my life," I shout over my shoulder, sprinting toward the stairwell. I fly down the stairs as fast as my legs will carry me, and I reach the underground level a couple minutes after the elevator. I slam through the doors into the parking lot, looking frantically all around me. I spot the top of Cheryl's blonde head over on my left, and I run after her. "Cheryl! Wait!" I holler.

Her shoulders stiffen at my words, and then she starts running, hurrying toward a rust-colored Audi that has clearly seen better days.

I reach her just as she pulls out of the parking space, prepared to drive off. I react on instinct, jumping in front of the car, and she slams on the brakes before knocking into me. My heart thuds behind my ribcage as adrenaline floods my system. I pound my fists on the hood of the car, glaring at her. "Get out of the fucking car, Cheryl." I am so fucking done with this running away shit. It fucking ends now.

She lowers her window and screams at me. "Get the fuck out of my way, or I swear I'll drive over you!"

"What the hell is going on, Kev?" Brad asks in an incredulous tone as he materializes at my side. His gaze bounces between me and Cheryl like we've both completely lost it. He lowers his head, squinting as he looks through the windshield. "Is that Cheryl Keeland?" He looks to me for answers. Brad also attended Old Colonial High, and he practically lived at our house growing up, so he knows her well. Walking around the side of the car, he peers into the driver's side window. "Hey, it is you, Cheryl. How are you here?"

"It's a long story," I answer on her behalf. "One I'll tell you if you can please fucking explain to Cheryl that she is fucking overreacting and that the redhead I was hugging at my door is *your* girlfriend."

Brad casually removes his cell, swiping the screen with his finger, and puts the phone in Cheryl's face. "That's me with my girlfriend, Rach."

She bites down on her lower lip as she studies the photo.

When she's done, Brad slides the cell back in his pocket, fixing Cheryl with a soft look as he explains. "We just had lunch at Kev's place. I left to drop our other friends, Gavin and Lauren, at the train station, and I was circling back to pick up Rach when she called and said there was some emergency and I had to return to the penthouse."

A car honks its horn behind Cheryl, and I glance up, noticing a line forming.

She jerks her head to me through the windshield. "Move so I can park," she snaps, equally as pissed as me, although she's probably feeling foolish for jumping to the wrong conclusion.

Again.

This is becoming a habit. One I need to stomp out pronto.

I step aside so she can park, using the opportunity to cool my jets. I don't want to lose sight of the important thing here—she was coming back to me, and that's all that counts.

"What's going on?" Brad asks as we both watch Cheryl park that piece of shit she's driving.

"I want her back, but the fucking past keeps getting in the way."

"You kept that quiet," he murmurs while Cheryl climbs out of the car.

"I had good reason to."

I walk away from Brad, toward Cheryl, reaching her before she's pulled her bag out from the back seat. Without giving her time to reject me, I reel her into my arms, hugging the shit out of her. She tries to protest, wriggling in my embrace, but it's a poor attempt. I close my eyes and hold her close. "Stop fighting this. And stop running the fuck away before I've had time to explain."

"I'm sorry," she sobs, clinging to my shirt. "I'm such a hot mess. Seeing you with your arms around her hurt so much."

I tip her chin up so I'm looking directly in her eyes. "I don't know what else I can do or say to make you see how much I love you. I only want you, Cheryl. There's never been anyone else."

She circles her arms around my neck, squeezing me tight. "I'm sorry I'm making a mess of everything, but I promise I won't run from you again."

"In the interests of transparency, you should know that Rachel and I kissed, before she got together with McConaughey, but it was only casual, on both our parts, and we are purely platonic friends now."

Her chest heaves as she peers deep into my eyes. "I believe you. Thanks for telling me, and I do love you, Keven. So, so much. I'm just scared."

I kiss the top of her head. "Don't be. It's going to be okay. *We're* going to be okay."

After Brad and Rachel leave, having satisfied an embarrassed Cheryl that the hug she witnessed was nothing more than a hug between two good friends, I run Cheryl a bath and force her into the bathroom while I make dinner.

She wanders into the kitchen a half hour later, barefoot, with damp hair, wearing gray sweats and a white tank, and she's never looked more beautiful. "Something smells good," she says, leaning her face in to sniff the sauce. "It's only chicken, noodles, and sauce, but it's all fresh, nothing out of a jar."

Tentatively, she wraps her arms around me from behind, resting her head on my back. A deep sense of contentment washes over me. Turning the heat off the stove, I turn around, lifting her up and setting her down on the island unit. I nudge her legs aside and step into her body, grasping the back of her neck and drawing her close to me. "You infuriate the hell out of me," I whisper before sweeping my lips against hers. "And we've got lots to discuss," I add before pecking her lips more firmly. "But I need to fucking kiss you right now."

"You won't hear any objections from me," she pants, and that's all I need to hear.

I kiss her lips thoroughly, devouring her mouth with my lips and my tongue, holding her tight body flush against mine as I reclaim her mouth over and over. When we finally come up for air, I lay my head on her shoulder, and she runs her small hand up and down my back. Neither of us speaks, but we don't need words to communicate.

At last, I think we're finally on the same page.

After we eat, we take our wine into the living area and sit on the couch beside one another. I take her feet into my hands, kneading her flesh as I begin explaining everything. She doesn't interrupt, letting me tell her how it all went down, and I hold absolutely nothing back, including classified stuff I shouldn't be telling her, but I know she won't breathe a word to anyone. When I get to the part about her ex and the underage girls, she turns white in the face.

"Oh my God." She puts her glass down, clamping her hand over her mouth, and a tormented look ghosts over her face. "I can't believe I was so blind. I can't believe he was doing that behind my back. It's horrendous. Those poor girls."

Tears roll down her cheeks, and I lift her up, placing her in my lap. I smooth my hand over her hair. "He's a master manipulator, honey. Most girls would've been fooled. It's not your fault."

"I feel responsible. I was living in that house, driving that new car he bought me, and it was all at the expense of others. I feel sick. And now I'll have to get tested too."

"Definitely, and if he's given you anything, I will fucking kill him." I'm seething at the thought of it, but I banish it from my mind because this is supposed to be about us moving forward, and continuing to fixate on her ex isn't helping either of us. I smooth my thumb over the furrows in her brow. "Stop blaming yourself. You didn't know. And, not to redirect the conversation, but where the hell did you pick up that rust bucket you're driving?"

"Lin's ex-girlfriend left it behind when she moved out."

"Gee, I wonder why."

"I didn't want to take anything he gave me, especially the Audi. I can get around the city just fine without a car, but I need one for getting to and from Walpole."

"You can't drive that car. It's a death trap. I'll fix you up with a new car."

"No." She turns around on my lap, and I groan, discreetly adjusting my cock in my pants. "Sorry." She sends me a sheepish smile. "You're not buying me a car. I have some money saved, and my dad will loan me extra if I need it. I'll buy my own car."

"Please tell me we're not going to fight about money? Because that's just plain dumb."

"I'm not taking your money. And I'll be paying you rent," she adds.

"You can try." I smirk. "But I'll just put it straight back in your account. And I'm getting you a car."

"No way, I won't—"

I shut her up with a kiss, and soon it turns very hot and heavy, and she's sprawled on top of me, writhing against me, almost making me come in my pants, but I stop it escalating further because we still have stuff to discuss. "We should talk," I rasp, holding her at arm's length when she leans in to kiss me again.

"Talking's overrated," she breathes in a raspy voice, and my cock is like a fucking brick in my pants.

I stare at her like she's just grown wings. "I swear you say shit like that to deliberately wind me up."

"I do not. I don't like arguing with you." She bends down, giving me a fantastic view of her rack and my cock fucking throbs. "I happen to think we can make better use of our time." She welds her lips to mine, sliding her tongue into my mouth and grinding on my hard-on.

It takes iron fucking willpower to pull away. "Woman, you will be the death of me. Can we get serious for a minute? Talking is *not* overrated. Not talking about things has led us to a world of pain and I'm not going to repeat the vicious cycle. We need to agree here and now that there are no more secrets. That we tell each other everything. That we don't run away from the other person if they've pissed us off or there's a misunderstanding. That we talk through our issues."

She nods. "I agree with everything you said, and I promise I won't run off again." She presses a sweet kiss to my cheek. "The only place I want to run to is straight into your arms."

Chapter 18

Cheryl

Kev and I still haven't had sex even though I sleep in his bed every night the following week. I've gotten the all clear—I'm clean, thank God—but he still won't go there. We make out like demons, and we've enjoyed rediscovering each other's bodies, but he's still hesitant to bridge that final step. Deep down, I know it's because he's giving me time to make sure I'm sure, but there's a small part of me that debates if he's having doubts.

Of course, he didn't listen to me about the car. I've no clue how he does these things, but I woke up for college on Monday morning to find a brand-new X5 waiting for me in the parking lot. The following day, he told me he'd moved *the rust bucket* to the parking lot at Kade's old place.

I went ballistic when he explained he's also bought Kade's apartment and put it in my name until he elaborated on the reason for it. He doesn't want Dan to discover I'm living with him in case he starts digging and uncovers the FBI connection. That could be dangerous for both of us, so it's best to let Dan believe I'm living in a new place. Kade was looking to get rid of his apartment because he and Eva have just moved into a new house, so it was a matter of signing some papers and transferring some money, and the deal was pushed through fast, or so I was told. There was no way I could hold onto my stubborn pride after learning all that. Kev is covering all the bases in his quest to protect me, and it only makes me love him more.

So, now I'm the proud owner of a stylish penthouse apartment in the best part of Cambridge that I'll most likely never live in.

Dan refuses to go away, hovering like a bad smell. He's bombarding my cell with texts and messages, so of course, Kev got me a new cell, depositing the old one in my empty apartment so Dan can continue sending messages to his heart's content, and I don't have to worry about them.

It was a good resolution until he showed up at the MassArt library on Thursday, demanding I speak to him. My bodyguard intervened, pretending to be a classmate, and he got Dan removed from the building, but not before he made a huge scene, embarrassing me in the process.

So, I'm a little stressed as we head for the airport on Friday afternoon although I'm happy to be getting away for a few days. "What's happening with the case?" I ask Kev when we are freewheeling it on the highway. "Did your boss get the warrant to search the barn?" Kev keeps me informed on a daily basis, which I really appreciate because I know he could get in trouble for divulging classified intel, but he trusts me not to tell a soul.

"No." He sighs, reaching out to thread his fingers in mine. "It was a long shot because we were using photographic evidence that's legally inadmissible, and we have nothing solid to link to the barn. The judge disregarded it straightaway. He said some stuff which leads the SSA to suspect he may be on Stanten or Mancusso's payroll, so he's concerned we've showed Stanten our hand, which means he'll be even more careful from now on. It's a fucking nightmare."

"That's not good. Where does the investigation go from here then?" I ask, rubbing soothing circles on the back of his hand.

"We'll keep digging. I know, in my gut, he's stashing stuff in that barn, but I can't figure out how he's getting it in. We have guys watching the house, and Agent Wentward is still following Stanten, but there's been no deliveries. I've pored over the plans of the house and the grounds, but there is no other way onto the property. It makes no sense." His frustration bleeds into his tone, and I wrack my brain for anything that might help.

I sit up straighter in my seat as a thought occurs to me. "I remember something," I say, twisting in my seat to face him. The leather squelches with the movement. "What plans have you been going over?"

"The one's Stanten lodged with his recent planning application."

Butterflies scatter in my chest, and the words rush out of my mouth in a hurry. "Check further back. Dan told me the house was originally built in the nineteen twenties. It had lain idle for the last eight years, having been neglected, and it needed a lot of work. He said he tore down most of the structure to build the current house, but if you check out the previous plans, including the grounds, maybe there was an old entrance somewhere that he's using."

"It's an intelligent suggestion, but I've already looked at the previous plans, and I didn't see anything."

"But have you looked at *all* the available plans? Maybe you need to go right back to the original plans."

His Adam's apple jumps in his throat, and he looks deep in thought. "It can't hurt to try." He smiles as he takes the turn for the airport. "Let me know if you have any other good ideas. You just might be on to something there."

I lean across the console and kiss his cheek. "Keep me posted if you find anything."

"You know I will."

Twenty minutes later, we walk hand in hand toward the Kennedy's private jet, and already I feel some of my stress flittering away. I remember flying to Nantucket with the Kennedys a bunch of times, but this plane looks much bigger. "Is this the same plane?" I inquire.

"Nope. Dad had to upgrade because the family keeps expanding." He squeezes my hand, smirking a little. "I hope you've prepared yourself."

"Prepared myself for what?" I ask, frowning.

"For the Kennedy reunion experience." His face breaks out in a wide smile.

"Tsk." I brush his concern away. "It's just like catching up with relatives I haven't seen in a while." Although, I'd be lying if I said I wasn't a little apprehensive. It's been years since I've seen most of Kev's family and I'm wondering how they've taken the news we're back together.

"If you say so." He winks, letting me ascend the stairs first. "Don't say I didn't try to warn you."

I've only taken one foot into the plush cabin when Alex—Kev's mom—jumps up out of her seat, rushes toward me, and grabs me into a mammoth hug.

"Cheryl. You've no idea how excited I was when Keven told me you were joining us for Easter." She beams at me, her eyes perusing me from head to toe. "Oh my." She plants a hand on her chest. "You've blossomed into a beautiful young woman. I always knew you would."

I blush a little at her compliment. "Thank you, and for the invitation. I'm looking forward to catching up with everyone."

"Be glad she isn't still at the helm of Kennedy Apparel, or she'd be roping you into modeling," Keaton says, coming up behind his mom. "Good to see you, Cher Bear," he adds—using the pet name he gave me when he was twelve—wrangling me into a hug.

"You too, Keats." I ease out of his hug, looking up at him. He's as tall as Kyler and Kaden now and every bit as good-looking as all his brothers. The Kennedy gene pool is something else and most unfair to the rest of the male population.

The stylish layer of stubble on Keaton's face and the tats creeping up one arm give him an edgy vibe, and it's not something I would've ever guessed I'd see on him. But I knew the triplets when they were young teens, and it only highlights how much I've missed. "Wow, you're definitely not a kid anymore."

"We're all grown up now, babe," Kent says, shoving his brother out of the way and yanking me into his arms. "I'd be happy to give you a full body demonstration, so you can see for yourself," he adds, copping a cheeky feel of my ass.

"I'm going to throw you out of this plane," Kev growls, pushing his brother off me. "While we're ten thousand feet in the air," he adds, narrowing his eyes at his younger brother.

"Don't be jealous, bruh. It's not my fault I'm younger and hotter," he retorts, winking at me in a deliberate attempt to piss Kev off. "Anytime you feel like trading him in for a newer model, I'm your man." He licks his lips suggestively, and I work hard to contain my laughter.

"Say that again, asshole," a girl with vibrant blue hair says, storming past me and pushing Kent in the chest.

"Whitney, baby." He reaches for her, but she folds her arms across her chest, glaring at him. "I was only messing around. Cheryl's with Kev, and I was just winding him up."

Kev gives Kent the middle finger before taking my hand and guiding me through the cabin.

"Hey, Keanu," I say as we pass the last of the triplets.

"Hey, Cher." He gives me a quick smile and a terse nod before popping his ear buds back in his ears and staring out the window.

"Don't take that personally," Kev whispers in my ear. "He's been a raging asshole for months, but none of us know why. He's as secretive as ever."

Kev pulls me into a seat beside him, facing off against his brother Kyler and a gorgeous dark-haired girl I'm guessing is his girlfriend. "Hey, Ky." I wiggle my fingers at him. "Long time no see."

"I know, right?" He unbuckles his seat belt, leaning over to give me a quick hug. "It's great to see you, and I'm glad you guys are giving it another go."

"Kyler." Kev's tone would stop traffic.

"I'd hoped his mood would improve with you back in his life, but I guess that was too much to ask for," Ky deadpans, slinging his arm around his girlfriend's shoulders.

She leans forward in her chair, smiling at me. "Hi, I'm Faye. I've been really looking forward to meeting you."

She has the most gorgeous, lyrical Irish accent, and I could listen to her all day long. "Me too. And congratulations on your engagement." My gaze bounces between them, and I catch the loving look they share. "How are your wedding plans coming along?"

"Great, it's all pretty much sorted. Alex is like a force of nature, she's so organized, and she keeps me on top of everything," Faye says.

"What Faye is too polite to say is Mom is like the craziest wannabe bridezilla you could ever meet," Ky faux whispers.

She tugs at his arm, fighting a smile while chastising him. "Stop it! She's just excited." Faye turns her attention back to me. "Alex has been feeling a little bored since she sold her fashion business, and I think she just loves being kept busy now with both weddings and her new interior design company."

"And speaking of ..." Ky trails off, grinning as he stands. "Hey, man." I glance over my shoulder, smiling at Rachel and Brad. I feel like such an idiot for jumping the gun last weekend, but Rachel was very gracious about it, and she went out of her way to ensure I didn't feel stupid, regaling me with stories of how contentious things were with her and Brad when they first met.

Ky and Brad do the man hug thing, and Faye hops up, squealing and clinging to Rachel as they both jump up and down.

"Changed your mind yet?" Kev teases, whispering into my ear.

"Not a bit," I tell him. "You know I love your family, and it's an added bonus having the girls on the trip. It's going to be great."

He wraps his large hand around the back of my neck, drawing me into him for a slow, unhurried kiss. My eyes flutter closed, and I hear nothing except the rapid beating of my heart. Kev makes love to my mouth, and I should care that we're not in private, but the heady feelings racing inside me overrule any sense of logic or decency.

"Ahem." A throat clearing breaks us apart, and I turn my head around, grinning at the good-looking older man crouching down over us. "I thought someone"—James shoots daggers at Keven—"would bring you into the cockpit so I could say hello, but I was fed up waiting, so I came to you instead. How are you, Cheryl? We're delighted you could join us."

I stand, giving Kev's dad a firm hug. "I'm great and really happy to be here."

"I hope you're still saying that after the weekend," he jokes, pressing in as an unfamiliar man and two young boys move past him to take the last of the seats.

"Dad!" Faye flings herself into the new arrival's arms, hugging him fiercely. "I was scared you were going to miss the flight."

"I was waiting at the office for Whitney and the twins to be dropped off. Their mother was running late, apparently." I don't know these people, but I detect the edge in his voice and sense there's some friction there.

"Right, I'd better head back. This plane won't fly itself." James grins before dropping a kiss on my cheek. "It's wonderful to have you back in the fold, sweetheart. Don't take any shit from this one." He jabs Kev in the shoulder, good-naturedly, before surveying the chaos in the cabin.

Hardly anyone is seated, and people are moving up and down the aisle or standing around casually chatting.

Putting two fingers in his mouth, he emits a shrill whistle, capturing everyone's attention. "We're talking off shortly, so I need everyone to sit down and buckle up. Kent!" James roars, and Faye's dad whips his head around, concern and frustration etched upon his face. "Get back to your seat. You too, Whitney!" he says, exchanging resigned looks with Faye's dad.

"What's that all about?" I whisper to Kev.

"Whitney is Faye's half-sister, and her and Kent usually screw around whenever they see one another. Christmas was the last time they were together, and they were caught fucking, and it did *not* go down well."

"Yikes. I'm so glad we're past all the sneaking around."

He pins me with a wolfish grin, sliding his arm around my waist and pulling me into his body. "Me too. It means I get to keep you by my side all night, and we don't need to worry about anyone catching us."

My mind goes back in time. "Do you remember that time—"

"When we were fucking our brains out in your bedroom thinking your parents wouldn't be home for at least another couple of hours," he continues, instantly thinking of the same incident.

"But Mom got food poisoning, and they came home early," I say.

"And I got such a fright I pulled out and came all over your stomach—"

"And on the bed, my pajamas"—I drill him with a look—"and you even managed to projectile into my hair."

He shrugs, his lips curving into a goofy smile. "What can I say? I've got mad skills." He waggles his brows, and I laugh.

"I can still see you, buck-ass naked, holding your clothes and practically tumbling out my window."

"It was a fucking close call," he admits, shaking his head.

"It sure was. I had just enough time to yank the covers up and hide my nakedness before Dad came into the room." My face scrunches up.

"Your cum was clinging to my skin while I was trying to keep a pleasant smile on my face. It was so gross."

"You think my cum is gross?" He feigns hurt.

"When it's gluing my skin to the comforter and strands of my hair are sticking together, hells yeah."

"I can't believe he jizzed in your hair," Kent says suddenly, looming above me as he leans over the back of my seat. My heart startles, and I clamp a hand over my chest, willing it to calm down.

"Quit eavesdropping!" Kev shoves him back down into his seat. "This is a private conversation, douche."

"You think I wanted to hear that shit?" Kent spouts at the top of his voice. "Keep your weird kink to yourselves this weekend."

I stare straight ahead as Kev continues to berate Kent. Faye and Kyler are struggling to contain their laughter, and when I look across the aisle at Rachel and Brad, and Kade and Eva—who must've arrived when Kev and I were talking a stroll down nostalgia lane—I spot them trying not to laugh too.

"He wasn't purposely trying to come in my hair," I say, feeling the need to explain, and they all collapse in fits of laughter.

"Fucking A," Kev says, plopping down into his seat and sighing. "Let's hope this doesn't set the tone for the weekend."

Chapter 19

Cheryl

"I'd forgotten how beautiful it is here," I say later that night as we stroll hand in hand along the shore of the private beach the Kennedys share with their neighbors.

"Or maybe you were too busy drooling over me to notice those other times you were here," he quips, darting in to dust his lips against mine.

"Wow, I didn't think it was possible, but your ego is even bigger than it was back in high school."

Without warning, he picks me up, flinging me over his shoulder and whacking my ass. "You're going to pay for that," he says, veering sideways and racing toward the ocean.

"I know the weather's warmer than usual for mid-April, but I definitely think a nighttime swim is out of the question," I joke, trailing my hands down his back and over his firm butt cheeks.

Hey, might as well take advantage of the situation.

"Perhaps you should've considered that before insulting me." He taps my ass again, sending a jolt of electricity firing through me.

"What if I complimented you now?" I suggest. "Would that negate the perceived insult?"

"It might if the compliment is on the same scale as the insult."

"You have the best ass I've ever seen on a guy," I supply, lifting my head up a little as we approach the water. A chilly breeze lifts strands of my hair, swirling them around my face as I warily eye the water. *He's not really going to throw me in there, is he?*

"Lame," he scoffs. "Is that the best you've got?"

"I can do better," I promise, running my hands over his ass again, squeezing and kneading his tight buns. "Yum. It's just so squishy and hard at the same time, and every time I see you, my eyes are drawn to your butt like lasers." I grab big handfuls of his ass, and a needy moan flies out of my lips, my panties dampening as my arousal roars to life. "I want to sink my teeth into your cheeks and bury my nose in your skin, and yeah, I could easily live there."

His body shakes as laughter rumbles through him. He stops at the water's edge and, very slowly, hauls me back over his shoulder and down over his body. Grabbing hold of my hips, he pulls my pelvis into his. "I should probably be very alarmed at that admission, because that was kinda freakish, but I'm turned the fuck on."

I lean up, circling my arms around his neck. "Me too, and now I really want to eat your ass." I make a gnashing sound with my teeth, and he throws back his head, cracking up laughing.

"Thank fuck Kent isn't around, or we'd never shut him up about this." He swivels his hips, thrusting his erection into my stomach, and stars explode at the back of my eyes. "And I'm beginning to think his comment about weird kink isn't too far off the mark." He tweaks my nose. "At least in your case."

"I have a butt fetish," I admit with a shrug. "Deal with it."

He lines our mouths up, and his warm breath fans my face as he speaks. "I fully approve as long as the fetish applies to *my* butt only."

"I only have eyes for your butt, I promise." I say it in my most solemn voice but totally ruin it by convulsing into a fit of giggles at the end. Kev watches me quietly, and I can't decipher the expression on his face. "What, too much?"

He presses his forehead to mine, holding me tightly against him. "I've missed you so much," he whispers. "I've missed this between us. Nothing has ever felt as right as you and me."

"You're the other half of my heart and soul, Kev," I whisper, peering into his eyes. "That's why it was always so effortless between us."

He grips my face in both his hands. "I fucking love you, Cheryl. And I want this for us for always. Please tell me you want that too."

Tears pool in my eyes. "Kev." I'm all choked up. "Of course, I want that with you."

He draws my face to his, closing the small gap between us, as his mouth latches onto mine. His kiss is tender and soft, and I hear everything he's saying with it. My heart is so full, and any tiny doubts that were hiding in the back of my mind disappear for good.

"Kev." It kills me to break this kiss, but I need him to hear this. "I've never loved anyone the way I love you. No one has ever held my heart the way you hold it. The only man I'll ever want is you. I know you worry that I have doubts, that I'm not sure, but I am. I don't need us to be back together for months to know what I feel. What I've always felt."

Taking his hand, I place it on my chest, in the place where my heart thuds wildly. "You have always been in here, just like I've always been with you. One day back in your company was all I needed to know the truth. I may have refused to open my eyes and see it at first, but I'm not blind anymore. I want you. Only you. For all time. And I want to pick up where we left off and start living our lives."

His eyes glisten with so much emotion, and a choked sob travels up my throat when a single tear cascades down his face. "I know we have lots of shit to deal with, but this right here." I clasp his hand more firmly to my chest. "This is the real deal. This is the culmination of what we've felt for each other in the past, what we're feeling right now, and what we have to look forward to in the years ahead. And once we both never lose sight of that, we can ride through the storm and come out the other side smiling."

"Cheryl." His voice cracks as he envelops me in his arms. "I promise to protect you and love you for the rest of my days. From the day I met you, my heart has only ever belonged to you. I love you so much, and I wish I could explain it better but—"

I press my lips to his mouth, cutting off his sentence. "No buts, unless it's the delectable one in your pants." I wink.

"You definitely have an obsession with my ass," he murmurs, smiling as he runs his fingers along my cheek.

151

"Do you have any objections?" I tease, sliding my arms around his waist and beaming up at him.

"I have zero objections when it comes to you. You can live in my ass if you want. That's totally fine by me."

"Although it might make it uncomfortable when you try to sit down," I joke.

He lifts me up, and my legs automatically wrap around his waist. "I have no plans to sit down right now. All I want is you and me, horizontal in a bed."

I feel like fist pumping the air. "Oh, God, yes." My pussy clenches in anticipation. "Let's go now."

We slip in the side entrance to the house, taking the long way around so we can avoid the kitchen and sitting room, where most everyone else is gathered. We're like sneaky thieves as we take off our shoes and tiptoe up the stairs to our bedroom.

Kev locks the door before stalking toward me with a dark, lust-fueled glaze in his eyes. Butterflies race around my chest like it's Derby Day. He backs me up to the bed, and I fall down on the mattress with him hovering over me. He braces his hands on the comforter, wetting his lips as his eyes drink me in from head to toe. It's like a sensual physical caress and one I feel all over. Kev leans down, capturing my mouth in a searing-hot kiss that has me moaning into his mouth and frantically trying to pull him down on top of me.

In a flash, he backs off, standing at the end of the bed, watching me. He pulls his T-shirt up over his head and tosses it aside. Saliva floods my mouth as I ogle his ripped eight-pack, bulging biceps, and the ink covering one arm, half his chest, and creeping up his neck. I've thoroughly explored his body from head to toe this past week, but I'm still mesmerized every time I see him naked.

He's magnificent. Like a chiseled sculpture begging to be licked.

I push up on my knees moving toward him, but he steps back, out of my reach. "You trust me with your pleasure, baby?"

"Always," I rasp.

"Then strip. Nice and slowly. One item of clothing at a time." He kicks off his jeans, socks and Vans, standing before me in tight black boxer briefs.

My panties saturate as I fixate on the massive bulge straining against the material of his briefs. "Now, Cheryl," he growls. "I need you naked now."

Staying in position on the bed, I peel my shirt off and throw it away to join his clothes on the floor. Then I draw my lace cami slowly up over my chest, my eyes locked on his the entire time. Fire blazes in his eyes as he watches me unclip my bra and fling it away. I caress my breasts as he watches, pushing my tits together and licking my lips provocatively. My nipples are like taut, hard peaks begging for his touch.

"Jeans off. Now," he barks, stroking a hand over his stiff cock through his briefs.

I climb slowly off the bed, tossing my hair over one shoulder and biting down on my lower lip as I shimmy the jeans down my legs. Flouncing around the bed, I stand in front of him, almost completely naked, keeping my eyes pinned to his while I hook my thumbs in my panties and slide them down my legs.

The dark look in his eyes sends a painful pulse throbbing through my core, and I sway on my feet as my knees buckle. He grabs my elbow, holding me steady. "Take my cock out," he demands, and I happily comply, yanking his briefs down. He steps out of them, kicking them away, as I wrap my hand around his hard base and start slowly pumping him.

"On your knees. Suck me off."

Oh fuck. The way he's bossing me around is such a turn-on and at this rate, I'll come before he's even laid a finger on me.

Sinking to my knees, I look up at his incredible body, trying to memorize this moment and the feelings surging inside me with the knowledge he's all mine again. His dick stands rigidly to attention, and I lean in, gripping his base as I slowly ease him into my mouth. I lick up and down his length, flicking my tongue over his crown, before sucking him deep, well, as deep as I can manage because Keven is huge, and there's no way I can fit all of him in my mouth.

Shuttering his eyes, he curses under his breath while his fingers delve into my hair, holding me in place. I blow him enthusiastically while he thrusts into my mouth, and it's a heady, powerful sensation. To have a guy like Keven at my mercy is the best confidence boost, especially when he groans or spews dirty words of encouragement.

He pulls out of my mouth unexpectedly, scooping me up and depositing me on the bed. "That was so good, baby, but I want to come inside your pussy tonight." He nudges my legs apart. "First, I'm going to make you scream." He doesn't waste time teasing me, and that's how I know he's eager to be inside me.

He devours my pussy with his tongue, sucking on my clit and thrusting into my channel over and over again. The moans coming out of my mouth are purely animalistic as his magical tongue worships my body. When he pushes three fingers inside me, pumping them in and out superfast, my head spins. Then his tongue returns to my clit, sucking and licking, and pressure is building inside me, almost reaching a crescendo.

The need to come has me whimpering and writhing like a woman possessed. Curling his fingers inside me, as deep as he can, he pinches my clit with his thumb and forefinger, and I detonate into a million exploding parts, my body arching off the bed as his fingers continue to milk me from inside.

My hair is a tangled mess all over my face, and I'm only starting to come down from the high when the rip of a foil packet reminds me the night is just beginning.

Kev crawls over me, and I push knotty strands of hair out of my face, opening my eyes and focusing on my man. He kisses me slowly and passionately. "I love you," he whispers.

"I love you too." I run my fingers through his hair, pulling his mouth back to mine as he strategically aligns our bodies. Then he's easing inside me, nice and gently, letting my body adjust to the hard, warm length of him. We continue to kiss slowly while he inches in farther.

When he's fully seated, he brushes hair back off my face, pinning me with the most adoring look. "Everything we've gone through has led us right here." He pecks my lips. "You're mine, Cheryl, and I'm yours. This is it."

"Prove it, baby." I cup one side of his face. "Make love to me."

Kev starts moving, slowly, in and out, and we find an easy rhythm. Our mouths and hands explore, and there isn't a part of my body he hasn't touched. Our lovemaking is slow and tender, at odds with his earlier domineering instructions and his usual alpha personality, but I know this is his way of letting me know how much he missed me, how much he adores and loves me.

Sweat coats my body, and it glistens off Kev's ripped abs as he picks up the pace, thrusting into me in long, deep motions. I wrap my legs more tightly around his waist and pivot my hips, feeling every movement as he fucks me harder and faster. I climax for a second time, and then he lets go, rutting into me until his orgasm hits and we're moaning together, kissing to cover our mutual screams.

After we've cleaned up, we creep under the covers, and I snuggle under his arm. "Don't ever leave me again, Cheryl," he whispers, running his hand up and down my arm.

"I'm going nowhere without you, Keven. I promise." I seal the deal with a kiss, and sometime later, after another round of lovemaking, we both drift off to sleep.

Chapter 20

Keven

I join my brothers for nine holes of golf the following morning while Cheryl stays behind with the rest of the girls to help Mom with dinner. Mom forced all the staff to take leave, wanting to cater to the family herself this time. It's just another example of how much things have changed since she sold Kennedy Apparel.

Kal, Lana, their son Hewson, and Lana's parents arrived on a commercial flight from Florida late last night, so I was expecting him to a be a no-show this morning, but he's here before all of us, grinning widely as he waits in the clubhouse.

We take turns hugging him, but there's little time for conversation so it isn't until after we've finished our round that I get to talk to him. "How's Hewson?" I inquire after my only nephew.

"Ah, man, he's the best. He's got so many words now, and the nurse at his developmental checkup said he's very advanced for his age." Hewson will be two next month.

"I'm not surprised," I say, grabbing my coffee and following him to the table where Dad, Adam, and the rest of my brothers sit. "You never shut the fuck up, and I'm betting you came out of the womb babbling crap." He grins, accepting it like a compliment. "I can't wait to see him."

"You'll be lucky if you catch a glance," Ky pipes up as we sit down. "Faye called dibs months ago."

"She can't monopolize him the whole trip," I say.

"Wanna bet?" Ky grins. It's no secret that Faye is head over heels for that little boy. The rest of us have bets on how fast Ky will knock her up after they're married in August. Being a young parent isn't something I want for myself, but I can see it with those two. While Kal and Lana have made it work, it's no cakewalk, that's for sure.

I definitely want kids, but I want to enjoy my time with Cheryl before we start a family. I almost fall off my chair at the surprising turn my thoughts have taken, but it's not an unpleasant or unwelcome surprise.

"We should make a schedule," Keaton suggests.

"I like the sound of that, bro," Kal says, winking. "Lana and I haven't had any time to ourselves lately, so knock yourself out. Spend as much time with the little guy as you like." He winks.

"Let me get this straight," Kent pipes up, and I stifle a groan. "You want us to devise a babysitting schedule so you can get laid?"

"Damn straight, dude."

"That's so very wrong." Kent shakes his head while Kade and I arch a brow. It's not like Kent to act all moralistic.

"Wait till you have a kid, and you'll get it," Kal replies.

"Ahem." Dad clears his throat, eyeballing Kal and subtly gesturing toward Adam.

Kal rolls his eyes. "I wasn't suggesting he go and knock Whitney up," he unhelpfully supplies as Adam's face turns ashen. "I was just stating he'll understand it when he's a dad. *Someday*."

"Someday very far, far away," Dad adds before poor Adam pukes.

"In a galaxy far, far away ..." Keaton's voice is gravelly and deep as he attempts to emulate the opening line to one of his favorite movies.

Ky bursts out laughing. "Dude, did you seriously just misquote *Star Wars*?"

"This family is so fucking weird." That's Keanu's first contribution to the conversation.

"And you're only just figuring this out now?" Kent slants an incredulous look at his triplet.

"Boys." Dad sends a warning glance around the table.

"Men." Kent corrects him. "We're all men now."

Kade tries to smother his laughter, but he can't. And I get it.

Kent has the maturity level of a three-year-old.

"While we're all here," I interject, figuring this is a good time to divert the conversation before it descends into the gutter. I hate having to do this while we're on vacation, but I'd rather say it to the guys than in front of the whole family. "You need to be aware of the situation with Cheryl as it potentially impacts everyone. And I want to discuss some precautionary safety measures." I proceed to fill them in on Stanten, his ties to Eva's ex, and the risks involved for both girls and anyone connected to them. Everyone listens carefully, even Kent, although he looks disinterested, but at least he doesn't interrupt. When I've finished explaining, they all agree to allow me to install the new tracking software on their cells and the girls' cells.

As we roll out of the clubhouse an hour later, en route to the house, Kal asks me about Cheryl. "What's the deal with you two? It sounds serious."

"It is. I'm not letting her go this time."

He thumps me in the arm. "Good for you, bro. I hope it works out for you as well as it's worked out for me and Lana."

Dinner is mayhem with so many of us crowded around the table, but everyone gets fed. Between Hewson buzzing around the place, Kent's and Whitney's antics, and Mom's frequent bouts of laughter—courtesy of a few glasses of wine—it's an entertaining afternoon.

I take a moment to appreciate it, truly grateful for my family. We've endured a tough couple of years, but we've come out the other side, stronger and happier.

My parents have a very amicable separation, and, it could be argued, they get along better than ever. Everyone adores Lana's parents and Faye's dad. And my brothers are happy with their respective others. It's only Keaton and Keanu who don't have anyone with them today.

Keaton's girlfriend Melissa is only seventeen, and she's spending the holidays with her family. And no one knows the status of Keanu's relationship with Selena or if it even is a relationship. He's always been really tight-lipped when it comes to the statuesque girl he models with. So, both my brothers are flying solo this weekend. Ordinarily, that would be me, and I hold Cheryl more tightly against me as that thought flits through my mind, so happy to have her here with me—back where she belongs.

The rest of the vacation passes by quickly, and before we know it, it's Monday evening and we're heading back to the city. Everyone else is hanging around for another few days, so we take a commercial flight back to Boston. Both Cheryl and I have work tomorrow.

"Did you have a good trip?" I ask her when we're in my car heading back to Chelsea later that night.

"I had the best time." She leans back in her chair, beaming. "Honestly, it was just what I needed. I was a little worried your family might hate me, but that couldn't be furthest from the truth."

"My family adores you almost as much as I do."

"And I adore them too. Hewson is so cute, and it was great getting to know Faye, Rachel, and Lana. I think we'll be good friends, and you already know how much I love Eva. I just ..." She trails off, and a faint blush stains her cheeks.

"What is it?"

"It's kinda silly," she sheepishly admits.

"Nothing that comes out of your mouth is silly, and you can tell me anything."

I watch a multitude of emotions flicker across her face. "It's just I love your family as much as I love mine, and being with everyone this weekend felt normal. And good. Really good. It felt like I belong," she quietly admits.

I pull my X5 into the shoulder and put it in park. Twisting around, I cup her beautiful face. "Honey, you do belong. You have *always* fit right in." I don't want her doubting her place in my life or her position in my family. A strange sensation invades my chest, and I exhale heavily as I gather my thoughts. I can't believe I'm actually going to say this, but it doesn't feel awkward or forced—it feels right.

"In case I haven't made it clear enough, you'll be an official part of my family someday. I'm not saying I'm going to propose right away, but we *will* be getting married, Cheryl. You are going to be my wife and the mother of my children. Unless you tell me you don't want that." My breath hitches in my throat as I wait for her to respond.

Tears glisten in her eyes. "It's what I've always wanted," she whispers. "Back in high school, I used to imagine it all the time."

I lean in, releasing the breath I'd been holding, and press a kiss to her forehead. "This is going to make me sound like a pussy, but I did that too. I pictured us together with the white picket fence and two point five kids."

I hold her hand, bringing it to my mouth for a soft kiss. "And we're going to have that, babe. When all this shit is behind us, and the time is right, I'm going to put a ring on your finger."

And as I fuck her later that night, I vow to find a way of eradicating Daniel Stanten from our lives so we can start making those plans for our future.

The next month passes quickly, and it's hard to remember the time when Cheryl wasn't a permanent fixture in my life. Nights are occupied curled up on the couch watching those crappy reality shows she loves while sipping wine. She makes it up to me when we go to bed, indulging my bossy side and subjecting herself to my every whim and desire.

I fall asleep, exhausted, every night after worshiping her body with my hands, my mouth, and my cock. Sex with Cheryl in high school was exciting because it was the first time for both of us, and we had fun exploring our mutual wants and needs. Now, it's out of this fucking world. Her body is my shrine, and I worship at her altar, finding imaginative ways to bring her to new heights. I'll never grow tired of watching her face dissolve in ecstasy as she falls apart in my arms.

However, Stanten continues to be a nuisance, showing up at MassArt and the studio where she works. No matter how many times Cheryl tells him she's done, he refuses to go away.

We've kept up our weekly sessions with Kade and Eva, in the gym and at the firing range, and Cheryl is much more confident handling a firearm now. She has a good grasp of basic self-defense moves, but there's more to learn, and I keep pushing her because as long as Stanten's sniffing around her, the danger is real. She doesn't disagree, and I know it gives her some peace of mind knowing she can defend herself.

The case is at a virtual standstill, much to my disgust. The hidden camera feed was evidently discovered because we lost access to the cameras in Stanten's house two weeks ago, and we still haven't found any alternate entry points onto his property. It's frustrating as fuck because I want to make him go away.

But I brush those thoughts aside as I wait for Cheryl to leave the bathroom, because there's no way I'm letting that asshole ruin today.

"Hon, we're going to be late if we don't leave soon."

"I'm sorry," she rasps, hurrying into the living room. "I was trying to pin my hair up, and I made a mess of it, so I had to invoke Plan B."

She's like a vision in a pink silky dress that hugs her voluptuous curves. The dress flairs out at the waist, falling to just above her knee, and I take a moment to appreciate her slim, shapely legs and the pretty silver sandals she has on. I step in front of her, smiling as I rake my gaze over her. Her beautiful blonde hair is wavy and falling loosely down her back, just how I like it. "If this is Plan B, I wholeheartedly approve." I move in to kiss her, but she slams her hands on my chest, keeping me back.

"I've got gloss on, babe." She points at her shiny mouth.

I grab hold of her waist, tugging her into me. "Do I look like I give a shit about lip gloss?" I don't wait for her reply, fusing my lips to hers and sliding my tongue quickly into her mouth. She gives up protesting, pressing her gorgeous tits into my chest and kissing me like I'm the air she needs to breathe.

"Damn you and your sexy mouth," she says, mock pouting when I reluctantly break the kiss a few minutes later. "Now you're wearing half my gloss." She swipes her thumb across my swollen lips, grinning.

"You can fix your makeup in the car," I say, grabbing her hand and hauling her out into the hallway. I stoop down to pick up our overnight bag and then hustle her out the door.

"How do I look?" she says when we pull into the church parking lot twenty minutes later.

She's spent the last few minutes touching up her makeup in the passenger side mirror. I pretend to notice the difference, inspecting her face meticulously. Cheryl always looks perfectly beautiful to me. "Like a goddess," I truthfully reply, and I'm rewarded with a big-ass smile.

"If I hadn't just reapplied my gloss, I'd totally kiss the shit out of you now," she says while I park the car and kill the engine.

"I'm holding you to that later." I jab my finger in the air.

"Deal, babe. And you know I'm good for it."

I help her out of the car, and we walk over to where my brothers and their girlfriends are congregating outside the front of the church. I notice a few paparazzi hovering around, and I wrap my arm protectively around Cheryl, advising her to keep her head down. I rush her into the church before any of those douchebags have time to take her picture. Faye and Rachel trail into the church behind us, and I leave Cheryl sitting with them, returning to my brothers.

"Everything okay?" Kade asks with a frown.

"Everything's fine." I don't want him worrying about any of this shit today. It's his wedding, and he doesn't deserve to be burdened with any of that crap now.

"You don't want the photographers to spot her," he surmises, refusing to let it drop.

"Definitely not. I've gone to huge lengths to hide our relationship so Stanten doesn't find out."

"You're worried he'll discover you're FBI?" His grave eyes fix mine in place.

I nod. "It's the only reason I haven't told him to back the fuck off my girlfriend. And the only reason Cheryl hasn't filed for a restraining order. Antagonizing that bastard wouldn't be good so we're trying to lay low."

"Both Eva and I would've been fine if you couldn't attend today."

I know he means that sincerely, but it still pisses me off. "There's no way I'd miss your wedding. Besides, who the fuck else could you trust to be your best man?"

Kade clamps his hand down firmly on my shoulder.

The motherfucker.

"No one. You're the only man for the job."

I gulp over the sudden wedge of emotion clogging my throat. "I'm happy for you, man. And glad to admit my initial interpretation of Eva was wrong. I can see why you love her, and you know I'm trying to keep her safe too. Everything I do is about protecting Cheryl and Eva."

"I hope someday I'll get to repay you for all you've done for us, Kev."

"You don't need to repay me, Kade. You're my brother. It's what brothers do."

He pulls me into a hug, and it's a weirdly emotional moment.

For once, Mom stages a timely intervention. "Boys!" Her shrill voice stabs my eardrums. "Over here!" She waves frantically at both of us, and we share a conspiratorial smile as we wander off to join the rest of our brothers in a family photograph.

The ceremony is beautiful, and Eva is a radiant bride. Her dress is white but nontraditional, quite simple but elegant, and it ends just below her knees. It's a custom Alex Kennedy creation, and that's one of the reasons why the numbers of paparazzi have swollen outside the church by the time the ceremony is over. Cheryl, watched over by her bodyguard, waits around the back of the church for me to bring the car around. I tell her to keep her head down as I floor it out of there.

The reception at the hotel is as extravagant as you'd expect it to be with no expense spared. Mom doesn't do anything by half. After the speeches and dinner are out of the way, I get rid of my tie and unbutton my shirt, finally breathing more easily.

Kade dropped a vast sum of money to secure singer Adele for the night. She's a well-respected British singer Eva is a huge fan of. Kade kept it a surprise, and Eva's screams of delight could be heard all over the grand ballroom.

"That'll be you next," I overhear Brad telling Kyler behind me as I watch Cheryl, Rachel, Faye, Melissa, and Lana shake their stuff on the dance floor.

"Not if Kev beats me to it," he quips, dragging my attention away from the girls.

"We're in no rush," I admit.

Ky's mouth hangs open. "I was joking, but you've already discussed marriage?"

I scrub a hand over my jaw, wondering how to phrase this. "I'm not sure if *discussed* is the right word. I told Cheryl I'd be putting a ring on her finger one day, and she was happy with that."

Brad chuckles, and Ky rolls his eyes. "I hope your proposal will be more romantic than that," he teases.

"It will be," I say with confidence, because if there's one thing I'm good at, it's planning shit. Ky went all out with his marriage proposal, whisking Faye away to the Bahamas to propose, so I've a lot to live up to. I look at Brad, happy to deflect the heat in his direction. "What about you and Rachel?"

"What about us?" he asks, running a finger under the collar of his shirt, starting to sweat.

Ky and I smirk. "Don't play shy, McConaughey. Will you be putting a ring on Rachel's finger any time soon?"

"Not any time soon, but someday, yeah, definitely." Brad rubs the back of his neck. "If she'll have me" he tags on the end.

"That's a given. She's crazy about you," I admit, because that girl never stops swooning over her man no matter how often I tell her she's making my ears bleed.

Ky smiles a wide smile, and it's good to see all the tension of the past few years has completely been laid to rest. "Faye will be over the fucking moon."

"Save me," Cheryl says, suddenly appearing through the crowd, clutching onto my arm from behind. "My feet are killing me!" She keeps one hand on my arm as she bends down, slipping her sandal off and rubbing the arch of her foot.

I don't hesitate, uncaring of the large audience. Scooping her up into my arms, I carry her to one of the velvet couches at the back of the room. I lay her down and flop onto the opposite end of the couch. Removing her other sandal, I start massaging her feet. She leans back, tucking her hands underneath her head and grinning at me. "Everyone's watching, you know."

"I couldn't give a flying fuck." I knead her feet with my thumbs, and she sighs contentedly.

"I'm nominating you for Best Boyfriend of the Year," she exclaims a few minutes later.

"And I'll nominate you for Best Girlfriend of the Year if you blow me in the bathroom," I joke.

She sits bolt upright, fire flaring in her eyes. "I'll do one better than that," she says, hooking the straps of her sandals through one finger and swinging her bare feet to the floor. She scoots along the couch until she's alongside me, fixing me with a lusty look. "I'll let you fuck me in the bathroom."

I wasn't serious, well, not much, but the instant she ups the stakes, my cock surges to life, answering for me. Jumping up, I grab her hand and lead her out to the bathroom, ignoring the knowing looks on my brothers' faces when they notice the direction we're heading in.

The minute we're locked in the wheelchair accessible bathroom, Cheryl drops to her knees, and I can't keep the smug grin off my face.

Best fucking wedding ever.

Chapter 21

Cheryl

"What's wrong?" I ask the minute Kev steps through the front door of the studio just before closing. "I thought we were going to meet *at* the firing range?" It's Thursday, and I usually drive myself there after work unless we've made other arrangements. We still meet Kade and Eva every week without fail. I never thought I'd enjoy firing a weapon, but learning to defend myself has given me a confidence I didn't expect. Plus, it makes me feel badass, so there's that.

"I need to talk to you about something," he says, looking solemn. "And then my boss wants to meet with you."

Blood thrums in my ears and a fluttering feeling breaches my chest cavity. "You're scaring me."

He comes around the front desk, placing his hands on top of my shoulders and squeezing. "What I have to tell you will probably enhance that feeling, and it's likely to upset you too, but I wanted you to hear it from me first before I bring you to my workplace." Kev's always so careful to never publicly mention the fact he works for the FBI. I've introduced him to my boss, but she believes he's a freelance tech consultant too. "Can we go somewhere private to talk?" he asks.

"Sure. Just let me square it with Sara." I walk over to my boss, quickly filling her in, and she has no issue with me taking Kev into the staff room.

"Okay. Hit me with it," I say the instant we walk into the empty staff room.

Kev takes my hands in his, bringing me over to the couch and forcing me to sit down beside him. "Hayley's body has been found."

I blink profusely as the words sink in. "Where?" My voice sounds remarkably calm even though I'm already quaking inside.

"In a seedy motel in Texas," he confirms, rubbing soothing circles on the back of my hand.

"And when you say found, do you mean she's ... she's dead?" I whisper the last words.

He nods. "I'm sorry."

I try to work out how I feel about this. I didn't know Hayley all that well, and half the time we were supposed "friends," she was lying to me and cheating with my fiancé behind my back. But that doesn't mean I wanted her dead. I *have* thought of her over the last few weeks and regularly asked Keven for any updates since she disappeared. My mouth turns dry, and a cold chill tiptoes up my spine. "And you think Dan did this?"

He nods again. "He wanted her out of the way so she wouldn't ruin his chances of winning you back."

I yank one of my hands out of his, pressing my palm over my mouth. Nausea swims up my throat, and I think I might puke.

"I know what you're thinking, and this isn't your fault."

"Isn't it?" I rise and start pacing the room. "If she'd never met me, then she'd never have met him. She'd still be alive."

"Stop." He stands in front of me and reels me into his arms, bundling me into his warm, strong embrace. "You didn't compel her to get involved with him, and you didn't abduct and kill her. Hayley's choices led to this. Not you." He holds the back of my head, keeping me tucked against his chest where I feel safe.

Silence descends, and we stay wrapped in our embrace, both of us locked in our own heads.

"Is there anything to connect her to Dan? Was there any incriminating evidence found?" I ask the question even though I already know the answer.

"Unfortunately not," he says in a clipped tone. I know how hard Kev's working to find something to stick to Dan but, so far, he's squeaky clean.

I sigh heavily, trying to stay strong, but I'd be lying if I said this hadn't shaken me. Since I discovered who Dan really is, I've been frightened although I haven't expressed that thought out loud. I know Kev will go to the ends of the Earth to protect me, and I've always believed that Dan wouldn't hurt me, but now I'm not so sure.

He may not have loved Hayley, but he still spent time with her. Still made love to her. Bought her expensive gifts indicating she was on his mind. If he can do that to *her*, he can do that to *me*, and that's what scares me.

"I want to help," I say, easing out of his embrace and looking up at him. "Whatever it is your boss wants me to do, I'm doing it. We've got to stop him, Kev. We can't live with this hanging over our heads."

"I know, but I'm not sure how you can help. Let's just talk to the SSA and see what he has in mind."

"Are you out of your ever-loving mind?" Kev roars, jumping up and knocking his chair over. This time we're talking with Supervisory Special Agent Clement in his office. Just Kev, me, and him.

"Keven." I tug on his arm, urging him to calm down. He can't speak to his boss like that even if he has just dropped a bomb on both of us.

"No way! She's not doing it! And I can't believe you've asked her to!" He grabs fistfuls of his hair and starts pacing the room.

I get up and go to him, forcing him to stop and placing my hands on his waist. "Keven, sit back down, and let's just hear SSA Clement out."

He grips my face tight. "You're not doing it. It's too dangerous."

I draw deep breaths, determined to keep a cool head. "No one has agreed to anything. Let's hear the facts, and then we can consider it. Please, baby," I whisper at the end.

I don't want to be the reason he loses this job.

He presses his forehead to mine, his chest heaving, and I am floored, once again, by the evidence of his love for me. I'll never take it for granted. Not when I thought I'd lost it, and him, forever.

He composes himself, keeping hold of my hand as we reclaim our seats.

"I don't ask this lightly of you, Cheryl," the SSA says, focusing on me, "but we are running out of options. We still haven't figured out how Stanten is getting supplies of guns, drugs, and young girls into the country, because any leads our undercover agents have picked up have been dead ends. We suspect he's on to us, which is why we've pulled our guys out; however, we're fairly certain he's hiding at least some of those things in that barn."

I shudder at the thought of kidnapped girls being kept in that barn while I slept only a couple of miles away. It makes me sick to the pit of my stomach.

The SSA leans forward on his elbows. "We know there's another entrance on that property, and we expect that's how Stanten is getting away with this, but we can't locate it. The old maps of the property show an entrance at the northwesterly side of the grounds, just off the smaller slip road, but it's not visible from the road, and we can't go snooping around without drawing attention. The drones haven't picked up any activity, which leads us to believe it's some kind of underground entrance. It's the only explanation that makes sense."

"Or he's not transporting anything to that barn," Kev interrupts.

"I know you don't believe that, Keven." The SSA drills him with a serious look. "Criminals don't appoint armed guards to an empty barn."

"There's got to be another way." Keven claws his hands through his hair, and frustration oozes from his pores.

"We've spent weeks brainstorming it, and there isn't. The old plans of the house clearly show underground tunnels, and that's why we need to get in there and see if we can locate them."

"I didn't see any evidence of that while I lived there," I admit with a frown. "And Dan never mentioned a word to me about them."

"I doubt he would, but I assure you they do exist. The original owner built the house during the prohibition era, and he became one of Boston's most notorious bootleggers."

"Dan said he gutted the house and pretty much rebuilt it from scratch," I continue, "so I wouldn't bank on any of those tunnels still being in existence."

"You may be right, Cheryl. It could be another dead end. But we've got to try." He slides a paper file across the desk to me. "Those are copies of email communications between the realtor and your ex-fiancé. The realtor said he was very keen to get his hands on the property, even offering an additional ten percent above the agreed price to close the sale quickly. I believe Stanten's decision to purpose that property was strategic. He wanted those tunnels."

Unease slithers over my body like fog. "Can't you verify it with the contractor who worked on the house?" I suggest.

"We can't play that angle," Kev replies. "Because the contractors are in Mancusso's pocket. They'll tell us jack shit, and we can't risk approaching them either. If Stanten discovers the FBI is on the case he'll re-strategize, making our job even harder."

"But I thought you said you had to pull your undercover guys out because of that very thing?" I direct my question to the SSA.

"We think Stanten knows someone is sniffing around, but it could be any number of government agencies or a plant from one of their enemies. We're confident he has no idea we're building a case against him."

Except for the corrupt judge. I think it but don't say it because I'm not supposed to know anything about that. I don't know how Kev deals with this stuff. All the unknowns would drive me demented, and constantly running into brick walls would deplete my patience reserves. Kev clearly has a higher tolerance than me.

"I can see where you're coming from," I add, eyeballing Kev's boss. "Getting into the house is the only way to prove or disprove the tunnel theory. I understand why you need me," I quietly add, not wanting to light Kev's fuse.

"It doesn't have to be Cheryl," Keven says in a restrained tone of voice. "Why can't you send in your undercover guys under false pretenses. Let them snoop around."

"Stanten is too smart for that old ruse," the SSA says. "He'll immediately smell a rat. Besides, it could take some time to locate the tunnel entry points, and it requires someone with unfettered access to the property."

"He'll smell a rat if Cheryl does a U-turn all of a sudden," Kev says, challenging his boss with a heated stare. "She broke things off weeks ago, and she's been rejecting all his advances. He'll be suspicious as fuck."

"Agreed, which is why this will have to happen gradually."

Kev shakes his head repeatedly. "No way. Cheryl's not dating him again just so she can get access to that house. It's too fucking dangerous."

"I know you're concerned, Keven, but we'll keep Cheryl safe."

"Like you kept Hayley safe?" he shouts, and I clutch onto his arm, willing him to calm down.

The SSA looks pained. "We couldn't get to her in time, because it happened so fast, but this will be different. We'll plan it meticulously, and Cheryl will be aware every step of the way. We'll ensure she's protected around the clock. Nothing will happen to her. I give you my word."

Kev swivels in his chair, turning to face me. "I don't want you to do this. There are too many things that could go wrong. No one can force you into doing this, so you can say no." He grips my face. "I want you to say no." His eyes drill into mine. "You promised you wouldn't leave me again, and I'm invoking that promise now."

"Kev, it's not the same thing, and you know it. If I agree to do this, I won't be leaving you. I'll be pretending to date him again, but it won't be real."

"If he finds out, he could kill you, Cheryl. Or force you into commercial sex like Hayley."

The team discovered Hayley had been routinely drugged and forced to have sex with different men from that seedy motel in Texas. A witness—a maintenance man at the hotel— came forward confirming he'd seen a rotation of different men going in and out of her room. He also confirmed there were at least three young girls working out of other rooms, all rented by the same man.

Of course, the ID they had on file was fake, and as the man had only ever paid cash, there was no way of tracing him that way. They had cleared out after Hayley OD'd, and that was the only reason the witness came forward. He was too scared to say anything while they were there.

"I know how to protect myself, and I can use a gun. Plus, I know what he's capable of. Hayley didn't have any of that knowledge which is why it was easy for them to take her."

"It sounds like you've already made up your mind," he snaps. "Don't my feelings count?"

I place my hands over his. "Of course, your feelings matter, and I *will* take some time to think about it, but I want to help." I peer deep into his troubled eyes. "This could put him behind bars, Kev. He could be out of our lives for good. Isn't it worth taking a risk for that?"

"No, baby." His eyes plead with me. "There is no risk worth taking when it comes to your life. None."

Chapter 22

Keven

I'm tired of arguing with her. I can see it's not going to make any difference. I was right when we were back in the SSA's office—she's going to agree to this madness. And I'm going to fucking lose it. I want to regret the day I agreed to join the FBI, but I can't because it brought Cheryl back into my life—even if I now want to pummel my boss in the face until he bleeds.

"You do realize if you go ahead with this, and it works, that you'll most likely have to go into witness protection?" I play my final card. "Is that what you want? For us to be permanently separated? To never see me or your family again?" Okay, I'm stretching a little, because there's no way I'd let her go into witness protection without me even if we have to have a quickie wedding to ensure the protection extends to me. But it's no word of a lie when it comes to her family.

"It won't come to that," she protests, knotting her hands in her lap.

"You'll be instrumental in putting Stanten behind bars. He's the son of the head of one of New York's most powerful crime families. You think Mancusso's gonna let you live if you take his son from him?"

Her hands shake, and her lower lip wobbles. I hate that I'm scaring her, but she needs a dose of reality.

"Then I'll go into witness protection." She stands, and a fresh layer of determination washes over her face as she walks over to me. She straddles my lap, forcing my back into the couch. "But only if you come with me. If you won't, then I'll take my chances. I'm not going anywhere without you." She runs her finger through the bristle on my chin, and I know what she's doing. Telling me I rank higher than her family. Trying to soften me up so I'll back down.

"You don't know what you're talking about." I glare at her, fueled by frustration. "You'd sacrifice your entire future by taking a risk that might not even yield any results? Do you hear how reckless that is? If my boss is wrong, if there are no tunnels, and no underground entrance, and Stanten figures out you are spying on him, he'll take you from me, one way or another, and I'm not okay with that Cheryl. The risk is not worth it. Please, baby." I cup her beautiful face. "Please tell my boss to fuck off. We'll find another way."

"I can't stand by while other girls are subjected to the same fate as Hayley," she whispers. "Don't ask me to be that selfish."

"Self-preservation is not fucking selfish!" I roar, struggling to keep my emotions in check. "It's survival one-oh-one." I grip her hips, pulling her in closer to me. "Listen to me, I know you feel guilty about Hayley, but her death is not on your conscience, and neither are any other girls that have fallen under Stanten's trap. It's not your responsibility or your job to stop him."

"But it's yours."

"Yes, it's mine and SSA Clement's, which is why it should be left up to us. He had no right to involve you." I've a good mind to report him. If Cheryl wasn't connected to me, I wonder would he have asked her to consider something so dangerous.

"I *want* to help." Her lower lip juts out, and I recognize the tell. She's getting ready to dig her heels in. Sliding off my lap, she sits alongside me, leaning back and looking up at the ceiling. A strained sigh escapes her lips. "When I first started volunteering at the residential home, I had a student named Camila," she starts explaining. "She was seventeen and severely troubled. She didn't speak except through the eyes of her camera. I could see she was hurting, and I wanted to help."

Of course, she would. Cheryl likes to fix things, and she always wants to see the best in people. It's one of the qualities I love most about her even if it does expose her to being taken advantage of. I still wouldn't want her to change. There are too many hardened, embittered people in the world. Cheryl's attitude is like a breath of fresh air, and it's a huge part of who she is. I'd never want to take that from her.

But wanting to help by putting her own life at risk is a step too far and not something I can condone or support.

"She came from a poor family in a small town in Mexico," she continues, "which made it easy for a predator to target her. I learned her story in part from her social worker and partly from Camila, once she learned to trust me and started opening up."

Tears stab her eyes, and I pull her into my side, unable to ignore the need to comfort her. "When an older good-looking American guy showed up in her village and started paying her attention, she was flattered. She was only thirteen, and she developed a crush on him. Rhett told her she was very pretty and she could get rich modeling in the U.S. She ran away with him because she thought she could earn enough money to provide for her family. As soon as she set foot on American soil, Rhett brought her to meet his 'family' which consisted of eight other young Mexican girls he'd kidnapped under false pretenses. She was shoved into a warehouse, handcuffed to a mattress, drugged, and raped by a succession of older men."

Tears cascade down her cheeks, and I wrap my arms around her, holding her tight. A lump forms in the back of my throat as I listen to the rest of her story.

"She was thirteen, Kev. *Thirteen.*" Her voice chokes, and I press a kiss to her temple. "They destroyed her innocence, and she lost her freedom. For three years, she serviced up to twenty men a day. She was kept drugged and weak and chained to that bed for hours at a time. They moved around, settling in different locations, and her pimp would bring her to homes and hotels, forcing her to have sex with various johns. One day, she was being dragged out of a hotel, screaming, when a woman intervened. The pimp drove off without her, and she was rescued, eventually ending up in the residential home when it was discovered the pimp had killed her family and she had no home to return to."

She sniffles, nudging her head into my arm and looking up at me with soulful, pained eyes. "She was tormented, Keven. She couldn't relate to any of the other kids. She'd been to hell and back trying to stay clean, and she blamed herself for her family's deaths." A loud sob rips from her throat. "She tried so hard, but it was all too much. She ran away one night, hitched a lift to the city, and jumped off the Tobin Bridge. Her body washed up on the shores of Mystic River a few days later. It's been four months since it happened, and I still think about her every day."

"I'm sorry, baby. I truly am." I press a kiss to her temple. "I hope you don't blame yourself for that because I know you did everything you could to help her, but sometimes, there is nothing we can do."

She stares at me with big, glassy eyes. "I understand that, but I *can* do something about this, which is why I need to do it, Kev. I couldn't help Camila, but I might be able to help stop others from being taken. Perhaps I can help rescue girls Dan's already trafficked, and that's why I've got to do this. I couldn't bear to live with myself if I had a chance to help and I did nothing. I'm tortured with the thought he might've kept girls in that barn while I was sleeping a few miles away."

I open my mouth to argue because it's not as cut and dry as that, but she places a soft hand over my mouth. "I know you're concerned, and I love you so much for wanting to shield me from this, but I also know you trust me and love me enough to make my own decisions."

She sits up straighter, wiping the dampness under her eyes. "I promise I'm not leaving you, Kev, and it's your love that'll ensure I make it through this. I want to do it. For Camila. For my own sanity. And because it's the right thing to do."

"I'm scared of losing you, Cheryl." I twist my fingers in her hair, pressing a soft kiss to her forehead.

She curls her hand around my arm, peering deep into my eyes. "I don't want to disregard or downplay your feelings. I completely understand where you're coming from, and if the tables were reversed, I'd be the same. I love how much you love me, Kev. And I'm sorry that me wanting to do this upsets you so much, but *not* doing this will upset *me*. Is there anything I can do or say that will make this any easier for you?"

"I want to put my foot down and tell you you're not doing it, but I don't ever want to be that man. The one who commands you to do things against your will, so, if you're hellbent on doing this, I won't stop you on one condition."

She kisses me softly and I just want to hold her against me forever. "Thank you. I know how much it takes for you to say that, and I'm not ungrateful. I've no problem agreeing to your condition if it'll help ease your worry. Name it."

"That you do everything in your power to keep yourself safe. That means rigidly following the FBI's instructions, staying alert, not taking any risky chances, and trusting your gut. If you feel like something's wrong, it probably is, and you need to react to that."

She nods. "I won't take any unnecessary risks. I want to catch the bastard and see him in jail. And then I want to move forward with my life, with you. Once we're together, nothing else matters."

I haul her into my arms, crushing her to me. My heart is racing a hundred miles an hour, and anxiety tightens my chest. I don't care what I have to do, but I'll do whatever it takes to keep her safe and ensure she comes back to me.

It's two weeks since Cheryl agreed to put her life on the line, and I'm close to breaking point. I haven't slept properly since she moved into Kade's old place, and our nightly Skype calls just aren't cutting it. I fucking miss her, and I hate this, but I also agree it's necessary. She can't be seen with me now she's "dating" that asshole again. The bodyguard I hired is watching over her, as is Agent Higgins. Plus, Agent Wentward is still shadowing Stanten.

All of them have assured me she's safe and that he's unaware of the FBI connection, but I can't rest easy. I won't until this is done. I have cameras all over her place and in her car, trackers on her cell and her shoes, and alerts set up, and I spend hours every night watching the feed, making sure she's safe, but it does little to ease my anxiety.

"You look tired, baby," she says when we Skype later that night.

"This is what I look like without you," I proclaim. "I miss you so much, and I just want this to be over."

"I miss you too, and if you think this isn't killing me, then you're wrong. I hate it, but it's working. He is so far up his own ass he honestly believes I've forgiven him." She rolls her eyes, and I know that's for my benefit.

An awkward silence filters between us, like it does any time *he* comes up in conversation. I trust Cheryl, which is why we didn't have this conversation before she moved out, but it's different now I can't see her in the flesh, can't touch her or hold her in my arms. I have to put this out there for my sanity. "You're not sleeping with him, right?"

A flash of anger flits across her face, quickly replaced with understanding. "Of course not, baby." She puts her hand up to the screen. "You're the only man I'll be sleeping with from now on. I promise."

"How is he accepting that?"

"I've told him I need to learn to trust him again before we start having sex, and he bought it. More than that, it lends authenticity to the situation. Any woman that would jump back into his bed after what he did couldn't be trusted."

Air whooshes out of my mouth in grateful relief. "Okay, and I'm sorry for asking, but it was eating me up inside."

"Well, it's not going to be for much longer."

My eyes pop wide, my heart accelerating at the exuberant grin on her face. "What haven't you said?"

"He asked me to come over Friday night after work, and I convinced him to let me cook for him. Told him I'd cook us a special celebration meal and leave work early to get a head start." She lifts up a bunch of keys, dangling them in front of her face. "He handed me back my keys without question."

"That is the best damn news I've heard in weeks."

"Thought you'd like that. Can you tell the boss man so he can put everything in motion? I'll drive to the house at four, and you can meet me there."

I nod buoyantly. "I'll call him immediately and oversee the plans myself. I'm going to double-and triple-check everything so there is no margin for error. We're ending it this weekend."

"I love the sound of that, and I'll be on a countdown till Friday." She places her hand back on the screen. "I need your arms around me so badly."

"I know, baby. Me too." I raise my palm to the screen, as if I'm touching hers. "I can hardly wait."

Chapter 23

Cheryl

Being back in this house again makes me sick, but I remind myself why I'm doing this, visualizing Camila in my mind's eye and allowing her image to bolster my courage. I trust Keven's prepared for any eventualities, but I'm still on edge, terrified something will go wrong and Dan will figure this out. Having to spend another second in his company will feel like a lifetime. These last few weeks have majorly tested my acting skills, but Dan's superiority complex works to my advantage. Any normal guy would be suspicious of my sudden U-turn, taking his time inviting me back into his life, but not Dan. His arrogance and misplaced self-confidence will be his downfall in the end.

A twisted part of me has enjoyed pulling the wool over his eyes, and I hope I'm there when the penny drops. I want to catch his expression the instant he realizes I've fooled him.

Glancing at the clock in the kitchen, I stick the pot roast I made last night in the oven on a low heat and hurry to set the table. Kev was adamant it needs to look like I'm in the throes of making dinner in case Dan shows up. Hopefully, he's too preoccupied with the planned distraction—a carefully controlled explosion at one of his warehouses in downtown Boston— to worry about being late for dinner, thereby giving us enough time to search the house from top to bottom.

The doorbell chimes just as I've finished setting the table, and I rush to let Keven in, my heart doing cartwheels at the thought of seeing my love in the flesh for the first time in weeks. I rein my excitement in, opening the door slowly and greeting him with a pleasant but disinterested smile, like I would any cable guy who materializes at my door.

Although he's in disguise, my heart is still careening around my chest as I drink in the welcome sight of him. Already, I feel my anxiety levels steadying, knowing he will protect me no matter how this goes down. He's dressed in workers pants and a high vis jacket, carrying a metal toolbox in one hand. I work hard to contain my mirth at the state of the longish dirty-blond wig and matching fake moustache which makes him look like a reject from the nineteen sixties. "I believe you have an issue with your cable, ma'am," he says, keeping up the façade in case any of the men at the barn are watching from a distance or the camera is picking up our conversation.

"Oh, I wasn't aware. My boyfriend didn't mention it to me." I purposely frown.

Trying hard not to scowl at my use of the *BF* word, Kev pulls a piece of paper from his back pocket, thrusting it at me. "You can inspect the order right there." He points at the falsified paperwork.

I pretend to inspect it before smiling casually at him. I step aside, ushering him in, discreetly checking the grounds outside for evidence of any prying eyes, but all looks quiet out the front.

The instant the door is closed, he pushes me up against the wall, and his lips descend on mine. I moan into his mouth, grabbing hold of his waist as our lips move punishingly together. I allow myself to enjoy his kiss for about ten seconds before I reluctantly shove him away. "The cameras," I rasp.

He grips my hips, pulling me into his hard, hot body. "I'll disable them in a minute." He leans his head down, lining up our mouths again, but I shove him back more forcefully this time.

"Shut them down *now*, Kev. We can't take any risks." I plant my hands on my hips. "Your rules, remember?"

"Fuck." He adjusts the bulge in his pants. "I want inside you so bad."

I send him my best school ma'am glare. "We need to focus, Kev. There'll be time for that later."

His lips kick up in a smile. "I'm going to fuck you so hard, all night long, so you won't ever remember being apart from me."

My core throbs with need at his filthy promise, and saliva pools in my mouth. I've missed being in his bed. Missed having him fill me up, eliciting earth-shattering pleasure from my body on a nightly basis. Every part of me hums at the prospect of having that again.

Walking swiftly toward Dan's office, he throws one last remark over his shoulder. "And that's a promise, sexy. Just you wait and see."

I stand dazed in the empty hallway for a couple of seconds until my head clears. Then I race after him in time to see him picking the lock and breaking into Dan's office. The instant his butt is on the chair and his fingers pound the keyboard, he's all business, flirting forgotten, for now. I stand over him, anxiously watching as he hacks into the camera system and shuts the feed down in mere seconds. He's a freaking genius when it comes to computers.

"Let's go." He jumps up, the chair making a screeching sound as it slams back against the wall. "Higgins and Wentward are keeping watch outside, and the team is on standby, a short distance away, ready to move in as soon as we have concrete evidence we can use against him," he explains before crushing his lips to mine. I cling to him, devouring his mouth the same way he's devouring mine.

Our tongues tangle, delighted to be dancing once again, but it's a frantic, fast-paced tango and one laced with an air of urgency and a dangerous undercurrent. All too soon, his lips are gone from mine, and I feel like crying.

"I could kiss you all day long, but you're right. We have a job to do." Taking my hand, he leads me out to the hallway. "Let's make this fast." He pecks my lips. "Call me if you find anything and I'll do the same." He swats me on the ass as I spin around, heading toward the stairs. "Stay safe, babe."

"You too." I walk backward, blowing him a kiss. "I love you!" I shout as I disappear out of sight, taking the stairs two at a time.

Per the agreed plan, I'm checking upstairs while Kev checks downstairs. If we can't find any hidden tunnels, then we'll have to venture outside, which is where it'll get tricky. Three heavily armed men guard the barn, and trying to snoop within proximity to them is risky as hell. I never remember Dan venturing outside, so I'm convinced there's an entry point to the tunnel, and the barn, from inside this house. I'm determined we're not leaving until we find it.

I examine every square inch of the master bedroom, opening and closing doors and cupboards and inspecting all the walls in the walk-in closet, coming up empty-handed. I move onto the guest bedrooms and bathrooms, one at a time, growing more and more agitated as my search reveals nothing. I call Kev, and he confirms he hasn't discovered anything either.

Sweat rolls down my back as I head into the second last guest bedroom, glancing at the time, starting to panic. By now, Dan is aware of the explosion at his warehouse. His cryptic text telling me he's running late confirms it, but I can't shake the nervous feeling that something's gone wrong.

I'm pulling out a pile of boxes stored in the closet of the gray guest bedroom when Kev races into the room, his eyes darting wildly about. "The asshole's pulling into the drive," he exclaims, his voice gruff. "Get down to the kitchen and pretend to be fixing dinner." He grabs my shoulders, steering me toward the door.

"What? How? He's texted me to—"

"Something must've spooked him. Go, Cheryl. Wentward and Higgins are watching, and they'll intervene if necessary, but you need to distract him. He can't find me here."

"What about—" I gesture toward the boxes I was in the process of removing.

"I'll fix it." He nudges me toward the door. "You're still wearing your wire, right?" I nod, as bile swims up my throat. "Good, I'll be listening, and I'm not going to let him hurt you." He cups my face tenderly. "You got that? He's not going to lay a finger on you."

"I love you," I whisper.

"I love you too, and if I hear anything I don't like, I'm coming to get you. I don't give a fuck." Removing a gun from his toolbox, he hands it to me. "The safety is on, but use it if you need to."

My hand shakes as I take the gun, slipping it under the band of my pants.

Kev presses his finger to the hidden device in his ear. "Go, Cheryl. He's getting out of his car. Play your part, baby." He plants a fierce kiss on my lips. "Be safe."

I race down the stairs, flying into the kitchen and turning the heat on under the pans on the stove. I've just tied the apron strings around my waist when Dan enters the kitchen.

"Oh my God, you startled me," I shriek, planting a hand on my chest as a smile forms on my lips. The only way I can do this is to imagine he's Kev. I walk toward him, fluttering my eyelashes and smiling coyly. "I thought you said you'd be late. Not that I'm in any way complaining." I giggle, circling my arms around his neck and stretching up on my tiptoes to kiss him.

"What did you do to the cameras?" he barks, turning away from my kiss and glaring at me.

My heart pounds in my chest, and it takes everything I possess to force my anxiety aside and act as expected in this situation. I frown, removing my hands from his neck and staring up at him in confusion. "What cameras? What do you mean?"

He grabs my face roughly, and the cold, harsh glare in his eyes sends shivers up and down my spine. "If you're up to something, I'll end you." He grips my chin, digging his fingernails into my flesh while his eyes flare menacingly. Terror has a vise grip on my heart, and bile swirls around my mouth.

"Dan, you're hurting me," I whimper, praying Kev doesn't come racing down the stairs yet. "And you're scaring me. What do you mean if I'm up to something? I'm making you dinner." I let a tear slip out of my eye, and he glances over my head, scanning the pots on the stove. Yanking me forward by the elbow, he stalks to the oven, aggressively pulling the door open. I rub my sore jaw as I silently coach myself to remain calm, hiding my free hand behind my back to hide my trembling. Dan is crouched down in front of the oven, staring absently at it, as if lost in thought.

When he straightens up, he releases his iron grip on me, smiling as if he's a different man. The dark, inhumane glare is gone from his eyes, replaced by a soft, adoring look that I now know is completely fake. He moves into me, but I step back, feeling off-balance. I start untying my apron with trembling fingers. "I think I should go."

"Darling, don't. I'm sorry." Slowly, he steps toward me, and I take another couple steps back.

"I don't even know who you are right now." I hold up my hand, keeping him at bay. "This was a mistake."

"No." He pulls me to him, hauling my hands up to his chest, and I feel nauseated. "I'm sorry I scared you. I've just had a really bad day, but I didn't mean to take it out on you. I love you, Cheryl. You know that."

Lying asshole.

His cell pings, and a flash of annoyance flares across his face. "Dinner looks delicious, and I'm starving." He rubs his thumb across my lips, and I shake all over. Thankfully, he mistakes it for desire, his eyes darkening with hunger this time. "That's not the only thing I'm starving for." He grabs my ass, pulling me flush against his erection, and I puke a little in my mouth. "How long are you going to make me wait?"

He leans in to kiss me, but I push him off. "I'm still mad at you. And if you truly love me, you'll wait."

He grinds down on his teeth as his cell pings again. "I've got to take this." He storms out of the room with the cell to his ear, walking toward his office with urgency. I collapse against the island unit as unrestrained panic consumes me. *What if he figures out Kev picked the lock?* I can't remember if he shut the door to his office after we left.

My cell pings, and I almost drop it on the ground as I scramble to open up the message from Kev.

I covered my tracks. Relax and stay calm. You're doing great.

A strangled sob escapes my mouth before I can stop it. I'm literally shaking with fright, and I've got to get a grip before he returns. I walk slowly to the stove, stirring pots and pretending like I give a damn about dinner.

Dan storms back into the kitchen five minutes later like a tsunami hellbent on destruction. "I've got to go out again." He presses a kiss to my cheek. "But I'll be back."

"Maybe we should leave this for another time," I say, playing along but silently hoping he won't call my bluff.

"No, babe. I promise I'll be back. Just make yourself at home, and I'll text you."

I wait an anxious few minutes after I hear the front door close before I break down. Then Kev is there bundling me into his strong arms, whispering words of reassurance and consoling me. I look up, glad to see he's removed the hideous wig and fake stache. I kiss his lips in one slow, lingering kiss, feeling my resilience return as his emotion and his strength pours into me. "Are you okay?" His face is creased with concern. "No one will blame you if you want to bail."

"I'm not bailing." I swipe at the moisture under my eyes, removing all trace of it. "I'm fine. The look in his eye just frightened me. He looked like pure evil."

"I was *this* close to charging down here and putting a bullet through his skull." Kev kisses my forehead, holding me tight. "I know Higgins and Mead would've covered for me, and it was tempting, but death is too easy for a bastard like him. I want to see him behind bars." He eases back, gripping my forearms. "Are you sure you're up to this?"

I vigorously nod. "I am. I'm not backing out now. I'm seeing this through to the end."

His eyes spark to life. "In that case, I've got good news."

My breath hitches. "You mean—"

"I found the tunnel baby. We're going to finish this tonight."

Chapter 24

Keven

"Oh my God." Cheryl's eyes are almost bugging out of her head as we stand in front of the open closet in the guestroom. A blast of cold air slaps us in the face as I pull the cord dangling from the top of the closet, and light floods the entryway to the tunnel below.

After I'd hurriedly replaced the boxes, I'd hidden in the closet, listening to the wire feed as that asshole terrorized Cheryl. Suspicion was clear in his voice, and I was on the verge of tearing down to the kitchen so many times, but I managed to restrain myself.

I had a feeling deactivating the camera feed might trigger a warning, especially so soon after the last time. I'm hoping he had it set up to receive automatic alerts. The alternative is that he pays for live monitoring which would be problematic, but I can't consider that now. I've got to keep my focus. There'll be time to consider the fallout after the operation has completed.

When I heard her say he was hurting her I slammed my fist into the back of the closet, my heart stuttering when I heard the hollow sound echoing back at me. I'd traced my fingers around the edge, feeling the small breeze blowing over my fingertips and I knew I'd hit pay dirt. But I couldn't risk exploring further, not with that bastard downstairs, so I had to bide my time until we enticed him out of the house again.

It seemed to take forever for news of the second explosion to reach Stanten's ears. We'd had a Plan B in case he showed up at the house, and once Wentward updated the SSA, he gave the order to detonate the second device at another one of his warehouses, over on the other side of the city.

I was confident once Stanten heard that another one of his warehouses had gone up in flames he wouldn't stay home even if he's now harboring doubts about Cheryl's reappearance in his life.

Or, perhaps, he's considering alternatives. Maybe believing the DeLuca family is making a reckless play. It's not a huge stretch at all. It's better if he believes the explosions and camera failures are connected to his Boston rivals; at least it will deflect suspicion from Cheryl. I make a mental note to leave a few crumbs pointing in that direction for him when I get back home.

The instant I brought Cheryl up to the guest room, I ripped the false panel off the back of the closet, exposing the stairs leading down to the tunnel. I wish I could do this alone so that I can keep her safe and out of harm's way. But the SSA was very clear. We need proof before the FBI can officially come barging in. Given what I suspect awaits us, there's no way I'm going down there without backup. Besides, I know my girl. There's no way she'd stay behind even if I begged her to.

So, it's up to the two of us to explore this tunnel.

I face my love, pinning her with a grave expression. "Stay behind me at all times, and once we reach the tunnel, take your gun out, and keep it armed and ready." She nods, visibly gulping. "Just keep calm and remember everything you've learned. I don't know if anyone is manning these tunnels, so expect the unexpected."

Determination glimmers behind her eyes as she straightens her shoulders. "I know what to do. I've got this, and you don't need to worry about me. Just concentrate on the path ahead and know I've got your back." She pulls back the chamber of her gun in one fluid, confident move, unlocking the safety and positioning her hands in the correct position before drilling me with a feisty, determined look.

"Damn, that's fucking hot," I admit with a smile, checking the knife is securely strapped to my calf and unlocking the safety on my Glock.

A muscle clenches in her jaw as she stares at the stairway to hell. "Let's go nail the bastard."

I descend the staircase slowly and carefully, my eyes and ears primed for any signs that we're not alone. When my foot hits the ground, it triggers some kind of electric sensor, and lights flare to life, illuminating the passageway in front of us. Cracked stone walls attest to the age of the tunnel, but the pathway looks new, and it's been swept clean. There's no mold, debris, or any obvious sign of rodents or water leakages.

Cheryl's breathing puffs out in audible spurts, but she's steadfast as she follows me. There only seems to be one route, one destination, although we pass by several older tunnels, jutting off to the left and right, that have been sealed behind iron doors. It's clear Stanten had this infrastructure upgraded to suit his purpose.

We walk for fifteen minutes, and I'm beginning to wonder if this is leading us anywhere when a piercing cry rings out up ahead. I slam to a halt, spinning around to Cheryl and placing my fingers to her lips. She nods, and I detect no outward fear on her face, only dogged determination. I tap the communicator in my ear, whispering, "Stand by" to Higgins and Wentward, but I'm met with empty static.

Fuck.

"What's wrong?" she whispers, seeing something on my face.

"We've lost contact with the guys. The tunnel must be disrupting the signal." I scrub a hand over my jaw, wondering if we should turn back.

"We're not going back," she says, as if she's read my mind. "We'll scout it out, and if it looks like something we can't handle, we'll go back and call for reinforcements."

I kiss her feisty mouth. "I fucking love you."

She grins. "I fucking love you too, now let's go. We don't have time to waste."

I inch ahead slowly, keeping tucked in close to the side of the wall with Cheryl at my back. The closer we get, the louder the pained cries become, and the more my rage builds. The screams are clearly feminine, and she's hurt or hurting. When I round the next bend, I instantly retreat, forcing Cheryl back the way we just came. Using hand gestures, I motion for her to stay put. I can tell she doesn't want to let me go by myself, but there's no way I'm letting her go any farther until I've checked it's safe.

I creep around the corner, scanning the space. We've come to a dead end, facing into a small rectangular room with four iron doors on one side and a wide set of stairs on the other. The wooden double doors at the top are sealed, but I've no idea if anyone stands guard outside them. I'm guessing we're underneath the barn, and this is where Stanten has been keeping the kidnapped girls until they're sent out to work. I creep past the first two closed doors, inching toward the only open one. Raising my weapon, I draw a deep breath and take a quick peek inside.

The room is tiny, and four girls are imprisoned inside, semi-dressed, sitting on dirty mattresses with their hands shackled to the wall. One of them looks at me with stark eyes, and I lift my fingers to my lips, urging her to stay quiet.

The fifth girl is naked, bent over a table in the corner of the room, as some asshole thrusts into her from behind. Her shrill cries slice a line straight through my heart, and I don't hesitate, reaching for my knife and tiptoeing up behind him.

Grabbing him by the hair, I yank his head back so his throat is exposed. Before he can call for help, I bring the knife straight across his throat, embedding it in one fluid motion, feeling zero remorse as his lifeforce drains out of him. This is a fight or die situation, and I'm not taking any chances with these thugs. He slumps to the floor, his hands frantically grasping his neck, a gurgling sound bubbling from his throat.

Two of the girls start crying, and the girl who was being raped looks over her shoulder and screams. I clamp a hand over her mouth—I have no choice—pleading with her to keep quiet. "I'm with the FBI," I say in a whisper, sliding my badge out of my back pocket and flashing it to the clearly terrified girls. "I'm going to get you out of here, and I promise I mean you no harm. Does anyone speak English?"

"I do," a skinny girl with beautiful brown eyes and a sad smile says.

"Okay. Can you explain to the others that they need to keep quiet? There are more men upstairs, and if they don't stop screaming and crying, they'll come down here to investigate."

She nods, speaking rapidly in Spanish as I search the pockets of the dead man for keys. I find them and quickly unlock the chains around the girls' hands and feet. Advising them to stay put and keep utterly quiet,

I run out and retrieve Cheryl, getting her to stay with the girls while I check out the other rooms. The girl who speaks English comes with me as I unlock the doors, one at a time. One room is empty, but the other two hold another nine girls between them, making it fourteen in total being held down here.

Once everyone is unchained and the little Mexican girl has translated for me, we start moving back down the tunnel in the direction of the house.

I keep guard at the rear while Cheryl leads. We run, needing to get clear before someone figures out they've escaped, but it's no easy feat for the girls as they are all barefoot and weak, and some of them are sporting minor injuries. However, their survival instincts are strong, and they don't complain as they run after Cheryl, shivering and whimpering but determined to get out of here.

A shot whizzes over my head from behind and the girls start screaming. Spinning around, I fire blindly in the direction the shot came from while roaring at Cheryl. "Keep going! Get them to safety, and I'll hold them off."

I remove my backup weapon from the waistband of my pants and walk back the way we came, firing both guns at the man ducking behind the nearest corner. Behind me, I'm aware of running footsteps growing more distant, and I'm glad Cheryl has taken my instruction and is sticking to the plan.

A shot embeds in the wall right beside me, and I lunge over to the other side, narrowly avoiding impact as the guy continues firing at me. Tucking myself into the small crevice in front of one of the old iron doors, I'm strategically firing while mentally calculating how many bullets I've got left. Then I get lucky, and one of my shots hits its mark. The man goes down, and he's not getting back up. Unwilling to take any chances, I run toward him with both weapons raised, firing another couple of rounds into his prostrate body.

When I reach his side, I prod him with my booted foot, but his rigid limbs and glassy-eyed stare confirm he's dead. I'm turning around to go after Cheryl and the girls when the cold metal barrel of a gun juts into the side of my head, and I freeze. A guy steps out from behind the corner, nudging me with his weapon. "Time to die, motherfucker," he says in a furious voice, and the distinct clicking of a weapon rings out before I've had time to make any move.

Everything happens in slow motion as my life flashes before my eyes.

A shot rings out, and my ears are on fire. I drop to the ground, clutching my head and roaring as pain explodes in my skull. My ears throb, and I rock back and forth on my heels as pain holds me captive. My stomach lurches violently, and nausea builds in the back of my throat.

It takes me a few moments to realize Cheryl is kneeling in front of me, her lips moving, but I can't hear anything.

I glance at the dead body lying by my side, the back half of his head missing and a pool of blood spreading outward. Bloody spatter coats my clothes, my face, and my hands. Cheryl pushes him away with her two feet, clearing a path for our escape. Helping me to my feet, she keeps her arm wrapped around my waist as we hobble down the passageway. I can scarcely keep myself upright. I'm staggering all over the place like I'm smashed. The ringing in my ears is affecting my coordination, and our progress is slow, but somehow, she manages to keep me moving. Sweat beads on my forehead and rolls down my back as we advance, and when we reach the stairs which lead back into the house, I slump against the wall, depleted of all energy.

Cheryl's lips are moving again, but I still can't hear over the ringing in my ears. Then Colin Wentward is there, forcing Cheryl up the stairs while grabbing my arm and slinging it over his shoulder. We climb the stairs slowly and awkwardly, and I wince as intermittent bursts of noise attack my eardrums while my ears struggle to regain their hearing.

It's mayhem when we step out of the tunnel back into the house. My FBI colleagues mingle with DEA agents and various medical personnel, searching rooms and attending to the frightened young girls. I drop down onto the ground, resting my back against the wall. It's like I'm a silent bystander, invisible as the madness swirls around me.

Cheryl hunches over me, worry etched across her pretty face. She's saying something, but I still can't properly hear. Fleeting words register too late, and I haven't a clue what she's saying. I point to my ears, shaking my head, and she nods in understanding, wrapping her arms around my shoulders and holding me tight. I rest my head on her shoulder, feeling her body shake with unshed tears. We cling to one another until an EMT forces us apart to check my vitals.

While he checks me out, I keep my eyes trained on Cheryl, watching as she momentarily leaves the room, returning a couple minutes later with an armful of T-Shirts. She walks around the room, distributing them to the girls. Gradually, my hearing returns, in more fits and spurts, and I wince every time, as pain darts through my skull, piercing my eardrums.

"Kennedy, you okay?" SSA Clement towers over me, extending his hand to help me up. I take it, struggling to my feet.

"I'm good."

"I want you to go to the hospital to get properly checked out."

I try to shake my head in protest, but moving it fucking kills.

"I'll go with him," Cheryl says, and the sound of her beautiful voice is like music to my ears. She loops her arm through mine. "Don't even think about arguing with me," she warns, already guiding me out of the room behind the EMT. "You know, if the tables were turned, you'd insist I was fully checked out."

"I'm not arguing," I say in a croaky voice, my throat feeling like it's been scraped with sandpaper. "And if I never see this house again, it'll be too soon."

Cheryl rides with me in the ambulance, holding my hand and staring at me with a look of pure relief. "I thought I was going to lose you," she says, tears streaming quietly down her face. "I've never been so scared."

I squeeze her hand tight. "Me too," I admit. "He was going to kill me, and I knew there wasn't enough time to react, but you took him out first." I gulp over the messy ball of emotion clogging my throat, staring into the face of the woman I love. My angel. My savior. "You saved my life, Cheryl."

"And I'd do it all over again if I had to." She sweeps hair back off my forehead, pressing a chaste kiss to my brow. "Even if the fact I killed a man today has me a little freaked," she honestly admits.

"You wouldn't be you if you didn't feel like that, and it's a normal reaction."

"But I have zero regrets, because he was going to kill you, and I didn't hesitate. I just pulled the trigger."

I pull her hand to my mouth, planting a soft kiss on her skin. "I'm so fucking proud of you, and, for as long as I live, I'll never forget what you did for me today."

Chapter 25

Cheryl

It's crazy when we arrive at the hospital. A bunch of doctors and nurses wait in the lobby for the ambulances transporting the Mexican girls, and I discover a crowded building downtown collapsed a couple hours ago causing several fatalities and copious injuries. So, the hospital is swamped, and the noise levels are deafening. Kev has his head in his hands while the EMT wheels him through to the emergency room.

I called Kaden just as we left the house, and he made it to the hospital before us. He's called the whole family, and slowly, they trickle in. Once Alex arrives, she immediately takes charge, getting us moved to the private wing where we await news of Keven. He was whisked away for examination the second we arrived, and we haven't heard a peep since.

"What happened?" Kyler asks, bursting into the room with Faye and Brad hot on his heels.

I offer them the same explanation I gave the others, and Kyler sinks into a chair in relief when I confirm he hasn't been seriously injured. Just then, the door opens, and Keven is wheeled in by the doctor.

Alex and James rush to their son's side, fussing over him. "He looks cranky," Kaden says, his lips tugging up at the corners.

"So would you be if a gunshot went off right beside your ear," Eva chastises him, nudging him in the ribs.

"That's just his resting bitch face," Kent unhelpfully supplies.

"You're lucky he can't hear you right now," Keaton says, thumping his brother in the arm.

"Don't fucking joke about that," Kyler says, glaring at Keaton. "We still don't know if there's any permanent damage to his hearing."

Kev stands, walking straight toward me and pulling me into his arms. He kisses the top of my head before turning us around to face his family. "Thanks for coming, but it wasn't necessary. I'm fine," he says, while contradicting himself by tugging on his earlobe.

"You need rest, Mr. Kennedy," the doctor says, narrowing his eyes at him. "We don't know what long-term trauma may have occurred or whether there is any permanent damage yet. My office will call you to schedule an appointment for two weeks. In the meantime, get this prescription filled. It will help with the pain, and the ringing in your ears should stop within the next twelve to twenty-four hours."

We say goodbye to everyone outside the hospital, and I promise to text updates regularly. Kade and Eva drive us back to Kev's, and I've never been more grateful for peace and quiet. After I grab a quick shower, I run a bath for Kev, making him some mac and cheese while he's cleaning up. We eat in silence and then head to bed, and I fall asleep quickly, enveloped in Kev's warm, strong arms.

The next morning, Kev's delighted when the ringing in his ears has faded and he wastes no time arranging a meeting with his team at the FBI building. Both of us are anxious to find out what happened after we left. All we know is his boss assigned a couple of agents to watch over our place last night, and I've avoided thinking about the reasons why.

A couple hours later and we understand the gravity of the situation.

"Unfortunately, Daniel Stanten is in the wind," SSA Clement explains once we are both seated around the conference table. The full team is here, and the expression on everyone's face is solemn.

"How the fuck did he get away?" Kev barks. "You said your team at the warehouse would bring him in."

"That was the plan, but Stanten's men opened fire the instant the team arrived. It was an ambush, and we lost three of our agents in the exchange of fire. During that time, Stanten fled, and it's clear it was a diversion executed purely so he could escape."

"Fuck it." Kev sighs, and a pained look stretches across his face. I reach under the table, giving his thigh a reassuring squeeze.

"How much can we assume Dan knows?" I ask, feeling remarkably calm despite the obvious threat.

"We have to assume he knows you were involved in this. I'm sorry, Cheryl. The risk to your life is considerable, and the offer of witness protection still stands. You can go into hiding, and we'll keep you safe until he's in custody."

"And what if you never capture him?" I ask, eyeballing him.

"Then you can't ever come back."

Silence descends on the room, and Kev's entire body is tense. I place my hand on his arm, his muscles rigid under the tips of my fingers. "Kev?"

His eyes lock on mine, and unspoken words pass between us. "If it comes down to that, I'll go with you."

The SSA clears his throat. "I don't think that'll be possible." He shoots him an apologetic look. "You're too recognizable and too well-known to just disappear. You would only place her in danger."

"Then we'll take our chances here," I supply, threading my fingers through Kev's. "I'm not leaving without you."

"Cheryl." Kev's voice is choked, and I watch the inner battle play out on his face.

I speak up before he says what's on his mind. "No." My tone carries considerable weight. "We're not being separated again. We will stay here and put additional precautions in place. We have the resources to do it. Dan is not taking me away from everyone I love. And I believe in you." I pin Kev with a confident look. "I trust you to find him and to keep me safe."

Uncaring that we're surrounded by his colleagues, Kev pulls me onto his lap. "Are you sure?" he whispers in my ear. "This isn't something that should be decided lightly."

"I'm one hundred percent sure, and I've already given it lots of thought. I understood it might come to this." I cup his face, gazing into his gorgeous blue eyes. "We're in this together, babe. Always."

He nods, and I visibly see determination and confidence return as he holds his head up, and resolve appears in his eyes.

"I have a suggestion," the SSA says, and we both give him our attention. "You graduate this week, right?"

I nod. "The ceremony is on Wednesday."

"Why don't you two go abroad for a while? You have the resources and contacts to hire a full security detail," he tells Keven. "Get out of the country and lay low while we track this bastard down. You can continue to work remotely, and we can conference you into briefings."

"What do you think?" Kev asks me.

I smile, instantly feeling some of the stress lift. "I'm thinking Europe sounds good. Plenty of amazing photo opportunities."

He runs a hand up and down my spine. "Okay, let's do it. We can make plans tonight."

The next few days are a hive of activity. Keven is making arrangements with his boss so he can work remotely from wherever we are. We're planning on spending the summer in Europe and moving around. It will make it harder if Dan, or his father, sends someone after us. We leave for Italy on Friday, and I'm so excited at the prospect of getting to photograph the Coliseum, the Leaning Tower of Pisa, the sites at Pompeii, the stunning cathedrals and architecture of Rome, the waterways of Venice, and so many other stunning locations.

Kev has hired a full team of private bodyguards to travel with us at enormous expense, and he's also reached out to some organization Kade made contact with last year who specializes in protecting expats overseas. I've called my parents and explained the situation, and Kev has assigned bodyguards to each member of my family, and Lin as well, in case Dan makes any move against them.

The SSA feels it's unlikely we are on Dan's radar right now—he has more pressing problems, like the international warrant that's been issued for his arrest—but I'm not naïve enough to assume he'll let this go. If the Feds don't capture him, he *will* come for me, but we'll be protected and ready, and we have the backing of the FBI behind us so I'm not feeling as scared as I was in the first few hours after everything went down at the house.

I still can't believe Dan bought that house purely for the tunnel infrastructure. All week, the major news channels have splashed pictures of the house, cordoned off with rows of tape, the street outside crammed with FBI and DEA vehicles, and agents swarming the property as they confiscate all the contraband discovered in the warehouse. Drugs with a street value of more than twenty million dollars have been seized along with box loads of weapons. The Feds found the underground tunnel Dan was using to transport the goods directly to the warehouse. The entrance was on that slip road Kev's boss mentioned, cleverly concealed behind a fake wall.

I can't believe I fell for someone like that. That he fooled me so thoroughly. And I'm glad Kev came back into my life, helping me to open my eyes before I made the biggest mistake of my life. I'd like to think I would have called the wedding off anyway. Things hadn't been right between Dan and me for months, but I shudder at the thought I could've ended up in a loveless marriage to a gangster with no easy way out.

"I wish we could go with you," Eva says later that day as we chat over a late lunch in a coffee shop a few blocks from Sara's studio. Both our bodyguards stand guard just outside the window, clearly visible from our table.

"I'd love that too," I admit, stirring my coffee with a spoon. "But it's far too dangerous, and Kev says it'd be harder to move around unnoticed with a larger group."

"Maybe we could fly out for a week and join you somewhere," she muses.

A shrill female scream outside has both of us looking up in concern. Butterflies invade my chest in a nanosecond, and adrenaline courses through my veins as Eva and I share anxious looks. All the blood leaches from her face as she glances over my shoulder. She reaches into her bag as I turn around in time to watch both bodyguards slump to the ground. I'm scrambling for my bag when an ear-shattering explosion rocks the small coffee shop.

High-pitched screaming echoes around us as the lights go out, and thick plumes of dark smoke sweep through the room in oxygen-restricting waves. Chunks of debris drop from the ceiling, falling on top of us. Something heavy hits me in the cheek, and a sharp sting slices across my skin. I drop to my knees the same moment Eva does, and we scuttle under the table together. Her hands are trembling as she rummages in her bag. My eyes burn, and my lungs throb as I cough repeatedly. Reaching out, I stretch my fingers as far as I can, grasping the strap of my bag and pulling it toward me.

I've just curled my fingers around my cell when I'm yanked out from under the table with force. A meaty arm slides around my neck from behind, keeping me in a chokehold. I can't see who's restraining me, but the butt of a gun prodding into my back tells me all I need to know.

"Hello, Cheryl. Mr. Stanten would like a word with you," a gruff voice says, nudging me forward, keeping a tight hold around my neck as I struggle to breathe. "Come willingly, and you won't get hurt. Try anything, and you and your pretty friend here will pay the price."

Chapter 26

Keven

I'm boxing up my things at work when I get the call. "Turn on the TV," Kade barks out. "Do it now, Kev, and please tell me that isn't the coffee shop the girls were having lunch at." Ice replaces the blood in my veins as I race across the room and turn on CNN, watching the news footage in horror.

"Fuck!" My shout reverberates around the room, drawing my colleagues' attention. Agent Cunningham gets up from her workstation, crossing to me in an instant. "I just received notification, and a team is on its way to the site, along with bomb disposal experts."

Black smoke billows out of the coffee shop, or what remains of it. The two large windows in front are completely open, shattered glass littering the sidewalk outside. The entrance to the shop has been blown wide open. Police tape cordons off the area, and several prone bodies line the area outside, draped in protective sheeting to protect the horrors from the crowds of bystanders who have congregated outside.

"Keven!!" My brother yells down the phone, reminding me he's still there.

"That was the place," I say in a scarily calm voice, walking urgently back to my desk, conscious that I'm ignoring whatever else Sinead is saying.

"Fucking hell, Kev. I can't get Eva or Rick on their cells. I've been trying repeatedly."

"Calm down. I'm checking their trackers right now." I say it, and I may look it, but I feel anything but calm on the inside. My fingers fly over the keyboard as I tap into my home surveillance system via VPN and pull up Eva's and Cheryl's trackers. "Both their cells are still at the coffee shop, but they're on the move." Thank God, I had the foresight to give all my family tracker chips for their shoes. The girls' trackers confirm they are super close to the airport, and I don't need to be a genius to figure it out.

"That means they're still alive, right?" My brother's frantic plea filters down the line.

"I hope so." I don't want to think about the alternatives. Shutting off my emotions is hard, but I'm of no use to Cheryl if I fall apart, so I compartmentalize, pushing my feelings away and looking at this objectively. My brain races like a computer as I scrabble a plan together. "They're close to the airport, so it's safe to assume he's taking them out of the state. Call Dad, Kyler, and Brad, and meet me at the private hangar at Logan. Tell Dad to get the plane ready, and I'll advise him of a destination as soon as I know where they're taking them."

I cut the call, pulling up the surveillance app on my phone and watching the little red marker as it moves. They've just pulled into the entrance for the airport, so I hack into the air traffic controller system scouring through all private flight plans.

"The coffee shop was a diversion to get to Cheryl?" Sinead surmises, materializing at my side.

"Looks that way. They have Eva too."

"Fuck. What do you need me to do?"

"Call the SSA." It's fucking shitty timing with the boss and the rest of the team out on an op. "They're at the airport, and I'm trying to locate their flight." I glance up at her briefly. "And can you call someone on the ground at the coffee shop for visual confirmation." Before I set this in motion, I need to ensure the girls aren't injured or lying dead back there. Bile floods my mouth even thinking the thought, and the trackers don't lie, so I'm sure they're not there, but I need to check. Sinead hurries back to her desk with her cell glued to her ear. My next call is to Paul, and he confirms he can't reach his men. It's safe to assume both bodyguards have been incapacitated, but he's going to check out the coffee shop and call me once he's there.

I sit down, scanning through all the documented flight plans, as I keep an eye on the app. The trackers in the girl's shoes haven't moved in the last few minutes which I'm guessing means they're on a plane. I pull up the list of approved planes for takeoff and find two private aircraft due to leave shortly. Snapping a pic of the flight details, I grab my jacket and jump up, stopping by Sinead's desk before I leave.

She's just ending a call as I approach. "I've good and bad news," she says, standing. "The girls aren't at the coffee shop, and a witness reported them leaving with two men shortly before local cops arrived on the scene."

I'm hoping that's the bad news, but no such luck.

"The bad news is the New York operation was a bust, and the team is on their way back, but the SSA said their ETA is two hours. However, he's placing a few calls to see what backup he can secure. He said you're to hold tight until he has a team in place."

Not fucking likely.

There's no way I'm cooling my jets here while Stanten has kidnapped Cheryl.

"Yeah, so not happening."

I spin around, but she clamps a hand on my elbow. "You could get kicked out for this."

"I give zero fucks. He has her, Sinead, and I'm not fucking sitting here waiting for a team when Cheryl's life is at stake."

"What are you planning?"

"I know where they're headed and I'm going after them." I send her a copy of my screenshots. "There are two private planes scheduled to leave Logan International shortly. It's one of them. Can you make some calls and see if you can delay both departures until I get there?"

"I'm on it. Go." She jerks her head to the side. "Good luck and keep me updated. I'll send backup as soon as I can."

Paul calls me when I'm battling busy Thursday afternoon traffic en route to the airport. He confirms both bodyguards are dead from fatal bullet wounds to the head. According to police, a shooter took them out from the high-rise building across the street. They didn't even get a chance to protect their marks. He chatted to the bomb experts, and they confirmed a small incendiary device was detonated from outside the shop. A bunch of people is being treated for minor injuries, and one civilian lost his life from a massive coronary brought on by the detonation.

This was a carefully planned and executed operation, and it leads me to believe Stanten's had eyes on Cheryl for quite some time. I've no clue how he managed to do it right under my nose, and I hate that he appears to be one step ahead of me.

I race across the asphalt to Dad's plane, climbing the stairs two at a time. Ky, Kade, and Brad all look up as I race inside the cabin, bypassing them and heading straight for the cockpit.

"The flight plan is logged, and you have a takeoff window in fifteen minutes," I say.

"It'll be tight, but I'll do it," Dad confirms, flicking a row of buttons on the dash.

"You still have that box on board I gave you?" I ask, and he nods. Call it pessimistic or forward thinking, but I had a feeling we'd need easy access to weapons one day, so I stashed a box of guns in the secure hold all, hidden underneath a fake panel.

"I brought it up to the cabin but told the others not to touch it until you arrived."

"Thanks, Dad."

He clamps a hand on my arm. "We'll get her back, Keven. Both of them."

I give him a curt nod before heading back to the cabin. "What's going on, Kev?" Kade asks, dragging a hand through his hair, strain clearly evident in his tone and in his pinched features

"All I know is they're on a private plane headed for Texas. One of my colleagues tried to stop it from leaving, but we were too late. They took off forty minutes ago."

"Fucking hell." Kade slumps into a seat, cradling his head in his hands.

I squeeze his shoulder. "We're going to get the girls back, and so help me God, if that bastard has laid a hand on either one of them, I'll kill him stone fucking dead."

"Not if I kill him first," Kade growls.

I turn to Brad and Kyler as the plane starts moving down the runway. "You don't have to do this."

"Yes, we do," Kyler snaps, looking pissed. "If this was Faye or Rachel, you'd be the first one jumping to the rescue. Cheryl and Eva are family, and we're not leaving you two to handle this alone."

"You sure, man?" I know I told Kade to bring them, but I really wouldn't hold it against either of them if they wanted to back out. I deliberately didn't mention the triplets because they're too young to get involved in this shit, and Kent would be more of a liability than an asset.

"We're sure," Brad replies. "And we know how to handle ourselves."

I know they do. All my brothers are skilled with guns. Because of the environment we grew up in, Mom and Dad felt it was important we knew how to protect ourselves. None of us are strangers at the firing range, and we're all competent with weapons. Brad too. That doesn't mean we're evenly matched with Stanten's hired guns, but we'll put up a good fight.

The plane slows down, and I crane my head out the side window as Dad's voice comes over the intercom. "We have company, Keven."

"Get the door," I shout at Kade, a big grin spreading across my mouth as I watch the four FBI agents racing toward us. Dad stops the plane, and Kade opens the door.

I step down, greeting Sinead on the runway. "I couldn't let you do this alone," she huffs out. "Clement will be pissed, but he's hardly going to fire all of us." She gestures at the three men behind her, quickly introducing them. I know if Wentward, Higgins, and Mead were here, and not on their way home from a busted op, they'd be here too, and it feels good to have a team at my side.

"You sure you're all okay with this?" I ask the men, and they nod.

"C'mon." Sinead brushes past me, ascending the stairs. "Let's go get your girl and nail this Stanten bastard to the wall."

Chapter 27

Cheryl

A metallic taste coats the inside of my mouth as I gradually come to. The room spins as I lift my head up, and my eyes fight to stay open. My arms ache and I try to loosen them, but they're tied firmly behind my back. My butt is numb from the hard chair I'm seated on. I gasp as I'm slapped in the face with ice-cold water, rivulets trickling down my hair, over my face, and seeping under my clothes.

"Wakey, wakey, baby." My head is yanked back forcefully causing me to cry out in pain. I blink my eyes open, shivering as I stare into Dan's harsh glare. He prods a gun into my temple, his eyes raking over me in disgust. "I had such high hopes for you, but you had to go and ruin it all." He moves the gun lower, along my neck, trailing it through the crease in my breasts, and down over my stomach before jabbing it into my crotch.

I'm still fully clothed, but he might as well have the cold steel pressed against my naked flesh. Inexplicable terror rips through my body, and I'm trembling all over. His lips kick up sadistically. "I could fuck you with this gun," he says, pressing it in hard. The denim rubs against my pussy, hurting me, but I force my scream back down my throat, focusing on glaring at my ex instead. "Ruin that tight cunt for Kennedy."

I'm not fast enough to hide my surprise.

He smirks again. "I'll admit you almost had me fooled." He twists the gun against my crotch, and I cry out as pain ricochets through my body. "I was naturally suspicious when you changed your mind about us, so I had one of my men follow you. I'm impressed at the lengths Kennedy went to in order to hide his presence in your life, and I'm pissed that I didn't find out in time to stop what happened at the house."

His nostrils flare, and he backhands me across the face. "That's for betraying me with him." Removing the gun from my crotch, he slips it in the band of his pants and leans into me, digging his knee into my pussy and sliding one hand up under my shirt. His fingers slip into my bra, and he tweaks my nipple so hard my eyes water. "And that's for setting me up." He leans into my face, and the look of pure evil in his eyes scares the shit out of me. He straddles my lap, gripping my chin and forcing my eyes to his. Then he licks my face, in long slow licks, like a dog, and a chorus of laughter breaks out behind him. I'm only now noticing the group of armed men standing at the back of the room with their arms folded looking at me like I'm their next meal.

I gulp over the panic wedged in my throat just as Dan shoves his tongue into my mouth, kissing me forcefully. I thrash about, but it's a feeble effort as I'm strapped to the chair with his full body weight on top of me. He grinds his disgusting erection against me, and I try not to think of what he has planned for me.

Without warning, he lifts off me, brushing has hand across his mouth. "How are you getting on?" he asks, glancing sideways as he strokes the bulge in his pants.

"I'm in fucking heaven, man," a familiar male voice says. I turn my head in Jesse's direction, and my stomach sours at the sight before me.

I know from stuff Eva's told me that Jesse—an ex-colleague of hers from when she worked at Harvard—was always sleazing on her and making inappropriate suggestions about the things he wanted to do to her, so the fact he's taking advantage of her now, when she's vulnerable and not in a position to defend herself, kills me on the inside.

"No!" Tears leak out of my eyes as I look at Eva, similarly restrained to a chair. I knew she'd been taken from the coffee shop as well, but they drugged me, and I lost consciousness until a few moments ago. They clearly gave the same treatment to Eva, except she's still unconscious, her head drooping forward, her chin resting on her naked chest. Jesse is fondling her bare breasts while stroking his exposed cock. Another man stands behind her chair, licking his lips as his hand moves underneath the waistband of his pants.

Nausea swims up my throat, and I turn my pleading gaze on Dan. "Please tell him to stop. Please don't hurt her. You can do whatever you want to me, but leave Eva out of this. This is between you and me."

Jesse grunts, his hand movements increasing, and he emits a primal roar as he comes all over Eva's bare flesh. Unfortunately, she starts to wake up at that exact moment.

"Too late." Dan's hungry gaze drops to Eva's chest, and he rubs at his crotch, not concealing his lust. "And you're wrong if you think this is just about you." He tears his gaze from Eva as she moans, trying to open her eyes, her head lolling back and forth. "She's the reason I was denied the pleasure of killing Garcia. He killed my best friend. Johnny had infiltrated the DeLuca family, risen to second in command, and he was ready to hand the whole business over to my father, when that asshole took him out in cold blood. I wanted to be the one to slit Garcia's throat, but that bitch robbed me of the opportunity."

"If you wanted to kill Jeremy," Eva croaks, finally opening her eyes, "you only had to ask. I'd have gladly let you do it."

"Hello, baby," Jesse says, grabbing her chin and forcing her gaze to his. "Miss me?"

"About as much as I'd miss a cockroach." She drills him with a vicious look, deliberately ignoring his limp dick.

"Careful, bitch," he sneers, tugging her head back. "Or I might come in your ass next."

A pounding on the door claims Dan's attention, forcing his focus away from Jesse and Eva. One of his men checks through the peephole before unlocking the door.

An older man in a loose-fitting black suit steps into the room flanked by two younger men wearing jeans, cowboy boots, hats, and shirts. Jesse pulls up his pants, tucking his hideous cock away. The man in the black suit removes his shades and steps up to Dan. "I've come for my order."

Dan nods his head at one of the armed men, and he exits the room. I surreptitiously scan my surroundings, trying to focus on anything but my mounting hysteria.

We're in a house, in an open-plan living area, with scuffed wooden floors, wooden walls, and overhead beams. A rudimentary kitchen resides on the far left-hand side of the room with a rustic log table and two long benches positioned in the center of the space.

"What about her?" the man in the suit asks, skimming his eyes over Eva.

"She's not for sale," Dan coolly replies before grinning at me. "We've much more exciting things planned for this one." He rubs his hands together. "I thought you liked them young and innocent, and that one's a fucking slut."

Eva looks over at me, and we share an unspoken communication, silently agreeing to stay strong, to stay alive, and to do or say anything we need to until our guys show up, because they will—there is no truth more assured.

"Pity. She has nice tits," the man says, ogling Eva with a predatory gaze.

The sound of sobbing fills the room as the guard returns with a scantily clad girl flung over his shoulder. He plants her on the ground in front of the man in the suit, and she cowers away from him, her lower lip wobbling. Her eyes are bloodshot and red-rimmed, her skin all blotchy, like she's been crying for days. She's young, no more than fourteen if I had to hazard a guess. Dan steps up to her, gripping her shoulders and pushing her in front of the buyer. "This one's yours."

Knots twist in my stomach, and bile floods my mouth. I have no words to describe what I'm witness to. Extracting a knife from his pocket, the man snips her bra straps and cuts her panties off her, leaving her naked, vulnerable, and shivering in a room full of vultures. Her sobbing turns into full-blown cries, and she tries to cover herself with her arms, but the man slaps her in the face, shouting at her to shut up. A lone tear slides down my cheek, and I'm thoroughly sickened.

The two men in the cowboy gear take hold of her arms, and one of them nudges her legs apart. I look away, too sickened to watch anymore, when the man in the suit invades her body with his fingers. "Tight. She'll do."

I look over at Eva, and my jaw pinches tight. That asshole Jesse is rubbing his cock up against her cheek, grinning as he tweaks one of her nipples. She looks straight ahead, displaying no emotion on her face, and she's so strong, but I realize with a heavy sadness this isn't her first rodeo. My entire body quakes as I think of all the horrible shit they can do to us, and I silently pray that the guys aren't far away.

The front door closes behind the men, and I try to drown out the pitiful cries of the girl. I dread to think what plight lies in store for her. Dan looms over me again, smirking, and I want to scratch my nails down his face and gouge out his eyeballs. He sickens me to no end.

"What's the matter, darling?" He grips my chin, digging his nails into my flesh. "Does that offend you? Or are you turned on?" He pops the button on my jeans, sliding his hand into my panties and roughly inserting one finger inside me. Tears threaten, but I force them aside, refusing to let him see how scared and vulnerable I feel.

"Not turned on," he murmurs, pulling his dry finger out. "Why doesn't that surprise me?"

The men laugh, and my eyes blaze with anger. I want to scream at him that he's a despicable excuse for a human being and a lousy, selfish lover, but no good will come from antagonizing him in front of his men, so I don't retaliate, letting the insult die in the air. A line of sweat rolls down my back, and tiny beads of moisture form on my brow. Now that the water has dried on my skin, I'm realizing how hot it is in this room.

"Let me fuck her," Jesse says, walking toward me with his erection on full display. "I'll get her so wet she'll think she's drowning."

"Fuck off," Dan says, shoving Jesse back. "And put your cock away. You've had your fun."

"I haven't had nearly enough." He leers at me, stroking his cock as his gaze rakes over me.

"I said put it away," Dan grits out, whipping out his gun and pointing it at Jesse's hard-on. "Or I'll fucking blast it to bits."

Jesse tucks himself away, frowning at Dan. "I don't get it. Why can't we fuck them up?"

Dan taps the gun off Jesse's temple. "Engage your brain, you imbecile." He rolls his eyes. "Kennedy will never agree to the plan if she's damaged in any way."

"You need to give him incentive," Jesse argues.

"And you need to shut the fuck up." Dan slams him back into the wall. "You are starting to get on my last nerve. Either shut the fuck up or leave."

Jesse holds up his hands. "Fine. Relax."

"What plan?" I ask when Dan comes back around to me.

"Still no patience when it comes to surprises." Leaning down, he tweaks my nose, and I growl at him. He laughs. "At first, I was going to sell you both, but then I discovered you were fucking Kennedy and that he'd joined the Feds. As much as I'd enjoy seeing the look on your face if I'd sold you to some pervert, a rat inside the Feds is a much more interesting proposition." He glances at his watch. "I'm expecting your *childhood sweet-heart* to show up soon, and then we'll see how much you mean to him."

I stare at him as if he's completely lost his sanity. "You're an idiot if you think Keven's going to agree to that."

He takes off his suit jacket, folding it neatly and placing it on the table behind him. Slowly, he rolls his sleeves up to his elbow. "Kennedy will do anything to save his woman, and he's not opposed to illegal activity. Your boyfriend has done some shady shit in his time, so I doubt it'll take much to persuade him." He glances over at Eva, and the devilish look in his eye twists my stomach into knots. "But I do have an incentive lined up in case he needs proof of how serious I am."

Rolling the bottom of his trouser leg up, he removes a dagger strapped to his ankle and stalks toward Eva. "Leave her alone!" I roar, thrashing about in my chair.

Dan moves behind Eva, tugging her head back and exposing the elegant column of her neck. He places the tip of his dagger underneath her chin, and goose bumps sprout on my arms. Eva has a neutral expression on her face, and I can't tell what she's thinking. Dan glides the dagger across her neck, slowly, barely touching her skin. A tiny trickle of blood oozes out, and a loud sob rips from my throat.

"Please, Dan. Please, don't hurt her. Kev will never agree if you kill her." I plead with my eyes. "I'll do anything you want. I'll marry you and never speak of this again. I'll do anything if you just spare her."

"Take over." Dan hands the dagger to Jesse. "Don't touch her until I tell you," he commands, giving him the evil eye. Jesse takes Dan's place, holding the knife to Eva's throat.

Dan crouches in front of me. "What makes you think I'd want you back? You're a lying, cheating whore who doesn't know the meaning of loyalty. The only thing you're good for now is collateral." He stands, grinning. "Kennedy will agree or you're dead. It's as simple as that." He nods at Jesse. "And he'll agree when he arrives and discovers his sister-in-law's lifeless body. He'll know I mean business." Dan puts his face right up in mine. "Eva's death will be on your conscience too. Just like that whore Hayley." He jerks his chin up, pinning Jesse with a wicked grin. "Do it. End the bitch."

I scream from the top of my lungs, and the steel glints as Jesse lowers the knife, positioning it midway across Eva's throat. My body floods with rage and adrenaline, and I rise, with the chair strapped to my body, and lunge at Jesse. He twists around to confront me, and a ray of light streams through a side window highlighting his form. I throw myself on top of Eva as a bullet whizzes through the window, instantly shattering the glass, embedding in Jesse's forehead. He falls back as the front door bursts open, and Keven charges into the room surrounded by FBI agents.

Eva and I fall to the floor heavily, the splintering of wood echoing around us as our chairs crack apart. Gunfire immediately breaks out in the room, and I keep myself pinned to Eva as we cling to one another on the floor. I offer up silent prayers, beseeching God to keep us all safe.

Eva trembles underneath me, and I see she was way more terrified that I realized. I don't blame her. This is the second traumatizing experience she's suffered in less than a year, not to mention all the abuse she suffered, for years, at the hands of her sadistic ex-husband. Locating her hand, I squeeze her fingers, relieved when she squeezes back. The gunfire seems to be easing off, but I don't look up, too afraid of being caught by a stray bullet.

"I'm going after him," Keven shouts, and it takes everything in me not to look around. "Get the girls!"

"I'm with you!" a female hollers, followed by the sound of multiple retreating footsteps.

The room is quieter when gentle hands land on my arm. "Cheryl. It's Kyler. Can I help you up?"

"Can you give me your shirt?" I ask, and he hands it over without question.

I slide it underneath me as he lifts me up, covering Eva's bare chest. Her eyes glisten with gratitude.

"Eva!" Kade's panicked shout bounces off the walls.

"Over here, Kade," Kyler hollers, helping me to stand.

Kade races by me, tears streaming down his face as he drops to his knees and pulls his wife into his chest. Eva is clutching Kyler's T-shirt to her chest and using her other arm to hug her husband. Both of them are sobbing, and tears prick my eyes.

"Can you walk, or do you want me to carry you?" Kyler asks, carefully inspecting my face.

"I can walk," I say, taking a tentative step forward and promptly collapsing. "Shit." I clutch onto his arm as Brad comes up, wiping sweat off his forehead. "I'm still weak from whatever drugs he gave me."

"I'll take her," Brad says, putting the safety on his gun before slipping it into his gun belt. He holds out his arms. "May I?"

Tears pool in my eyes as I nod in agreement. Very carefully, he scoops me up, and I lean back against him, exhausted as I come down from the adrenaline high. I survey the damage in the room as he walks outside. Several bodies are slumped on the ground, eyes glassy, bodies motionless, and blood pooling under wrinkled shirts. I loop my arm around Brad's neck and look behind me to see if Eva is okay. She has Kyler's shirt on now, and Kade is rocking her in his arms, whispering in her ear. A guy in an FBI vest is talking animatedly on his cell over in the corner, but other than that, there is no one else in the room.

Scorching-hot sun beats down on us as we step outside, and it's like stepping face-first into a giant hairdryer. "Where are we?" I inquire, lifting my hand to shield my eyes from the glare.

"West Texas," Ky says, pulling a ball cap out of the back pocket of his jeans and offering it to me.

I smile at him as I pull it on, tucking my hair underneath. "Holy shit." I had no idea we'd even left the state of Massachusetts although the stifling heat in the house should've been a clue.

"Cheryl," James says, coming up to us on the dirt road outside the house. "Are you okay?" I nod, opening my mouth to speak when a row of blacked-out SUVs bearing the FBI logo come tearing around the corner, screeching to a halt. Doors swing open, and armed agents pile out of the vehicles. They split up—some going into the house while others race off down the road.

"Fucking A," Kyler says, a big grin spreading across his mouth as his gaze travels in the direction of the agents on the road.

I crane my neck to see and immediately burst out crying.

"Hey," Kyler's voice is intentionally soft, and Brad hugs me a little tighter. "He's okay, Cheryl. He's safe."

"I know," I sob, watching as Keven strides toward us, escorting Dan in handcuffs. Agent Cunningham—Sinead—has a hold of Dan's other arm, and they are both steadfastly hauling him forward as he tries to wriggle free. "It's just … it's over. It's finally over."

Ky nods, smiling. "I knew Keven would deliver. He never lets us down."

"No, he doesn't," Kade says, standing beside us with Eva nestled in his arms.

We reach for each other at the same time, linking hands, and I know, in this moment, that our experience today has bonded us forever. We look at one another, both conveying so much with our eyes, and we subtly nod in agreement. The guys don't need to know the shit that went on back there. It will be our secret to keep.

A round of applause breaks out as Keven and Sinead bring Dan forward, handing him over to the local FBI for processing. Dan pins me with a chilling look, opening his mouth to say something, when Keven steps in front of him, blocking his view of me. "You don't get to look at her or speak to her ever again."

"You're welcome to the cunt," he says. "But enjoy her, because you won't have long." Kev roughly shoves him into the back of an SUV as all the tiny hairs lift on the back of my neck, and a shudder works its way through me.

"C'mere, baby." Keven slides me into his arms, nodding his thanks to Brad. The family disperses, giving us some alone time. He presses his forehead to mine. "The plane journey seemed to take hours, and I never thought we'd get here. I was terrified, baby. If anything had happened to you …"

"I'm okay, and I knew you would come." I offer him a soft smile. "I knew you were tracking me and that you'd get here as soon as you could."

"I was so scared I wouldn't reach you in time. I never want to go through that again." Keven caresses my cheek while examining my face. "Did he hurt you?"

I shake my head. "No. He tried to intimidate me, and I was scared, but he didn't hurt me."

"You'd tell me if he ... if any of them did anything to you, right?"

I nod. "He didn't hurt me because he was planning on using me for leverage with you. He thought you'd agree to be his FBI bitch if he handed me back."

Kev blinks repeatedly. "He's one crazy motherfucker. I was so fucking tempted to put a bullet through his skull when he ran off, but I meant what I said before. He deserves to be punished for his crimes. Death would be too easy."

"There was a girl," I say, and I proceed to tell him what went down. He takes me with him, and we talk to the local FBI guy in charge. He confirms they found ten other girls locked up in one of the back rooms, and then he takes details from me and Eva in relation to the men who left with that poor, terrorized girl.

All I want to do is go home, take a shower, clean up, and snuggle in bed with my man, but there are procedures to follow first, like formal statements and medical examinations. It's past midnight when we are finally in the air on our way back to Boston. I insisted we let Kade and Eva take the only bedroom on board, so Kev and I are lying facing one another in the main cabin with our chairs reclined fully and comfy blankets thrown over us. Brad is snoring his head off across the way, and Kyler is in the cockpit, keeping his dad company.

"Thank you for coming to get me," I whisper, lifting my hand and running it across the stubble on his face.

"I will always come for you, Cheryl. Always." He kisses me softly. "You never have to doubt that."

"I don't, Kev. I have zero doubts where we're concerned. No one has ever loved me the way you do."

His kiss is more insistent this time. "And no one else ever will," he whispers over my mouth. "Because it's you and me forever. There's nothing standing in our way now."

"I like the sound of that," I whisper back with tears gleaning in my eyes.

"Me too." He pulls my head into his warm chest. "Now sleep, honey. And when you wake up, I'll be right here. Like I plan to be every single day. With my arms wrapped around you. Hugging you close because you are my heart, my life, my whole world."

Epilogue
August

Cheryl

"You may now kiss the bride," the celebrant says, amid whoops and hollers from the small assembled crowd. Kyler and Faye rented the entire castle and the grounds for the weekend so they could have a completely private wedding without any unwelcome media intrusion. Guests were limited to family and close friends, and apart from immediate family, no one knew the details of the venue until they rocked up to the Kennedy house in Wellesley to be transported here. I didn't think such a place existed in Massachusetts, but Faye said they found several similar venues in the state before settling on the Brookline venue.

It's worked like a dream and, so far, the day has gone without a hitch.

I dab at my eyes as Kyler lifts Faye's veil and tenderly cups her face before drawing her into him for a very long, very slow, extremely passionate kiss. Faye throws her arms around his neck, clinging to him like he's her life support, and my heart swells in my chest. I just love seeing people in love, and I've always adored weddings.

Faye looks absolutely stunning in a couture Alex Kennedy dress. The lace bodice is fitted to her beautiful curves, and the chenille skirt flows in delicate layers to the ground. It's dreamily romantic and like something I'd pick for myself. Her hair is styled in an elegant bun with

221

a few wispy strands framing her face. Tiny little diamonds glisten in the hairpiece she wears.

"They make such a beautiful couple," Eva whispers at my side. Our men stand proudly in the row across from us, all dashing in their black Armani tuxedos.

I was delighted when Faye asked me to be a part of the bridal party along with Eva, her half-sister Whitney, her best friend Rachel, and the other Kennedy girlfriends. Keanu was the only brother without an official date, so he's escorting Faye's other Irish friend Jill. Alex designed all our gowns too, allowing us to choose our own personal design, so even though all the dresses are in the same blush pink material, each looks unique. I opted for a classic, strapless, fitted gown with a fishtail, and it's the most gorgeous dress I've ever worn. "They are going to make such beautiful babies," I whisper back to Eva, noticing her hand automatically moving to her flat stomach. My eyes pop wide as I stare at her, and her entire face lights up.

"Don't tell anyone," she whispers. "We don't want to take away from Faye and Kyler's day."

I can't resist giving her a quick hug. "Oh my God. I'm so happy for you both. When are you due?"

"March fifth. I'm so excited." Kade looks over at that exact moment, beaming at his wife, and I give him a subtle thumbs-up.

"Does Kev know?" I whisper as the celebrant draws the ceremony to a close.

"Kade's going to tell him today. But we're only telling you two. We'll tell the rest of the family next week."

Warm arms wrap around my waist from behind, and I almost spill my champagne down the front of my dress. "You look fucking ravishing," Kev says, nipping at my ear. "And I can't wait to devour you later." My core floods with warmth at his words. It's almost embarrassing how horny I am for my man. The last couple months have been utterly blissful, and I never thought I could feel this much happiness.

Dan's trial concluded this week, and he was put away for life. The last vestiges of stress lifted from my shoulders at the news that his father had a massive stroke the same day, and he's not expected to pull through, so it looks like we're completely in the clear. I'm most definitely in the mood for celebrating tonight, and I have a few ideas in mind. "We could always take a secret bathroom rendezvous like we did at Kade and Eva's wedding?" I suggest, sending him a seductive smile.

Very discreetly, he nudges his hips against my ass, and I feel his growing erection. "Now look what you've done to me. Naughty girl." His lips suction on my neck, and delicious tremors slick over my skin.

"You know I'll look after you. All you have to do is ask."

He spins me around in his arms, holding me tight to his chest, and his eyes glisten with so much emotion, taking my breath away. "If I asked you to elope with me tonight, what would you say?"

"I'd say yes." I circle my arms around his neck. "A million times yes." I peck his lips. "But we're not bailing on your brother's wedding. I wouldn't miss this for the world." I turn us around to look at the beautiful room. Circular tables dressed in crisp white linens cover the hardwood flooring. Tall bouquets of white and pink roses make up each centerpiece. The room has a succession of double glass doors that open out onto a beautiful terrace overlooking the magnificent gardens. Light streams through the glass illuminating the room. Guests mingle between the inside and outside space, and waiters float around the room offering champagne and canapes.

"Is this something you'd like?" he inquires, probing my eyes with intensity.

"I'll be happy with any kind of wedding if it's you I'm marrying."

"I'll take that as a yes then," he teases, capturing my lips in a steamy kiss.

"We have plenty of time to decide, and I'd prefer to get married when we have enough time to focus on our future." Right now, we're both crazy busy with work. Kev is working a new case and he's been given elevated responsibilities. SSA Clement also confirmed he's completely off the hook in relation to any of his past illegal endeavors, so he can breathe easy now that's not hanging over his head.

I'm working more hours at the studio, but I'm also in the process of setting up my own freelance photography business. Eva and Kade are helping me pull a website together, and in return, I'm taking photos for their new online business, so it's a win-win.

I've also set up a part-time studio at the residential home with the owner's backing. I thought it would be good for the community to see firsthand the good work done in the home, and it's a fantastic learning experience for my students, so once a week, the little makeshift studio is open to members of the Walpole area. They can book in for a session, and all we ask in return is that they make a small donation to help with the running costs. So far, we've done mainly family portraits and a few new baby sessions, but word of mouth is growing, and I'm expecting it to get busier and the requests to become more varied.

Kev offered me the money to lease my own studio, but I declined. I want to do this myself. With my own money, and I'm happy to build it up bit by bit. I'm still learning, and I'd rather stay with Sara Lewis until I feel I've learned everything I can and I'm ready to go it alone. Then, once I've established a solid business, Kev and I can focus on getting married and having kids. We're both still young enough to achieve it all. And I do want it all—I want the man, *and* the career, *and* the family.

"Does that mean you wouldn't be opposed to a long engagement?" he asks, leading me toward our table as the manager summons everyone for dinner.

"Not at all." He pulls out my chair for me, and I peck him briefly on the lips before sitting down. "I don't care what we do once we do it together."

"I want my ring on your finger," he whispers in my ear while his hand slides low on my exposed back. "I want everyone to know you're mine."

I fling my arms around his neck, beaming at him. "Have you any idea how much I love you?"

"About as much as I love you, so that's a fucking lot." He kisses me sweetly. "I'm hereby putting you on notice. You can expect a proposal sooner rather than later."

"You could just ask me right now, and I would say yes. I don't need any extravagant gestures. I've only ever needed you."

He kisses me again. "I know that, honey, and it's one of the reasons I love you so much, but I'm not proposing to you at my brother's wedding. Imagine the horror of explaining that one to our kids." I giggle, rubbing my fingers along the back of his neck. "And I want it to be special and a memory we'll always cherish."

"Every moment with you is a memory to cherish," I say, tears welling in my eyes.

He pulls me into his arms, pressing a fierce kiss to my head. "I wholeheartedly agree. I'm so glad you came back into my life, Cheryl, and I never take what we have for granted. I'm so lucky you decided to give me a second chance, because I never imagined I'd feel this happy in my life. You make my life complete in every conceivable way."

I can't hold my tears at bay anymore, and it's true what they say, weddings bring out the romantic in everyone. I ease back, peering into his eyes and cupping his handsome face. "Forgiving you was the easiest decision of my life because loving you is effortless and timeless. As long as I live, I will love you so completely because you mean everything to me, Keven."

He links our fingers together before raising them to his lips, planting a soft skin on the back of my hand. "It's you and me forever, Cheryl."

"Forever," I whisper, leaning in to kiss his lips.

Keanu

"Dude, check out the ass on the blonde," Kent says, elbowing me in the ribs and yanking my head up from the table.

The dark room spins, and my vision is blurry as I attempt to focus in the direction of his pointed finger. The club isn't crowded tonight, but it's still pretty busy for a Monday night. We only got home from Brookline this morning, and it was Kent's idea to head to Torment, talking shit about curing our post-wedding hangovers by drinking our body weight in beer. Hence why I'm now seeing triple of his face. Torment is notorious for turning a blind eye to fake IDs and underage drinking, so it's our usual go-to spot when we want to get trashed.

"And those legs." He whistles, adjusting the front of his jeans. "I'm already hard thinking about those legs wrapped around my neck."

The fact he just spent the weekend with Whitney's legs wrapped around his neck seems to already have been forgotten. "You've got a problem," I slur.

"The only problem I have right now is you. Seriously, bruh. You're a fucking mess."

"She broke me," I mumble, always too talkative when I'm smashed. "I *am* a fucking mess."

He clamps his hand on my back. "She only broke you if you let her. Screw Selena. She fucking led you on for years and then tossed you aside like garbage. No one does that to a Kennedy."

I rub at my pounding temples, wondering why I thought it was a good idea to unburden myself to Kent. It's not that I don't trust my brother to keep my confidence, because I do. Despite what my older brothers think about him, Kent knows how to keep a secret. While he's loyal, and he's gone out of his way to cheer me up, he's not exactly an advocate for relationships. I doubt Kent even knows how many girls he's hunched, but it's a lot. He meant well, but he gave me the worst advice when Selena and I first broke up, and I regret throwing my virginity away on the first girl that came along.

I'd been saving it for Selena. Patiently waiting until she was ready. But then she broke up with me. And I'm so fucking angry. With her. And with me. Because I can't get her out of my head, and it's killing me inside.

I should've asked Keaton for his advice. He's been in a relationship with Melissa almost as long as Selena and I were together, if that's what it was, because now I wonder what the label really was.

Were we ever truly boyfriend and girlfriend, or was I just a crutch for her to lean on?

"C'mon." Kent yanks me off the stool, and I almost face-plant the ground. "You're on wingman duty."

He keeps hold of my elbow, stalking toward the girl at the top end of the bar. She has her back to us, and all I can see is long, long legs and long, long almost-white blonde hair resting above a peachy ass. Damn. Kent sure knows how to spot them. She's got that thin, angular model shape, and she's tall too. If she were a brunette, she'd be a mirror for my ex, and I hate that my mind automatically goes there. *Why won't my stupid brain just get with the program?*

As we draw nearer, I notice the girl is already talking to a guy, and I fist my hand in Kent's shirt, pulling him back. "She's with someone."

He arches a brow, or at least I think he does. Can't properly tell because my vision is still a little wonky. "And your point is?"

"You can't hit on someone's girlfriend, right in front of them."

He smirks. "Says fucking who?"

I roll my eyes. "No wonder you have such a shitty rep."

"I've earned my rep, and I'm not ashamed to admit that." He glances over his shoulder at the girl. "And that nerdy freak isn't any competition." He yanks me forward by my shirt. "Watch and learn, bro."

If I wasn't so smashed, I'd leave him to his own chaos, but I'm too fucking drunk to fend for myself, so I trail after him, watching as he struts up to the girl and confidently taps her on the shoulder. "Hey, baby girl. Is it hot in here, or is it just you?" he says, and I slam my palm into my forehead, groaning. Kent has the worst pickup lines. And the awful thing is, he has a never-ending list of them. I'm getting ready to apologize for him when she turns around, and my world tilts sideways.

"Fuck. Me." Kent steps back, his eyes blinking profusely as if he can't believe what he's seeing.

Neither can I.

"Selena?" I don't know if it's my alcoholic-influenced eyes playing tricks on me or if she's really here, because that would be so out of character for her.

"Keanu." Her soft voice tears a new strip off my heart.

"What the fuck did you do to your hair?" Kent asks.

She ignores him, looking up at the tall, nerdy geek by her side, and I'm betting she's giving him those vulnerable girl eyes, begging him to extricate her from this situation.

My blood boils, and my hands ball into fists at my side.

There hasn't been any occasion where I doubted the stuff she'd told me. I've witnessed her anxiety up close, and her vulnerability always made me want to wrap her in cotton wool and protect her from the outside world.

Until now.

Now, I'm beginning to wonder if I haven't been an even bigger fool.

"Don't fucking look at him," I snarl. "Or is he your new savior?"

"Back off, man," the nerd says, attempting to stare me out of it.

I push my chest into his, pleased that I tower over him, and shove him back a few steps. "Fuck you."

"Keanu, please." Selena touches my arm.

"Don't touch me!" I snap, turning around to face her and instantly regretting it, because we're way too close, and it's the worst form of torture.

Hell.

Why does she have to be so completely and utterly stunning? And why does she insist on looking at me with those beautiful hazel eyes, pleading with me to understand?

"I know you're angry with me, but please don't take it out on Todd," she quietly beseeches.

"Todd." I snort. "Figures." Asshole name if ever I heard one.

"Don't be mean, K. Please."

"Leave us alone," Todd says, brushing past me and pulling Selena off to the side.

A raging jealous beast possesses my body, and I glare at both of them, torn between wanting to pummel my fists into his smug face and longing to grab her into my arms and kiss the shit out of her until she remembers she's mine. But I do neither. I tap into my inner Kent instead, because jerk mode requires little effort when I'm trashed. "It's like that, I see. You fucking him? Huh, Sel? Did you spread your legs for him the minute you kicked my ass to the curb? Or were you fucking him behind my back?"

"Keanu. No. Stop. Please." Her voice is barely louder than a whisper, and her lower lip wobbles.

"No." I fold my arms and stare at the girl who was once my everything. "I want to know why I wasted years waiting for you. Supporting you. Helping you. *Loving* you. And for what?" I throw my hands in the air as Kent smirks. Of course, he'd approve of the dramatics—he practically invented the word. "So you could dump me and start fucking around? How are you even here? Was everything a fucking lie?" I roar that last part, and several heads turn in our direction.

Tears pool in Selena's eyes, and she looks crestfallen. I instantly feel like the biggest dick. But I'm hurting so bad. I don't want to believe she used me, but that's what it's starting to seem like, and I can't handle that.

"Did I ever mean anything to you, or was it just convenient to lean on me?" I ask in a softer tone, because I'm still clueless as to what I did wrong. How it all fell apart.

"Of course, you meant something to me," she cries, her tone impassioned. "How can you even question that?"

"Because you tossed me away like I didn't matter."

"No, Keanu. That is not what happened." She adamantly shakes her head.

Kent snorts, but I ignore him. "Then enlighten me because I still don't fucking know how we ended up here."

She steps closer, tipping her chin up, and her gorgeous eyes radiate with determination. "I loved you enough to know I had to set you free."

Kent fakes a cough, muttering, "Bullshit" under his breath.

"I didn't want to be set free," I pathetically murmur.

"I'm sorry you're hurting, K. Genuinely, I am, because you're the last person I ever wanted to hurt. Someday, you'll understand why I did what I did, and you'll realize I did the right thing."

I reach out and cup her beautiful face, knowing I'll pay for this later, but unable to stop myself. "I miss you so fucking much, Sel. I can hardly breathe." My chest tightens, and a lump the size of a football clogs my throat.

A lone tear treks down her face. "I miss you too, K. Every single day." She places her hand over mine, smiling for a second before she pulls away from me. "But it changes nothing. We can't be together. I'm sorry."

Then she gestures to Todd, and they walk off together, leaving my heart ripped apart all over again.

TO BE CONTINUED.

Releasing Keanu is slated for publication in May 2019.

Subscribe to my romance newsletter to read an exclusive bonus chapter of Faye and Ky's wedding from their prospective. Copy and paste this link into your browser: https://smarturl.it/WeddingBonusScene

Adoring Keaton and *Reforming Kent* are the final two books in the Kennedy Boys series, coming 2020.

About the Author

USA Today bestselling author **Siobhan Davis** writes emotionally intense young adult and new adult fiction with swoon-worthy romance, complex characters, and tons of unexpected plot twists and turns that will have you flipping the pages beyond bedtime! She is the author of the international bestselling *True Calling*, *Saven*, and *Kennedy Boys* series.

Siobhan's family will tell you she's a little bit obsessive when it comes to reading and writing, and they aren't wrong. She can rarely be found without her trusty Kindle, a paperback book, or her laptop somewhere close at hand.

Prior to becoming a full-time writer, Siobhan forged a successful corporate career in human resource management.

She resides in the Garden County of Ireland with her husband and two sons.

You can connect with Siobhan in the following ways:

Author Website: www.siobhandavis.com
Author Blog: My YA NA Book Obsession
Facebook: AuthorSiobhanDavis
Twitter: @siobhandavis
Google+: SiobhanDavisAuthor
Email: siobhan@siobhandavis.com

Books by Siobhan Davis

TRUE CALLING SERIES
Young Adult Science Fiction/Dystopian Romance

True Calling
Lovestruck
Beyond Reach
Light of a Thousand Stars
Destiny Rising
Short Story Collection
True Calling Series Collection

SAVEN SERIES
Young Adult Science Fiction/Paranormal Romance

Saven Deception
Logan
Saven Disclosure
Saven Denial
Saven Defiance
Axton
Saven Deliverance
Saven: The Complete Series

KENNEDY BOYS SERIES
Upper Young Adult/New Adult Contemporary Romance

Finding Kyler
Losing Kyler
Keeping Kyler
The Irish Getaway
Loving Kalvin
Saving Brad
Seducing Kaden
Forgiving Keven
*Releasing Keanu^*
Adoring Keaton*
Reforming Kent*

STANDALONES
New Adult Contemporary Romance

Inseparable
Incognito
When Forever Changes
*Only Ever You^*
*No Feelings Involved^*

Reverse Harem Contemporary Romance

Surviving Amber Springs

ALINTHIA SERIES
Upper YA/NA Paranormal Romance/Reverse Harem

The Lost Savior
The Secret HeirThe Warrior Princess
*The Chosen One^*

^Releasing 2019
* Coming 2020

Visit www.siobhandavis.com for all future release dates. Please note release dates are subject to change based on reader demand and the author's schedule. Subscribing to the author's newsletter or following her on Facebook is the best way to stay updated with planned new releases.

Printed in Great Britain
by Amazon